VINTAGE VILLAINY

VINTAGE VILLAINY

A VINTAGE BY VIVIAN MYSTERY

EILEEN WATKINS

LEVEL
BEST BOOKS

Author Photo Credit: Glamour Shots

First edition

ISBN: 978-1-68512-912-5

Cover art by Level Best Designs

This book was professionally typeset on Reedsy.
Find out more at reedsy.com

To Robert and June Anderson, who introduced me to the romantic, offbeat charms of 1940s Barkcloth fabrics, Roseville pottery and Turner bird prints!

Chapter One

I dragged the last of my burdens inside and shut the barnlike door behind me, snuffing out much of the sunlight. After the mid-May warmth outside, I shivered at the sudden chill. The building's gloomy lower level spread out to either side, the stone floor and sooty brick walls more than a century old.

Everything down here reminded me that this structure, which covered an entire city block, originally served as a parachute factory to equip soldiers during World War I. Just one of the many less-than-glamorous roles it had played during its lifetime.

I'd already done a lot of lifting and hauling that morning, and the underarms of my cardigan sweater—worn to make me look professional—had grown damp by now. I pushed up the sleeves a little as I turned to face my next challenge. At least I had on dark-wash jeans and updated Keds sneakers today, for this strenuous and potentially messy job.

Up ahead now, a big, soot-stained chamber yawned open and waiting, as if to devour me.

I dragged my three super-sized storage bins another fifteen feet or so, and over the metal threshold of the freight elevator. Original to the factory building, it still operated on a manual rope pulley system. I'd been assured that this did not require too much brawn to operate. A good thing, because I stood only five feet, four inches tall and weighed only about one hundred ten pounds. These days, too much heavy lifting also reminded me, sometimes, that the big 4-0 lay not far in my future.

I pushed an ornate Victorian lever to roll the steel mesh, accordion-style door shut. A single overhead bulb sent down only a very dim glow. Musty basement smells wafted in. I wondered if any rats hung out on this level.

If this were a set for a movie or a play, it would be the ideal spot for the naïve female victim to come to A Very Bad End. I shuddered. *Whatever, Viv. Just don't spend any more time down here than you need to!*

From pulleys high above my head hung two long, sturdy ropes, on my left and right. I tried to remember my instructions—which to pull?

Left to go up, I think, and right to go down.

A tug on the left rope produced no effect at all, even when I hauled with both hands. I tried the other rope with the same lack of result.

Could my load possibly be too heavy? Absurd. Surely, over the past hundred-plus years, hauling military-grade parachute silks, the lift had handled a lot more!

I'd never suffered from serious claustrophobia, but it started to creep up on me now. I checked the primitive control panel and didn't see any kind of alarm button. Of course, I wasn't really *trapped* in this sooty conveyance. I could always exit the way I came in and go for help.

On my first day, though, I didn't want to stand out as "the newbie," and certainly not as a helpless female.

C'mon Viv. What would one of your old-time movie heroines do, like Katherine Hepburn? Or your sort-of namesake, Vivian Leigh? Or even Emma Peel from The Avengers?

Just keep a cool head, and think!

My new landlord, Fred Palasinski, had assured me that despite its age and appearance, the elevator still operated well. Its original designers had equipped it with all the latest safety features of that time, including...

The brake! He told me to always set that when I finished using the lift, and that it wouldn't move either up or down as long as the brake was on.

I searched for a less-obvious third cable, found it, and easily released the car to move. After that, with a moderate pull on the right-hand rope, my merchandise and I began to rise. The brick-lined shaft, framed by ancient steel girders, slipped past so slowly that the trip felt like more than just two floors. And still unnerving, because the mechanism creaked, groaned, and

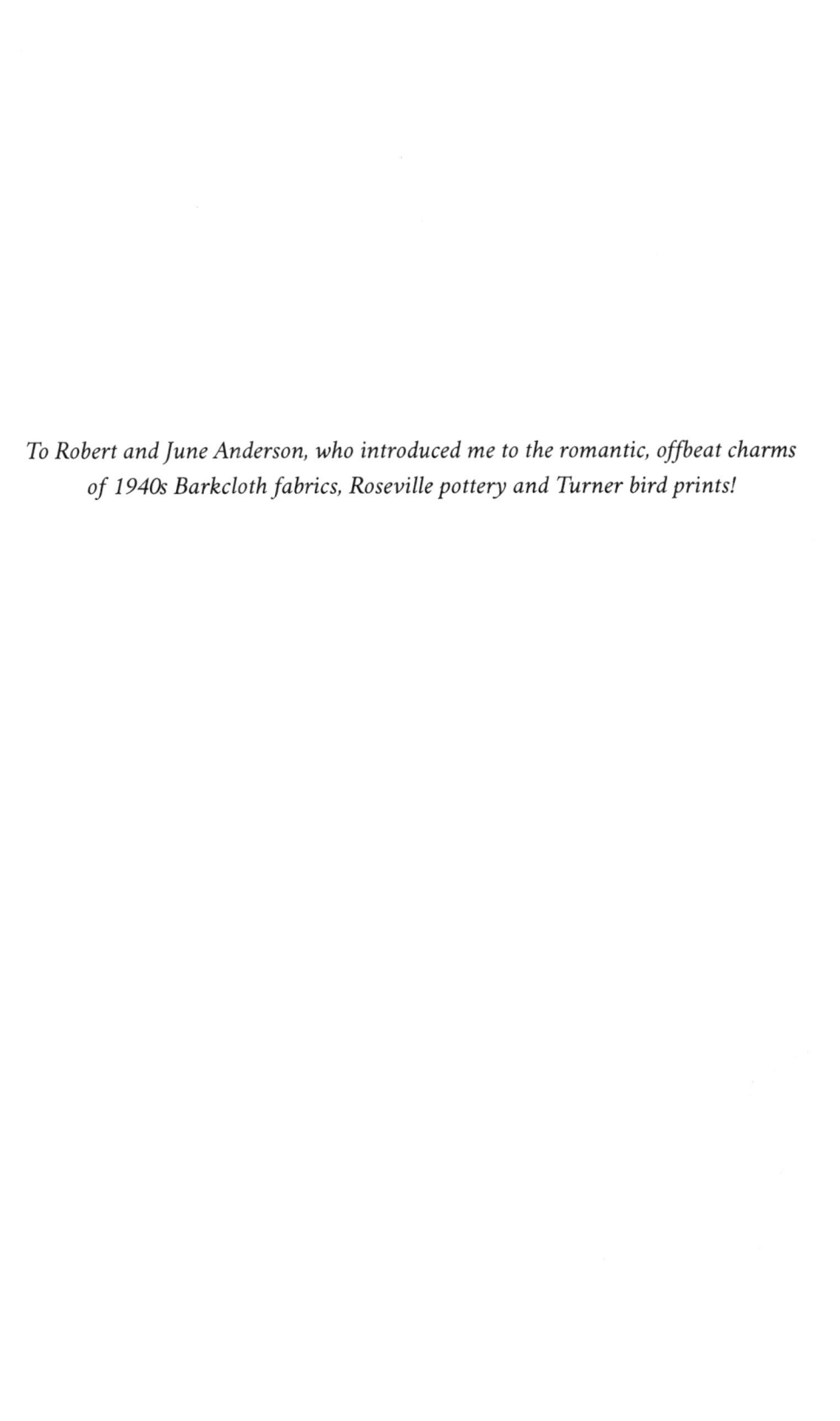

To Robert and June Anderson, who introduced me to the romantic, offbeat charms of 1940s Barkcloth fabrics, Roseville pottery and Turner bird prints!

Chapter One

I dragged the last of my burdens inside and shut the barnlike door behind me, snuffing out much of the sunlight. After the mid-May warmth outside, I shivered at the sudden chill. The building's gloomy lower level spread out to either side, the stone floor and sooty brick walls more than a century old.

Everything down here reminded me that this structure, which covered an entire city block, originally served as a parachute factory to equip soldiers during World War I. Just one of the many less-than-glamorous roles it had played during its lifetime.

I'd already done a lot of lifting and hauling that morning, and the underarms of my cardigan sweater—worn to make me look professional— had grown damp by now. I pushed up the sleeves a little as I turned to face my next challenge. At least I had on dark-wash jeans and updated Keds sneakers today, for this strenuous and potentially messy job.

Up ahead now, a big, soot-stained chamber yawned open and waiting, as if to devour me.

I dragged my three super-sized storage bins another fifteen feet or so, and over the metal threshold of the freight elevator. Original to the factory building, it still operated on a manual rope pulley system. I'd been assured that this did not require too much brawn to operate. A good thing, because I stood only five feet, four inches tall and weighed only about one hundred ten pounds. These days, too much heavy lifting also reminded me, sometimes, that the big 4-0 lay not far in my future.

I pushed an ornate Victorian lever to roll the steel mesh, accordion-style door shut. A single overhead bulb sent down only a very dim glow. Musty basement smells wafted in. I wondered if any rats hung out on this level.

If this were a set for a movie or a play, it would be the ideal spot for the naïve female victim to come to A Very Bad End. I shuddered. *Whatever, Viv. Just don't spend any more time down here than you need to!*

From pulleys high above my head hung two long, sturdy ropes, on my left and right. I tried to remember my instructions—which to pull?

Left to go up, I think, and right to go down.

A tug on the left rope produced no effect at all, even when I hauled with both hands. I tried the other rope with the same lack of result.

Could my load possibly be too heavy? Absurd. Surely, over the past hundred-plus years, hauling military-grade parachute silks, the lift had handled a lot more!

I'd never suffered from serious claustrophobia, but it started to creep up on me now. I checked the primitive control panel and didn't see any kind of alarm button. Of course, I wasn't really *trapped* in this sooty conveyance. I could always exit the way I came in and go for help.

On my first day, though, I didn't want to stand out as "the newbie," and certainly not as a helpless female.

C'mon Viv. What would one of your old-time movie heroines do, like Katherine Hepburn? Or your sort-of namesake, Vivian Leigh? Or even Emma Peel from The Avengers?

Just keep a cool head, and think!

My new landlord, Fred Palasinski, had assured me that despite its age and appearance, the elevator still operated well. Its original designers had equipped it with all the latest safety features of that time, including…

The brake! He told me to always set that when I finished using the lift, and that it wouldn't move either up or down as long as the brake was on.

I searched for a less-obvious third cable, found it, and easily released the car to move. After that, with a moderate pull on the right-hand rope, my merchandise and I began to rise. The brick-lined shaft, framed by ancient steel girders, slipped past so slowly that the trip felt like more than just two floors. And still unnerving, because the mechanism creaked, groaned, and rattled along the way.

But it got me where I needed to go. Rolling back the big door on the second floor felt like a hard-won victory. *Vintage by Vivian*, Booth No. 17 at the Addamsville Antiques Center, would open for business this morning, after all!

This level had a more pleasant aroma, of seasoned old wood, from its scarred oak floors to its high rafters. Over the peacetime decades, it had served various commercial purposes. About ten years ago, it had taken on new life as a mecca for lovers of moderately priced antiques and other collectibles. Now, its two stories accommodated almost fifty booths that overflowed with nostalgic merchandise.

Of the twenty-some vendors who shared the second level with me, most occupied similar twenty-by-twenty spaces along the exterior walls, lit by overhead skylights and whatever lamps we chose to supply. A few who wanted to showcase larger and more valuable pieces paid for extra square footage in the middle of the vast space, where they could create period room settings and other special effects. In spots, you could see and hear what was happening across the way, hampered only by the occasional highboy dresser or decorative screen.

The week before, Fred had helped me bring my the biggest stuff—a 1930s "waterfall" dresser, a rattan loveseat, and a six-foot-tall folding screen. Now I just needed to add the contents of several heavy blanket bags, stuffed with draperies, bedspreads, and tablecloths, and three large plastic storage bins filled with smaller, decorative pieces from the 1940s.

At least the door of that old-fashioned lift didn't close automatically—it stood patiently open while I dragged all of my merchandise out into the aisle. From there, I only had to transport the containers another twenty feet or so. If I had to make a few trips, so be it; I'd already blown my image as a polished, sophisticated antiques dealer. Passing a dresser mirror in another vendor's booth, noticed that my dark, shoulder-length, somewhat retro bob had lost some of its bounce during my labors.

Why the heck hadn't I brought along a hand truck? Oh yeah, because there wasn't room to also fit that into the hatch of my ten-year-old "crossover"-

sized SUV.

I glanced around to see if there might be such a thing nearby, and locked eyes with a sturdy guy who looked in his late twenties. He smiled and crossed the aisle to ask if I needed a hand.

"Oh, thanks." I added, "I'm just moving in, and it took me a while to get the hang of operating the elevator."

"Yeah, she's quite a relic, isn't she? Which is your booth, Seventeen?"

It was a logical guess, as the only display space on this floor was currently untenanted. He hitched one of the bins up to his chest, briefly hiding his T-shirt's garish image of Godzilla on the rampage, and carried it to my space with ease. I toted the second tub, but let my helper also deal with the third. The garment bags presented less of a problem, especially between the two of us.

By then, I must have looked pretty wilted, because my fellow vendor offered me some water. He disappeared back across the aisle, obscured for a moment by other partitions and displays, and returned with two chilled bottles.

"I keep a cooler at my booth," he explained, handing one to me. "There's a vending machine downstairs, by the restrooms, but it runs out a lot."

I thanked him, twisted off the bottle's top, and took a deep swallow.

Much less winded than me, he brushed a thatch of bronze bangs out of his eyes with one hand and offered me the other to shake. "Anyway, welcome to the center. I'm Gerry Rubello."

I returned the gesture. "Vivian Joyce."

Gerry massaged his scraggly blond beard and scanned the larger merchandise I already had on display, as if trying to guess my overall theme. "So you're into…"

"Home décor from the late thirties to early fifties. As you see, I have just a few pieces of furniture, but I'll also carry vintage drapes, artwork, pottery, barware…anything else from the period that's eye-catching and different."

"Cool! We've got a guy downstairs who deals in Mid-Century, but I guess that's a little later…"

"It is, though there's some overlap." I eyed Gerry's campy T-shirt. "What's

your specialty?"

"Pop culture collectibles, early sixties up to the nineties. I've even got kids' lunch boxes and waste baskets that tie in with old cartoons, stuff from TV shows, horror movies…" He puffed out his chest, in case I'd missed the shirt. "I also do pop and rock music memorabilia, from the Beatles on."

"Sounds like a good market," I said.

"It's turning out to be. I started collecting for myself, but ended up with so much stock that it only made sense to get into selling. I sold online first and put myself on the waiting list for a spot here. Most of my customers are Baby Boomers who owned some of that stuff the first time around, but a lot of young kids today are fascinated by it, too. I'm Number 25, over there."

He pointed directly across the vast space, as if he knew I probably couldn't see his booth at the moment. Even standing on my tiptoes wouldn't have helped, because the pegboard walls of many booths reached almost to the ductwork of the ceiling. Only in a few spots could you easily see, and walk, across the expanse of the building's second story.

"My background's pretty much the same," I told Gerry. "I've been selling online for a few years, too, and on consignment through a couple of smaller antique stores. But I live not far from here and have always had my eye on this place. Last week, this booth opened up and I finally got lucky."

"You'll do great, I'm sure," he said, with a grin.

When an old R&B tune sounded from his jeans pocket, Gerry pulled out his cell phone and checked the screen. "I gotta take this. Nice meetin' you, Viv!" As he ambled back across the aisle, I heard him tell someone in a hushed tone, "Yeah, I can talk. What's up?"

Meanwhile, I sifted through my memory bank and identified the distinctive ringtone: "Money," the Motown hit made even more famous by the Beatles.

My own phone told me it was almost quarter to eleven. I'd hoped to have more time to arrange these last pieces before the center opened to customers. *That's assuming they'll arrive in a horde, and all stampede straight for my booth.* I frowned at my own optimism. No doubt I'd still have plenty of time to get organized.

My college art courses, and past jobs in interior design and retail, had not quite prepared me for this challenge—cramming as much merchandise as possible into a fairly tight space, while still making it attractive to customers. I glanced around at the other booths on this floor, which accommodated more than a dozen, and saw about half currently occupied by the proprietors.

Fred, a rangy, mustached man in his sixties, ran the place and handled all sales through his cashier's window downstairs. He only required the vendors to tag each piece of merchandise by booth number and price, and be present in person a few days a week.

When I'd first talked to him about renting a space, about a month earlier, Fred noted that frequent attendance was mostly important for the booths that had locked cases: "Otherwise, if someone wants an item of yours that's locked up, either I or another vendor has to run to get the keys, which takes us away from our own jobs."

I'd assured him he didn't have to worry about that with me, because at the moment, I didn't have any secured cases. It made me wonder, though, if I would need some. The Arts & Crafts booth on this floor, for instance, displayed some of its pottery and silver serving pieces in locked Plexiglas cases, just above eye level.

I had asked Fred tactfully if the antiques center had much of a problem with theft.

"Very little," he'd told me. "It's pretty relaxed here, and the vendors all kind of look out for one another. They do have insurance for their own booths, but few carry anything that's extremely valuable and also easy to steal. Everyone is responsible for the security of their own booth."

Today, I had extra reason to wonder about the effectiveness of that system. The previous week, two masked robbers had knocked over a shopping-mall jewelry store, right across the river in Delaware. A smashed display case had tripped an alarm, and security guards had responded, but the thieves still escaped with a haul of men's designer wristwatches. They'd even shot and wounded one guard in the process.

I remembered all of these details because my sister Mona, a news reporter for the *West Jersey Herald*, did a follow-up with a local angle. She had interviewed shopkeepers in our area who sold similar merchandise, asking if they were concerned and taking any precautions against such robberies. Now I reflected that, for anyone expert and brazen enough to rob a well-guarded chain store in a shopping mall, our antiques center would be child's play. Maybe our best defense is that we didn't sell any of those high-end Rolexes and Omegas.

I shrugged off such worries and got busy staging my display for the hoped-for influx of customers. My rattan loveseat, dressed up with three barkcloth pillows, already occupied a central spot. I unfolded the tall screen, slid it behind the loveseat, and tossed a single barkcloth drapery over it as a backdrop. This thick, pebbly cotton, popular during the World War II era, was one of my specialties. Originally, it had been produced in baroque florals, but during the war years, it sprouted hibiscus flowers, banana leaves, and other exotica that soldiers saw in the Pacific Islands. Toward the 1950s, it also began to include "atomic" and boomerang shapes, as well as surrealistic human figures inspired by the artworks of Jean Arp and Salvador Dali.

I figured whether you were an old-fashioned romantic, an adventurer, or a sci-fi nerd, you could find a barkcloth design to suit your taste. Besides, the stuff was just plain fun!

For spring, I decided to mix various tropical motifs. Against one wall, I had already placed a blanket rack to display folded draperies. Above this, I hung a framed print, in soft, grayed tones that resembled watercolor, of graceful white egrets browsing in a lagoon. The Turner Manufacturing Company of Chicago mass-produced these artworks, which sold through "five and dime" stores in the 1940s and '50s. With their unique, easily recognizable style, they commanded serious prices from collectors today.

On top of a sleek walnut dresser from the thirties, I created a small grouping of floral Roseville pottery, another specialty of mine.

Finally, I felt satisfied that my ten-foot-square booth overflowed, almost literally, with exotic, nostalgic romance. High on one pegboard wall, the only spot that remained empty, I used hooks to hang a three-foot-wide wooden sign. In black art deco lettering on an aqua background, it branded my space as *Vintage by Vivian*.

As I stepped down from my folding stool to judge the effect, I heard a high female voice exclaim from across the aisle, "Ooo, I like!"

Not a customer (rats!), but a fellow vendor, Cindy Metcalf. We had met on one of my earlier visits to scope out the antiques center. A plump, rosy-cheeked woman who might have been fifty, she specialized in Shabby Chic décor and accessories. Personally, I felt that style had become a little clichéd, but since Cindy could afford two adjoining booths the size of mine, I had no right to criticize—she must be doing well.

I remembered one day, when I'd still been browsing as a customer, I had asked Cindy how she got into her specialty.

She smiled at the memory. "I used to work as a secretary in a law office. Very cut-and-dried stuff, but it paid well. Anyway, I lived alone in a small apartment, and found myself collecting these old pillows and throws in faded, soft colors. They really helped me relax when I came home at night—made me feel as if I were living out in the country, or at an earlier time."

"I can imagine." The pieces that I collected and sold certainly give me a taste of romance and adventure, usually missing in my everyday life.

"You might think this style would appeal to sentimental older ladies," Cindy went on, "but often it's the opposite. I have a repeat customer, a computer technician in her twenties, who says she loves to sink into her faded-floral sofa cushions at the end of the day. She drinks tea, watches old-timey mysteries on Acorn, and leaves her work day far behind."

Now I stowed my stepstool and moved to one side, so Cindy could assess my display. "Does this look okay? I've decorated temporary booths before, at some outdoor shows, but I wanted to kick it up a notch for this location."

"It's fun," she reassured me. "So tropical, which will be great for the spring and summer! I like the way you mixed the different floral drapes and pillows, and the birds and the Roseville...even though nothing really *matches*, it all works together."

At that point, Fred also dropped by, in his usual garb of a flannel shirt and corduroy pants, to see how I was settling in. He joked to Cindy, "Doesn't she seem too young to be interested in this era? Most of us here are retirees, like me, who grew up living with the stuff they sell."

I smiled. "Maybe because I *didn't* grow up with it, the period always fascinated me. The designs are so different from anything today! One of my grandmothers had Art Moderne furniture from the 'forties, and flowered barkcloth draperies and pillows. When I visited her as a kid, I always admired them." The memory sobered me. "That could be why, when Nana passed on a couple of years ago, she left most of those things to me in her will."

Cindy's blue eyes rounded. "Wasn't that kind of her!"

"It was. Since my parents didn't want any of it, I moved some into my first apartment and put the rest in storage. That's how I got the idea to start selling vintage."

"Well, welcome aboard," said Fred. "I hope you have a great first week."

Cindy tapped his arm. "Hey, aren't those people from the playhouse supposed to come by one of these days?"

"That's right." His face lit up. "Viv, you could be in luck! They'll be looking for props and costumes for their spring production, some old-fashioned comedy."

"It's a modern play, but it *is* set in the 'forties," Cindy said. "A takeoff on one of those *noir* detective movies. Yes, you definitely need to connect with them!"

"Sounds terrific, thanks for the tip."

Growing up in the next county, and always interested in movies and theater (if only for the set designs), I'd gone to several productions over the decades at the Addamsville Playhouse. The picturesque western New Jersey town, close to the Delaware River, attracted tourists year-round. Back in the heyday of live theater, the playhouse had mounted its own summer stock productions and hosted touring companies from Broadway. Now that people could easily watch heavy drama on cable TV, it still drew decent audiences by offering light, wholesome fare. Such shows appealed to vacationing families and residents of the area's active-adult communities.

"I'll go check what day they said they were coming," Fred told us, as he retreated toward the stairs. "I know I wrote it on my calendar."

While we listened to his steps trotting down to the first floor, Cindy shook her head indulgently. "Fred will only get dragged into the electronic age kicking and screaming, I'm afraid. He even keeps all the accounts in an old-fashioned ledger book." She pulled out her own cell phone and tapped and scrolled until she found the website for the playhouse. "Here's the show they're doing for spring, *Murder Most Noir.*"

She passed me her phone so I could appreciate the play's colorful poster. Sketched in melodramatic 'forties style, it centered upon a dark-haired man and a sultry redhead, both in glamorous evening clothes à la Nick and Nora Charles. He gripped her shoulders angrily, and she raised one hand to ward him off. From the upper right corner, the close-up face of a detective spied on them both, while holding a magnifying glass and wearing a fedora. His chiseled jawline struck me as somehow familiar, but maybe just because it was a common stereotype.

"Looks like a hoot, doesn't it?" said Cindy. "The Broadway production ran for a couple of years and got pretty good reviews. I'm sure this is a different cast, of course."

I scanned the names of the three leads and got a jolt.

*No way! Must be some other—*but when I studied the sketch of the detective's face more closely, I realized it could very well be the same "Edward Kiernan."

My pulse picked up speed. How long had it been, now? Seventeen, eighteen years? If I still thought of him at all, I imagined his life had taken a much different turn than mine, and that our paths would never cross again.

Now, suddenly, he had resurfaced, practically on my home turf. The first guy who had broken my heart.

Chapter Two

All right, I'm being melodramatic...and unfair. Even if "Eddie Kiernan" did break my heart, way back then, I'm sure the poor guy never realized it. That was the problem, in fact—I'd never even been on his radar.

Still fixated on the screen of Cindy's phone, I muttered his name under my breath.

"Yes, how about that? Well, I guess *Boulevard Blues* got canceled—that was his TV series on Starflix. So...now he's doing a play out here in the boonies."

Another surprise. I had heard *of* the series, but never watched it. Starflix was a premium channel, and on my sporadic income, I didn't subscribe to many of those.

"He actually grew up around here," I told Cindy.

"Did he?"

"We went to the same college. He was in all the school plays then, too."

"No kidding!" She took back her phone. "I caught a few episodes of his series. Well, he wasn't *the* star; it was kind of an ensemble cast. Come to think of it, though, he also played a detective in that." She shrugged. "I thought it was pretty good, but you know how fast cable shows come and go these days. Guess it just didn't get the ratings."

Fred tramped back up the wide wooden stairs, his date book in hand. "The theater folks are coming Wednesday morning. At ten, so they'll have an hour to shop before we open to the public."

Cindy elbowed me. "If they use any of your stuff, Vivian, you'll get a mention in the playbill and a half-price ad."

That certainly gave me an incentive. When I'd gone to Addamsville Playhouse shows in the past, I had come home with a substantial pamphlet that credited everyone involved in the production, as well as area merchants who had contributed in some way. With so many businesses trying to save money by going all-digital, I was glad to hear the theater still printed such things.

"A show usually runs three weeks, so those playbills get seen by a few thousand people." Fred also sounded eager to get the name of the antiques center in front of all those eyeballs.

I laughed. "I don't need any more encouragement. I'll be here nice and early on Wednesday!"

Once Cindy and Fred had gone back to their posts, I logged the appointment into my phone's calendar...as if I was likely to forget it. Then I marveled that, in less than twenty years, Ed Kiernan from college had almost faded into the mists of my memory. True, he'd graduated two years before me, and once I entered the work world, I went through a lot of changes that might have left me a little jaded. Trying to "find myself," I'd taken a series of different jobs, moved a few times (thought never too far from my family), and dated several guys not-too-seriously.

Most recently, I was in a relationship with Steve Osler for almost three years, though I never committed as far as to move in with him. We'd never totally clicked, but I tried to make it work. Steve's lack of any real compassion while my mother was dying from cancer, though, had finally convinced me I was better off on my own.

Mom's death also made me reassess my lifestyle up to that point, always at the mercy of unpredictable bosses and landlords. With some money she left me, plus my hoard of Nana's heirlooms, I'd purchased my current condo and decided to go into business for myself.

Five o'clock drew near, and I saw my neighboring vendors closing up shop for the day. I tossed a few fleece throws over my own display and slipped my cash box, with that day's modest take, into my trusty tote bag (crafted from a flowered, early-fifties tablecloth). On my way out the building's front door, I passed the cashier's window, topped by an arch of Victorian millwork, where

Fred sat jotting something in his ledger. I stopped to say goodnight to him, and he asked how I'd enjoyed my first day.

When I told him I'd actually made one sale, he congratulated me. "Towards the weekend, you'll do better," he promised. "Saturday is always busiest. You'll see."

* * *

I had only a fifteen-minute drive home to Hunterdon Village, a condo community populated mostly by youngish professionals. I never used to think of myself as the "condo" type, and after leaving my parents' suburban colonial nest, I'd lived in a succession of older apartments. But when I broke up with Steve, I got the urge to own a home where I'd have a few more amenities and no landlord who could toss me out on a whim.

Now I lived almost equally distant from my father, my sister, and my new workplace. My unit was on the ground floor, but because the community was gated, I didn't worry much about security, and I could easily haul merchandise out to my car in the nearby lot. Hunterdon Village even provided an outdoor pool and a "park-like setting" (according to the brochure), where I could stroll when I needed to chill out, or swim or jog if I felt more ambitious. Neighbors sometimes waved when we crossed paths, but mostly kept to themselves, which was fine with me.

My two-bedroom unit had come as a blank slate, but with my love of quirky décor I soon livened it up. The guest bedroom also served as my sewing/computer workspace. My patio gave me room outdoors to garden a bit, something I had missed while living in apartments. Now, in warm weather, I grow hibiscus and hydrangeas in pots, and ferns and spider plants in hanging baskets. In winter, I could just move these inside the glass slider doors.

The community did have an ordinance about letting animals run loose, but I was used to that kind of thing—at my last walk-up, the landlady had forbidden any cats or dogs. To get around that rule, I'd acquired Aramis, a classic gray-and-white cockatiel with a yellow face and orange cheeks.

Definitely an indoor pet, as long as I made sure to shut him in his cage before I opened those patio sliders!

And the bright little bird had proven to be great company. Tonight, as I unlocked my front door after a full day of "vending," he greeted me with a shrill wolf whistle.

I had to laugh. "Aramis, you always make me feel appreciated!" I hung my shoulder bag on a foyer coat stand and headed for the dining alcove of my kitchen. There, the setting sun that streamed in through the sliders seemed to gild his five-foot-tall cage.

At my approach, Aramis shrieked with delight, or maybe just impatience to be fed. Of course, he'd get his dinner before I got mine. I set down my tote and poured him some seed; as he started to eat, I lightly stroked the crest of gray-and-yellow feathers that stood straight up on his head. (This flamboyant headdress had inspired me to name him after one of the Three Musketeers.)

I left his cage open at the top, so whenever he finished eating, he could go for a whirl around the condo. Heck, I wouldn't want to be confined to a cage all day, either. Though maybe his spacious enclosure actually gave Aramis more "wing room" than my ten-by-ten booth at the antiques center gave me!

I didn't feel like cooking, so I chose a savory Greek-inspired frozen dinner and popped it into the microwave. Once it was ready, I dished it out onto one of my "everyday" plates, part of a 1950s Franciscan Starburst ceramic set that also had belonged to Nana, my paternal grandmother.

By that time, my feathered friend took advantage of his freedom to cruise around a bit. He knew better than to bother me while I was eating, but alighted on the back of the kitchen chair opposite mine, where he warbled happily to himself. The lonely little dude obviously felt like conversation, so while I dined on my casserole of broccoli, chickpeas, sweet potatoes, and feta cheese, I filled him in on my day.

"Yes, everybody at the new place was very nice to me, thanks for asking. I talked with two of the other vendors. Only made one sale, near closing time, but it *could* lead to another. A very handsome guy around my age, wearing a pink polo shirt and khakis, bought one of my throw pillows."

Beady eyes riveted to my face, Aramis fanned his crest in excitement.

"Good start, huh? He was getting pretty serious about some draperies, too, so he must be a barkcloth fan."

The little bird bobbed his head eagerly, counterbalanced on the chair back by his long, slim tail.

"Finally, he said he didn't want to make such a big purchase without input from his partner, Jim, but they both might come by this Saturday."

My cockatiel's crest deflated.

"I know, bad news for my social life, right? But still promising for my bank account." I finished my light meal and deposited my plate in the sink, since modern dishwashers can be rough on vintage dinnerware. "How was your day, buddy? I see the landscapers finally got around to mowing the lawn. Hope that wasn't too noisy for you."

He answered with a series of sharp clucks, which might have expressed his annoyance.

I opened my laptop on the kitchen table to check for any online orders or responses to my latest blog. Before I could even power it up, though, my phone played the cheery, ragtime strains of my latest ringtone: "Everything Old is New Again," from the movie *All That Jazz*.

At least one actual human being also wanted to hear about my first day at the antiques center—my dad.

Maybe because I was a few years younger, a few inches shorter, and a bit more introverted than my sister Mona, my parents always had been more protective of me. She got to take more risks, while they always urged me to play it safe.

Mona grew up while my father was still a news editor at the *West Jersey Herald*, sometimes tagged along with him to the office, and eventually followed him into journalism. When my talents led me in a different direction, Dad saw me as an artsy daydreamer who'd probably never be able to support herself. He liked it best when I was apprenticing with some well-known interior designer or had a steady job with a big chain furniture store. If I complained about being bored or frustrated in those roles, he accused me of having my head in the clouds. Mom's death had only made him more concerned for my welfare, especially when I'd decided to strike out on my own.

My recent decision to take a space at the antique center did seem to calm him down a little. Tonight I gave him about the same rundown as I had to Aramis, and Dad sounded satisfied. "Well, that place has been in Addamsville for at least twenty years, I think, so they must do a good business. And you can sell some of your Nana's stuff there?"

"I brought in her highboy—you know, that little walnut dresser she kept in the hall?—and some of her pottery. A few of her Roseville pieces I'm always going to keep for myself, because I like them so much."

I'd been named for his mother, Nana Vivian, who in turn had been named for *Gone with the Wind* actress Vivian Leigh. Early on, my parents started to call me Viv, to avoid confusion between Nana and me.

"Should be a nice, quiet place to work, anyhow," Dad said. "I wish your sister would find something to do at the *Herald* besides the crime beat."

Our father had spent more than a decade with the paper as an investigative reporter, himself, even garnering a couple of statewide awards for his stories. Now he was trying to rein in Mona? *Good luck with that!* "C'mon, Dad. You know she loves covering hard news, even the late deadlines. She gets a rush out of it."

"Maybe too much. She's got a story in today about a pawn shop that was robbed, just a couple of towns away. Two guys with masks and guns came in, middle of the day, and made the owner open up his cases. I guess while they were shoveling the stuff into a bag, the owner managed to trigger an alarm. But by the time the cops showed up, the robbers were long gone."

"That is unusual, for this area," I admitted.

"The cops think it's a ring, that these same guys pulled the smash-and-grab last month at Martinson's Jewelry, across the river. That place had better security, but it was also right on the highway. They shot it out in the parking lot with the security guards."

"So I heard, that sounded pretty scary. But like you said, it was in Delaware. Why would you be concerned that Mona—"

"Her byline's on today's story, Viv. What if one of these robbers thinks that she knows too much? She works out of the main *Herald* office. They could wait for her some night, and—"

"Dad, I doubt that a couple of guys on the lam would attack a reporter and call even more attention to themselves. They've probably gone deep into hiding, or even left the area."

He sighed on the line. "I guess you're right. And at least she's got Artie there with her, even if they don't always work the same hours."

My older sister had been married for about two years to Art Rodriguez, a sports writer she'd met at the paper. At least that had relieved Dad's fears that Mona would be an "old maid," though now he worried that both she and Artie kept themselves too busy to start a family.

Since my adolescence, I had envied Mona's courage, independence, and even physical style. She took after Dad with her tall, lean frame, and on her more stylish days reminded me of the classy-but-tough dames from the old movies that she, Nana, and I used to watch together on cable TV—an updated Katherine Hepburn or Rosalind Russell.

In spirit, too, Mona took after our mother, who had organized a few protests about public issues, in her day, and would call out a local politician at a town meeting for promising changes he had never delivered. Our mom had shown the same kind of courage in her long, valiant battle against ovarian cancer.

I recalled now that even Nana Vivian, whom I resembled more closely, served as an army nurse in France during WWII. She had saved lives over there, survived to tell the tale, and came home to New Jersey to start a family.

Whether or not Dad appreciated it, we Joyce women seemed to be a tough breed. I reminded him, "Mona's just following in your footsteps."

"I know, but that's why I got out of the business after I had you kids. With the crazy hours and the pressure, and the phone calls I got from some of those sleazebags I exposed..." Accepting Mona's choices, for the time being, he swung his attention back to me. "What about the antiques center, Viv? Do they have any fancy stuff these guys might come after?"

I'd scoped out the place pretty thoroughly before I'd even signed the lease, and had a ready answer. "Very little. There's one woman who carries a lot of flashy costume jewelry, but it's all fake. She doesn't even keep it in cases while she's there, just spreads it out on a couple of tables." I also repeated what Fred had told me earlier, that the vendors didn't carry much that would tempt a really discerning thief.

Except when it came to furniture, which could hardly fit into a pocket or even a tote bag!

My father didn't sound totally convinced. "Well, the sellers and you may know that, but not someone from the outside. Anyway, be careful. You and Mona are all I've got now, and I don't want to lose either of you."

Ironically, Dad still had a lot going for him—a full head of silver hair, a firm jawline, and even a trimmer waist since he had retired from his high-pressure desk job. Now that he'd been windowed for years, Mona and I often wished he would turn more of his attention toward some females his own age, instead of micro-managing our lives.

I told him, "I appreciate your concern, Dad, but—*ouch*! Aramis is tugging on my earring..."

"Who? Oh, the bird."

"He gets some chopped fruit at night, and I guess I'm behind schedule. Anyway, I gotta go. Love you!"

My cockatiel, perched decoratively on his cage several feet away, tilted his head at me.

"I know, you didn't do a thing," I apologized. "I just wanted to get off the phone."

This time, his staccato clucks definitely sounded like laughter.

Chapter Three

When I parked at the antiques center the next morning, I spotted Gerry Rubello in a far corner of the lot, talking with a taller man who also looked a few years older. Gerry leaned against what I assumed to be his own black Trans Am, a golden Firebird spreading its wings across the hood. His dark-haired friend seemed to have left a beefy motorcycle parked half under the trees. They talked in low tones, and as I passed on the sidewalk, Gerry shot me a wary-looking glance over his shoulder.

Remembering how helpful he had been when I moved all my merchandise in, I smiled as I passed him. "Hi, Gerry!"

He reacted with a start, then a brisk nod. Almost as if he had never seen me before, or wished I hadn't seen him. He and the other man then retreated farther back toward the sports car to finish their conversation.

Weird. Does Rubello think the straight-arrow new girl might report back that he was goofing off, instead of manning his booth? As if Fred, or anyone else, cares what Gerry does with his time!

It's not like I even overheard what he and his pal were talking about.

Inside and upstairs, at No. 17, I started the work day with a flourish by stripping off the fleece throws. Then I took both still shots and a short video of my booth to post on my website and my blog. It seemed a good time to take care of that chore, as I'd been told that mid-week days tended to be quiet in terms of customers.

Next, I took a stroll around the rest of the second floor. I was already familiar with most of the other booths, having visited the center as a customer in the past. The displays varied widely in terms of neatness, organization, and professionalism. Some gave off a rummage-sale ambience, as if the vendors had just emptied their attics, selected anything quirky, and labeled it with a rock-bottom price. The more interesting booths, though, emphasized at least two or three specialties, such as old sheet music, magazines, and books; country-kitchen furniture and utensils; or vintage dolls, toys, and games.

One vendor concentrated year-round on 1950s Christmas ornaments, Santa and reindeer figures, and other types of Noel nostalgia. Another displayed old, salvaged railroad signs and a multi-level Lionel track with two highly detailed model trains. When activated, they chugged through miniature forested hills and past a quaint, European-style village.

Beneath the banner of *Baubles and Bangles*, I paused to admire a glittering array of costume jewelry. Here and there, a mannequin bust wore an especially nice necklace, or a swatch of velveteen stretched within a gilded frame showcased assorted scatter pins. I noticed, though, that even the fanciest designs bore very reasonable prices. Across the rest of the table, stone and bead necklaces and bracelets lay grouped according to color (turquoise, coral, ivory) or era (Art Deco, ladylike-glam fifties, psychedelic seventies). A tiny easel held the vendor's business cards, and I read her name—*Ronnie Holbrook*. I already knew the shaggy-haired, twenty-something woman by sight, but she didn't seem to be around at the moment.

I heard Gerry's voice from the next booth over and glanced that way. He stooped beside a boy of about twelve, explaining the significance of a bright-yellow *Camp Crystal Lake* T-shirt.

"I can't believe you've never seen *Friday the 13th!*" Gerry laid it on a bit thick. "You've got to check it out—it's awesome!"

"Maybe." The boy sounded noncommittal. "I'm more into sci-fi monsters."

Gerry pawed further through his rack of T-shirts. "How about *Rodan*? Way before your time, but it's still fun. Or *The Thing*? This is the remake from the '80s…"

"Yeah, I saw that one." More enthusiastically, the boy added, "It was really sick!"

Before long, Gerry had made the sale and even stuck to his price when his young customer tried to bargain him down. Well, I guessed if you were a soft touch, you wouldn't last long in the childhood-nostalgia business. I also recalled, from the day before, Gerry's blatantly capitalistic ringtone.

Crossing back to booth 17, I passed a more expansive display in the middle of the floor. This one concentrated on high-quality Arts & Crafts pieces—ceramics, textiles, and sturdy oak furniture—all from the early 1900s. Like me, this vendor had given her space the look of a furnished room. William Morris draperies mounted on a pipe frame served as a backdrop for a Mission-style bookcase, settee, and rocker. A few pottery bowls rested on top of an old trunk, and a group of vases topped the bookcase; I could see other fine pieces displayed inside.

Roseville. Older and pricier than the period I collected, with symmetrical designs and earthy tones that blended well with the Craftsman pieces.

From one shallow bowl, I picked up the vendor's card. *Kaye Burrell, Antiques,* plus a website address and email. I had seen the chic, mid-fortyish proprietor in her booth on one of my earlier trips, but so far never had a chance to talk with her.

Back at my own post, just after noon, I settled on my loveseat to eat the sandwich and drink from the thermos I'd brought with me. (After Gerry's warning, I'd decided not to rely on the center's vending machines.)

If a prospective customer paused by my booth, I got up to greet them and recited my chirpy line about how everything dated from the early 1930s to the early 1950s. That fanned the interest for some. Now and then, a visitor would comment that they'd seen draperies or a side table like that in their grandmother's living room. But while they might smile fondly at those memories, none stayed very long that day or even checked the prices on my wares. My earlier buoyant mood darkened somewhat, but the antiques center stayed open until five, and I was determined to stick it out to the end.

I reminded myself that tomorrow should be more promising, providing the set and costume people from the playhouse did show up. If they intended to come by ten, I'd make it in by nine-thirty. Fred had said lending even one or two pieces to the theater for its spring production would get me a credit line and a discounted ad in the playbill, great publicity for both my booth and my online sales. Plus, I might hear some more gossip about Eddie Kiernan, and how he'd segued from a cable TV series to doing community theater back on his home turf.

As closing time neared, I settled once again on my loveseat, bolstered by plump pillows in exotic floral prints, and checked my text messages. One from Mona brightened my outlook.

Sorry, I was out of touch yesterday—breaking story. Dad told me your first day went pretty well, though. Treat you to dinner tonight?

Sounds wonderful, I answered. *Just let me stop home first to freshen up and feed Aramis. Maybe six-thirty at Applegarth's?*

A minute later, I got her response. *Great, meet you there. It'll take me a while, anyway, to wrap up here. Meanwhile, in case you missed it, here's my front-pager from today.*

I opened the attached link to her story:

LOCAL PAWN SHOP HEIST MAY BE LINKED TO DELAWARE ROBBERY, by Mona Joyce.

I'd read only a paragraph or two before the article struck a more personal note for me. When Mona identified the victims of the attack as Betty and Al Kramer, I realized I knew the couple. I'd only driven past their Jonesburg shop once or twice, I guess, without making the connection. But I'd taken a table next to theirs one summer at a street fair, and another time I'd run into Betty at an estate sale. In each case, we'd chatted and I'd gotten the impression of them as interesting, well-traveled, funny, and all-around-nice people.

On an impulse, I searched for their number online, but found only the one for their business. When I called that, I got no answer and couldn't leave a message—the mailbox was full.

They're probably besieged right now! Not only by press, but by friends and relatives who, like me, just read the story in the paper. I'd like to tell them how sorry I am, but why add to the chaos? I'll wait and try again to reach them after the excitement has died down.

* * *

An hour later, at the restaurant, my sister and I toasted each other with glasses of Chablis.

"To your new job," she said.

"And to your front-page byline," I added.

A fully liberated 21st-century woman, Mona had kept her maiden name after marriage. She sometimes joked that Artie had kept his, also. Except for our coloring—pale skin, dark eyes, and hair—Mona and I contrasted in appearance. I had always envied her elegant, almost Kate Hepburn features. At a good five-eight, she looked great in the tailored pantsuits and smooth, bobbed haircuts that worked for her fast-paced job.

"Happy as I am that you got a front-page story, it upset me to hear the Kramers got robbed." I explained how I'd gotten to know them, a bit, over the years. "They're both such sweet people. Do the cops really think the guys who hit their shop are the same ones who robbed that highway store?"

"There were differences, for sure," Mona admitted. "In the Delaware job, the pair worked fast. The one with the gun threatened to shoot anybody who tripped an alarm. Meanwhile, his buddy used a hammer to smash just one case, with high-end watches. What he didn't know was that it also set off an alarm at the security company. Anyhow, he scooped the watches into a bag, and both guys ran back out to their car. Two security guards pulled up, shots were fired on both sides, and one guard took a bullet in the stomach. But the thieves got away in a plain, dark sedan, and no one noticed the make of the car or a license plate."

I shook my head in wonder. "Don't those places have security cameras? Wouldn't they at least have video of the break-in?"

"The guys both wore masks over their lower faces. And they mostly stayed near the one case, so I guess the cameras didn't get much."

Over our salads, Mona added that the wounded security guard in the first robbery had surgery and was expected to recover. "So at least the shooter won't be charged with murder."

"If those Delaware thieves were looking for top-notch merchandise, why would they hit a pawn shop?" I wondered aloud.

"The cops are thinking this is part of a larger ring, and maybe they have buyers for different types of jewelry," Mona explained, while stabbing a forkful of romaine lettuce with blue cheese dressing. "At any rate, the pawn shop made an easier target. It has security gates at night, but the robbers came during the afternoon. They grabbed the wife and forced the husband to open the cases they wanted—jewelry, again. At least they didn't hurt anyone this time, but after they left, and the wife called 911, the husband was taken to the hospital with chest pains. Last I heard, he's doing better, so he should survive, too."

"Glad to hear that, anyway!" No surprise that the Kramers weren't picking up their calls, if Al had to be rushed to the ER. I hated to think of my elderly friends going through such an ordeal. They'd probably have to shut down their business, at least for a short while. Though they were around retirement age, no doubt they still depended on that shop for at least part of their income. "Were they able to describe the robbers?"

"Masked, again. But by their heights and builds, they do sound like the same two who did the Delaware job."

"I don't like the thought that they're getting closer to Addamsville," I told her, with a grimace. "Jonesburg is just a mile away. Dad's afraid the robbers will come after you, now, because you're writing the story."

Mona scoffed at this idea, as I'd known she would. "More likely, these jerks are thrilled to be on the front page of the *Herald*. After all, they pulled off a pretty big job without too many hitches. They did wound a security guard, but it could've been worse."

Yes, I thought, the robbers probably would take that cynical attitude. "And I guess big mall jewelry stores have insurance to cover this kind of thing."

"They do, so they'll get their money back. Your friends with the pawn shop may not be so lucky."

The waitress brought our dinners, and we ordered more wine to go with them. I savored the first few bites of my Cajun Salmon, and Mona started on her Chicken Parmesan. Meanwhile, I finally gave her the rundown on my colleagues at the antiques center and my few sales so far. I also told her some news I hadn't shared with our father—that staffers from the Addamsville Playhouse would be coming to scout for props and costumes Wednesday morning.

"They want stuff that looks like it could be from the 'forties." I also explained about the advertising perks.

"That would be so cool!" said Mona. "And I'm sure it would be fun to see some of your things used onstage, too. Almost like having someone you know in the cast, right?"

"As a matter of fact…" I'd been of two minds whether to bring up Edward Kiernan, but couldn't resist this opening. I told Mona about his starring role in the upcoming stage play, and reminded her about my tenuous college connection with him.

She stopped a forkful of cheesy chicken on the way to her mouth. "It's the same guy? I remember in college you were always working backstage on the theater productions, painting sets, or sewing costumes. Mom, Dad, and I went to a couple of the shows. But even if I saw this Kiernan in some of them, after all these years, I probably wouldn't recognize him or even make the connection."

"Did you ever watch *Boulevard Blues*?" My sister was a bigger fan of cop shows than me and subscribed to more cable channels.

She chewed and swallowed before nodding. "Artie and I caught that a couple of times and liked it all right. One of those ensemble casts, so the emphasis shifted among the characters. If you had a picture of Kiernan, I probably could tell you what role he played."

I found the theater's promo on my phone and showed her.

"O-kay, yeah…he was the police detective," she confirmed. "Not the biggest role, but pretty important. Too bad the show got canceled, though I guess it's a nice break for the playhouse to get him." As she handed back my phone, Mona squinted shrewdly at me. "I get the feeling you had a thing for this guy. Did you date him?"

I felt heat rise to my face. "Are you kidding? He was a senior when I was a sophomore. Besides, if you remember, I was a mess back then. About twenty pounds heavier, with a bad, bushy haircut and still wearing braces."

"Gee, I forgot you had braces for that long. Mom always said you got her small jaw. They weren't that bad, though, Viv. You were still cute, hardly 'a mess'! Was this Ed such an Adonis?"

"Well, no…at least, not the way you probably mean. He wasn't very tall, and not the jock type or even your typical leading man. But he had his own kind of charisma, especially onstage. He could sing, do physical comedy, anything. And he was just…popular."

Mona smiled sympathetically. "Had all the other girls chasing after him?"

"Enough of them, and he also had a steady girlfriend. We didn't see her much, because she went to some private college in Philadelphia, but everybody knew Ed was taken. It was kind of a joke that he didn't run around on Janet." I smiled sadly at the memory. Just one more way in which he had seemed almost too good to be true.

In fact, I had sighted Janet a couple of times, when she'd come to see Ed backstage after our shows. I'd been surprised that she was so plain—as short as me, with straight, mouse-brown hair, drab clothes and no visible makeup. She also seemed very quiet, not mixing easily with the more outgoing theater types. In the back of my mind, I think I realized, even then, that Janet and I had some things in common.

But oddly, that made me even less eager to try to steal Ed away from her. If she'd been lucky enough to win his heart, who was I to mess that up?

"Well, that was a long time ago," Mona pointed out. "You're not that shy college girl anymore, Viv. You've made a good life for yourself, and even looks-wise you got it goin' on these days! Unless he ended up marrying this mysterious Janet, maybe give Ed another try."

"Oh, please." *A Hollywood actor? If he was out of my league in college, he'll be much more so now! At this point, the closest I can hope to get to him will probably be a mezzanine seat for* Murder, Most Noir.

To cut off any more suggestions, I told Mona, "Frankly, after all the crap I went through with Steve, I'm not in a hurry to get involved again with anyone."

26

Mona had listened to me complain about Osler and had backed my decision to cut him loose. Now, having made better progress on her meal than me during our conversation, she offered more reassurance. "I could see early on that you two weren't a good fit, Sis. I think even Dad ended up sorry he ever pushed you two together. Steve was kind of...well, a bore."

"You thought so, too?" I felt a little betrayed. "Why didn't you ever say so?"

"Hey, I wasn't going to interfere in your relationship. You seemed pretty into him, at first."

Steve worked for the firm that handled our family's, and Dad saw him as a solid, sensible guy and a potential good provider. The fact that he was also tall, dark, and good-looking biased me in his favor, initially. But Steve turned out to be "old-fashioned" in a much different way from me—traditional, unadventurous, unimaginative. He didn't like me challenging any of his opinions, and thought it childish if I did anything quirky or impulsive. I'm sure when I finally called it quits, that just convinced him he'd been right all along.

I finished off the last of my wine and complained to Mona, "Why is it so hard to find a guy who's creative, imaginative, and just...fun?"

My sister smiled. "You forgot to add, 'and also straight.'"

"True. Gay men make great friends, but—! Of course, I also want to date men in my age bracket. It seems like even guys who have some spunk when they're younger get it all pounded out of them by forty."

"I hear you," said my sister. "What attracted me to Artie was his energy and enthusiasm, even if he usually directs them toward the latest win by the Devils or the Giants. But occasionally he does aim them towards me!"

"More than occasionally, I'm sure," I told her, with a laugh.

Also, halfway through her second glass of wine, Mona turned philosophical. "Remember, Dad introduced you to Steve not long after Mom got sick. That news threw you into a tailspin—we could all see it—and Dad probably thought you needed someone who could take care of you."

Looking back, I could see how my emotional state at the time might have influenced my father's choice. "But that was five years ago, and I'm well over thirty now. I make my own living, I'm in good health, and I have my own home! What I need most is someone to hang out with, have fun with…"

In my mind, I added…*and to love*.

A nod from my sister. "You're not his timid little girl anymore, and you're perfectly able to take care of yourself."

"Thanks for the pep talk, Sis." I toasted her with the last of my wine. "And the best way to do that, right now, will be to make a success of my business. Tomorrow, I'll try to persuade the folks from *Murder Most Noir* to borrow some of my wares for their production. That could get my new venture off to a roaring start!"

Chapter Four

The next morning, after showering and eating breakfast, I stepped back into my tapered, black ankle-length pants and low platform sandals. They would let me stand, walk, and bend comfortably during my six-hour shift,which could stretch to seven that day, since I planned to show up early. I added a retro red cardigan, with three-quarter sleeves and a beaded appliqué of a long-tailed bird diving down from each shoulder. Even if I buttoned it all the way up, the bird design still made it a little sexy.

Ordinarily, I didn't wear much makeup. I'd never smoked, imbibed heavily, or spent much time sunbathing, so my skin had held up pretty well. But today I accented my eyes with a little liner and mascara, fluffed some pink over my cheeks, and went for redder-than-usual lipstick to match the cardigan. For hectic, no-nonsense days, I often pulled my thick hair into a topknot, but today I parted it deep on one side to play up the natural waves. A pair of red Bakelite hoops on my ears capped off the 'forties vibe.

In my dresser mirror, I looked right at home against the backdrop of my bedroom, with its pastel chenille spread, Turner print of cockatoos over the headboard, and barkcloth draperies patterned with oversized fronds. Steve used to turn up his nose at my vintage décor, complaining that it reminded him of an old lady's house. He'd even suggested it switched off his libido, and after a while, his criticisms started to switch off mine.

A glance at the clock told me not to linger on those unpleasant memories or to fuss any more with my appearance. I wanted to be at the antiques center by at least nine-thirty!

In the kitchen, I grabbed a sandwich, an energy bar, and a water bottle from the refrigerator, tucked them into an insulated lunch bag, and dropped that into my flowered tote. I stopped by the birdcage to give Aramis a little more seed, then posed for him and asked, "What d'ya think, boy?"

His distinctive wolf whistle sent me off in high spirits.

Not having any merchandise to load in that day, I enjoyed the luxury of entering Addamsville Antiques by the ground-level front door. I figured it would be left open, since Fred expected the theater folk at ten. He already puttered behind the sales counter, hunting for something in one of his black metal file cabinets. As Cindy had mentioned, he was analog all the way in his record-keeping, though the vendors admitted that he very rarely made an error.

Fred and I traded cheery good mornings. On my way to the wide main staircase, I took stock of which first-floor tenants had come in early. Ben and Sally Lederman already bustled around their double booth, which made sense. They specialized in vintage clothing—no doubt, the theater's costume designer would head their way immediately.

I climbed the weathered oak stairs and found the second level nearly deserted, though at least Fred had turned the lights on. One of the burly Randolph brothers, who specialized in old-style military and police memorabilia, opened the tentlike flaps in front of that space. At No. 22, just down the row from me, dapper, silver-haired Adrian Marcus polished the top of an oval Art Deco coffee table. He might be my toughest competition today, since a lot of his items also would be the right period for *Murder Most Noir*.

I reached my booth, gave it a quick glance to make sure nothing looked disturbed, and dropped my tote out of sight in a corner. I was fluffing up the loveseat's pillows for best effect when a piercing voice behind me cried out, "There you are!"

That baffled me. Since the center did not open to the public for another hour and a half, I could hardly be considered late for anything. But Kaye Burrell, in flowy gray pants and a matching jacket, approached me across the aisle. Her finely chiseled face wore an acid smile.

In case she might have mistaken me for some arch-enemy from her past, I put out my hand and introduced myself.

The taller brunette ignored my gesture. "I know who you are. And this is your booth, of course."

With the art deco *Vintage by Vivian* wall sign and the bowl full of business cards, I couldn't exactly deny it. "Is anything wrong?"

"I'm just curious about something," Kaye purred, more like a leopard than a pussycat. "That's an impressive display of pottery you've got, on that small dresser. I'm surprised you don't have it in a more prominent spot."

"Thank you…well, it's a tight space. I'll probably keep moving things around to see what works best. This is only my second day."

"Mmm. You work fast, don't you?"

I could tell she didn't mean that as a compliment and felt more confused than ever.

Kaye eased behind the loveseat for a closer look at the highboy dresser and squinted behind her rectangular-framed eyeglasses. "I was especially intrigued by this piece. Where on earth did you find it?"

She pointed to a vase near the front, about eight inches tall with slender handles down each side; they flanked small yellow flowers that rose on delicate stems, against a clay-pink background. The craftsmanship and depth of color marked it as authentic Roseville. But I'd never seen this particular vase before, or even one quite like it.

I stammered. "Gosh, I-I don't know how… That's funny! I mean, I didn't—"

Kaye snatched the piece from my display. "I saw you nosing around everyone's booths yesterday. Obviously, you saw this among my things and decided to add it to your collection! Maybe you thought you could sell it before I realized it was gone?"

Her accusation unnerved me almost as much as if it had been true. "No, absolutely not! I would never—"

"You've got a good eye, for sure. This is a rare, experimental piece, worth thousands. It doesn't even have the Roseville name on the bottom, just a serial number. But you probably already checked that, didn't you? When you removed my label!"

Her angry tone must have carried throughout the vast, quiet building, because a second later Fred came jogging up the stairs, "Hey, hey, what's going on up here?"

My face felt hot with shame, and I struggled against tears of outrage. "Kaye seems to think I stole one of her pieces and was trying to pass it off as mine. That's not true! I guess it somehow got mixed in with my vases, but I was just as surprised to see it there as she was."

"Oh, I'll bet." The older woman planted one hand on her hip and scowled at me.

Fred seemed unsure which of us to believe. "Even if you'd tried to do that, Vivian," he reminded me, "it wouldn't have worked. Every piece is noted, with the vendor's name and the price, in my record book. If a customer brought it downstairs to purchase it, Kaye still would have gotten the sale."

He had explained that system to me when I'd leased my booth, though I'd temporarily forgotten. Feeling bolstered, I turned back to Kaye. "You see? It wouldn't even have done me any good!"

Gloating, Kaye upended the vase to show Fred the bottom. "But the label for this one is missing, see?"

"Did you forget..." he began.

"Of course not. I've had this vase for at least two months, and I distinctly remember labeling, recording, and photographing it."

I saw no way to prove I hadn't removed her label, but Fred remained unruffled. Turning away, he carefully scanned the expanse of rough-hewn floor between my booth and Kaye Burrell's. In less than a minute, he spotted the small white adhesive label curled up and hiding under a footstool...near the front of Burrell's booth.

Fred handed the scrap to Kaye so she could confirm her own printing, and she flushed.

"That sticky backing does dry up over time," he reminded her. "Tell you what I think happened: A customer wandered through picking things up at random...maybe looked at Roseville in both of your booths. They were thinking of buying this vase, and carried it around for a while, but at the last minute changed their minds. So they went to put it back..."

I finished the thought for him. "But they didn't remember which booth it came from, and the label had fallen off, so they just stuck it in front of *my* Roseville pieces. Sure, that makes perfect sense."

We all heard the bells above the front door jingle, and a robust male voice called out, "Hello-o!" Since it was still before our regular hours, and casual customers usually didn't announce themselves, that got Fred's attention.

"Coming!" he called back, then told us, "I've got to go deal with the theater people, but...are we all good here, ladies?"

Though Kaye seemed disappointed not to have caught me in any criminal activity, she relented. "The lax security in this place, Fred! Your hypothetical customer could just as easily have stashed the vase in a bag and walked out with it."

His reply, while tactful, carried some bite. "Then maybe you shouldn't leave something so pricey out in the open, Kaye. Put it in one of your locked showcases."

She seemed to be in a fighting mood and wouldn't let the issue drop. Even as Fred turned to go back downstairs, she scolded him, "Our surveillance system is outdated and half the cameras don't work anymore. I hope you heard, Fred, about that robbery across the river this week. 'Locked showcases' didn't stop those thieves."

He clasped one of Kaye's slender hands between both of his own, in a fatherly gesture. "I don't think you need to worry about either of those gentlemen causing trouble here. I really can't see them holding you at gunpoint and stealing one of your vases! Rolexes are a lot easier to fence, my dear, on the open market."

I faced back toward my own booth to hide my smile from Kaye.

Knowing she had been put in her place, Burrell finally retreated to her own side of the aisle and let Fred continue down the main staircase.

Back in my own area, I sank down on my loveseat, still a bit shaken. I'd faced some sniping and competition when I worked for interior designers, and even at big furniture chains, but I had expected things to be more congenial here.

Thank God for Fred's low-tech accounting system! A pretty smart way, really, to make sure no vendor can benefit from selling someone else's wares. As Cindy suggested, though, he might at least computerize it.

It took me a few minutes to remember that the customers I most wanted to deal with had already started doing business on the lower level of the center. I presumed I could safely leave my booth for a while—Kaye wouldn't dare play any nasty tricks on me, after Fred had just put her in her place. En route to the main staircase, I passed Cindy's booth and checked my reflection in the ornately framed mirror of a Shabby Chic dresser. At least being accused of grand larceny hadn't smeared my mascara or made my hair actually stand on end.

In front of the sales counter, Fred was talking with a tall, slender black man who wore dark jeans and a zip-necked, fleece pullover—casual but well-tailored at the same time. I heard our landlord call him "Tom" and knew I'd lucked out. This must be Tom Richardson, the set designer for the playhouse; I'd read his name in programs but had never seen him in person.

Unfortunately, Adrian Marcus had gotten to him first, and in cultivated tones described the mint-condition Art Deco and Art Moderne furniture he could provide.

"Much of the play takes place in the apartment of a wealthy Hollywood couple, doesn't it?" he asked.

"It does," Tom confirmed, with a smile. "But they don't have the best of taste, so some of your things might be a little *too* high-quality. We'll see, though..."

Fred, bless him, gave me a little push between my shoulder blades. "Vivian here is our newest vendor, Tom, and you'll also want to have a look at her booth. She's got some terrific accessories from that period, very colorful."

I described my draperies, throw pillows, and wall art. "If you want a Hollywood vibe, Tom...some of it's very theatrical. I think it would make a great impact onstage."

That seemed to interest Richardson even more than the pedigrees of Marcus' French imports. "Sounds promising! Are you two both upstairs? Well, first let me have a quick look around down here..."

I watched him go with a little more confidence, reminding myself that

Murder Most Noir was a comedy, and just might call for some décor on the wild side. Meanwhile, I'd grown aware of some lively conversation halfway down the aisle from us, in the Ledermans' curtained twenty-foot-square space. Their booth featured menswear on one side and ladies' fashions on the other, though Sally had once joked that customers could try on whatever they wanted, no questions asked. I assumed Lauren Murdock, costume designer for the playhouse, must be browsing through their offerings.

I had never met her and wouldn't have recognized her voice, but a woman declared in lilting tones, "The hat is key, really. It's got to be iconic…very Bogie, very Sam Spade."

"Oh, we've got fedoras of all kinds," said Ben. "What's your size?"

"Darned if I know!" said another man. "Can't remember the last time I wore anything but a knitted, winter hat. Medium, I guess."

That voice was familiar. *Could it be—?*

"Try this one," said Sally.

As if killing time until Richardson was ready for me, I drifted casually down the aisle, past mostly unoccupied booths. The Ledermans kept their area curtained on three sides, so they could hang more clothes for display, and customers could try things on in privacy. At first, I could see only Lauren—a slim, fortyish blonde, elegant even in faded jeans and espadrilles—because she had backed into the aisle. I shifted my vantage point until I could spy on long-skirted, Bohemian Sally, who adjusted a gray fedora on a man with wavy auburn hair. He wasn't too tall, so she had no trouble reaching his head. From my angle, I couldn't even see his reflection in the full-length mirror. Still, there was something about the set of his shoulders, and the way he planted his hands on his slim hips…

"You thugs figger y'er pretty smart, doncha? But I'm onta ya, see?"

The other three chuckled. "That one's a good fit," Lauren told him. "But try the brown, too."

"Yeah," the actor said, in his own voice, "Danny's more a brown kind of guy."

Dan McDougal, I remembered from the play's synopsis, was the hapless detective in *Murder Most Noir*.

Ben Lederman peered over the heads of everyone else and spotted me in the aisle. "Viv, you have an opinion?"

They all glanced my way, and my heart thudded.

"Oh, I'd never intrude on your costuming decisions," I told him, lightly. "I'll save my input for the set design."

"Cute sweater!" Sally trilled. "Love the birds. Where did you find it?"

While I told her, the actor in the fedora also faced me, and I confirmed it was Ed Kiernan. He'd definitely matured since I'd last seen him, in his early twenties. Though still compact, his build seemed stronger, his cheekbones and jaw more clean-cut, even his skin tone a little deeper. Still, I easily recognized him.

I could tell, though, that the reverse was not the case. His pleasant, open expression, as Sally introduced us and he shook my hand, gave no sign that he'd ever met me before. Not at any time, anywhere.

Meanwhile, Sally reminded me, "You bought a terrific dress from me a couple of years ago, that 1950s sheath. I think it was a deep purple, with a curved, 'sweetheart' neckline."

"I'm amazed you remember that!" I told her.

She waved a hand. "It was a favorite of mine, and I was so happy that someone else appreciated it. It had a kind of tough-dame swagger to it, and the color looked great on you. Did you ever find anyplace to wear it?"

I felt a pang of guilt. "Sorry to say, I'm still looking for the right occasion."

"And maybe also for the right escort?" Sally leaned closer to whisper, "The guy with you that day acted like a bit of a stuffed shirt about it. If you don't mind my saying so."

"I don't mind," I assured her. "He's history."

Sally pivoted back toward Ed and Lauren. "Vivian has a great booth upstairs.Lots of crazy fabrics and knick-knacks that could work for your show."

"And speaking of crazy fabrics..." Ben pulled out a selection of men's ties, in some of the wildest retro designs I'd ever seen.

Ed howled, in a combination of glee and agony, and Lauren looked delighted as she tried to choose from the tasteless neckwear. She plucked out a red tie printed with gold banana leaves, a rust-toned one with dancing lime wedges, and a couple more in clashy, geometric patterns.

"C'mon," Ed begged her. "Danny may be an idiot, but he isn't blind!"

Ignoring his protests, she tied the rust one around his neck—since he was wearing a collarless pullover—and swapped the gray fedora for the brown one.

"That works," Ben suggested, and Lauren and Ed had to agree.

They still had to decide on a 1940s suit when Fred called to me from the front of the shop. "Richardson's going upstairs, hon. Don't miss your chance with him!"

"Okay, thanks." Reluctantly, I dragged myself away from the spectacle of Ed and his attendants trying to evoke his clueless detective character through their costume choices. I struggled to pull myself away from Ed's presence, period.

Give it up, Viv, I told myself. *You already "missed your chance" with him... eighteen years ago.*

Chapter Five

B y the time I reached the second floor, it sounded as if Adrian Marcus had already talked Richardson into borrowing a roll-armed sofa, upholstered in dusty-rose mohair, for the upscale "living room" of his production. That didn't bother me in the least, though. I didn't deal in such large pieces of furniture, at least not yet, and figured several of my flashy throw pillows would look spectacular against that upholstery. While the set designer considered adding Adrian's coffee table to the deal, I waited alertly but patiently in my own booth.

As soon as the two men shook hands and Tom appeared ready to move on, I flagged him down. My booth did the rest. The handsome black man grinned ear-to-ear. I knew it was not my own charms but those of my backdrop that attracted him.

"Oh yeah, *this* is what we need." He stopped a few feet back in the aisle to survey all my colors, patterns, and kitsch at once. "Gloria DeWitt, all the way!"

That was a designer I'd never heard of, much less collected. "Who?"

"The character who gets murdered in the play, a famous actress. The original New York production made her place very streamlined Art Deco, but I think it should be more like this—lush tropical flowers and plants everywhere." He ventured closer and picked up a pillow. "These are in nice shape, for the age of the fabric. Make them yourself?"

"I do, and I can tailor any of the drapes, if you need me to." I mentioned my professional design credentials before adding, "I also worked on props and sets for my college theater."

Of course, that led him to ask which college.

When I told him, Tom nodded in approval. "That's not too far from here, right? Good theater department. A few people on our crew came from there."

"Actually, Ed Kiernan went there, too. He starred in several of our plays." There, I thought, it was out.

"No kidding!" Still holding the pillow—exotic magenta blooms exploding across a black background—Tom walked to the top of the stairs. "Hey Kiernan, did you know this lady went to your alma mater? Bet she's got a lot of old dirt on you!"

Okay, now I was seriously embarrassed. Before long, Ed and Lauren both came jogging up the stairs. "Say what, now?" he asked Tom.

"You don't remember, I'm sure," I said. "It *was* almost twenty years ago."

Ed grimaced. "That long already, eh? But how..."

I explained, then, about my backstage roles for four of "his" plays in college. "I worked on sets sometimes, costumes other times. But I would have been up on a ladder with a paint brush, or in the costume shop behind a sewing machine."

"And I might not even have been around the theater at the same times as you. Although if you worked in the costume shop..." He searched his memory and nodded slowly. "Yeah, I think I do remember you, Vivian. But if so...you've changed a bit!"

He said nothing more along that line, but his slight smile suggested that I'd changed for the better.

Lauren had drifted away from us, across the aisle, and lingered now by the costume jewelry. At least Ronnie had gotten herself to work that day in time to pitch her wares to the designer. If I paid tribute to the 'forties with some of my work outfits, Ronnie seemed more influenced by the 'eighties. She favored overblown hair—usually streaked with some color not found in nature—and sporty/sexy *Flashdance*-type outfits, though she probably wasn't even born when that movie was made.

Richardson, meanwhile, grabbed a couple more of my dramatic pillows and tried them out on the rose sofa. Though Adrian looked as if he'd swallowed one of his faceted lead-crystal candlesticks, Tom grinned over his shoulder at the rest of us. "Y'think?"

"Definitely," Ed told him.

Tom brought the pillows back to my booth, where he also browsed through my quirkiest Roseville pieces. He mumbled, "The way they combine all these dusty, romantic colors and flowers with these weird notches and angles..."

"That's what I love about them, too," I said. "They're never quite what you'd expect."

Lauren rejoined us and suggested to him, "You should borrow something big that can be seen from the audience. Like an urn!"

That hadn't occurred to me. "I don't have anything very large here, but I've got a jardinière at home." In case she or Ed didn't know the term, I added, "A big planter on a pedestal."

In the end, Richardson made out a request form for two sets of draperies, six throw pillows, and three framed Turner prints. He told me if I could bring the planter to the antique center by the following week, he might borrow that, too. I almost worried about being cleaned out of merchandise, until he explained that these were all on spec. Some definitely would be coming right back to me, after he saw what did and didn't work with the set design, lighting, and blocking for the play.

The theater folk worked efficiently and said their goodbyes promptly at eleven, when the other vendors and regular customers began to arrive. I promised Richardson I'd have the jardinière available the next day, in case he wanted to pick it up that soon. Lauren half-joked that she might be back as an actual customer to purchase some of my smaller Roseville items. She did take along one of Ronnie's flashiest pieces, a big rhinestone brooch in the shape of a curling feather.

Ed lingered long enough to apologize for not remembering me sooner and promised me good, free seats for the show. With a breezy wink, he added, "Maybe we'll even see each other again before that."

I had given Tom my business card, so I seized the chance to do the same with Ed. I had no idea whether he was currently involved with somebody— how would he not be?—but no harm in letting him know how to reach me.

For professional reasons, of course.

The rest of my workday went almost as well. I don't know if word got around town that the playhouse had been scouting costumes and props at our establishment, but we saw a little more traffic than usual. I apologized to a couple of people for not having a wider range of barkcloth throw pillows on hand by saying, "The set designer for the Addamsville Playhouse was here this morning, and couldn't decide on the fly, so he grabbed quite a few." I showed them some of the substantial remnants I'd stacked off to one side. "If you see anything here you like, I can make pillows to order." One browser did choose that option.

Toward mid-afternoon, I heard Kaye grumbling again to Fred, across our aisle. "You could at least have steered them over to my booth, as well! If this character in the play is supposed to be wealthy, I have much more upscale pottery and glassware."

"Well, if you wanted to be considered, you could've come early like other people did," he threw back. "I figured you didn't want to risk lending your things to the theater for the whole run of the show. They probably have no place there to lock up the really good stuff."

That finally settled Kaye down, and again I felt sorry that Fred had to put up with her high-strung, slightly paranoid temperament. At least she hadn't targeted me this time.

I got the feeling Kaye rubbed many of her fellow vendors the wrong way when Cindy sidled over to my booth for a chat.

"I heard about the run-in you had with Ms. Burrell this morning," she said in a hushed tone. "Don't let that witch get under your skin! She's always been full of herself, but it's even worse now because she's going through a messy divorce."

"Oh, really?" Most of the time, I wouldn't care about the details of a coworker's personal life, but after all, Kaye had taken her bad temper out on me.

"I gather her husband feels she's been spending too much time and money on her antiques business, and he's using that as an excuse to cheat on her. I'd almost feel sorry for Kaye, except she's such a snob. She's also bitched to Fred about some of the vendors here being low-class, that their booths look like yard sales. She snipes all the time about Gerry, calling his stuff 'juvenile comic-book crap.' Of course, he's also had some choice words for Kaye behind her back."

"I can imagine." I hoped that I hadn't landed in a wasp's nest of bickering colleagues.

"Still, I was surprised when Fred took your side against her today," Cindy went on. "In some ways, the fact that she keeps such a sharp eye on the rest of us makes his job easier. Kaye and Adrian are the only people he trusts to open up in the morning if he's going to be late or on vacation."

So I still should be wary of bad-mouthing Ms. Burrell around our landlord. "Thanks for the heads-up, Cindy. I don't want trouble with anybody."

"Smart girl." She patted my shoulder. "Sorry you've gotten off to such a rough start at this place."

"I've coped with worse, but I do appreciate the support."

I packed up for the day, then, telling myself sales tomorrow should be better. *My toughest challenge probably will be transporting that Roseville jardinière safely from home, and up here to my booth, without any mishaps. At least now I know how to use the elevator!*

On my way past the cashier's window, Fred hailed me. "Viv, I'm letting everyone know…I've got a doctor's checkup tomorrow morning that could run to about noon, so Kaye will be here at ten to open up."

Had he made a special effort to warn *me*? With a chuckle, I confided to him, "Thanks. I'll be sure to give her a wide berth."

* * *

That night after dinner, I yielded to a temptation I'd been battling all day. With Aramis reading over my shoulder, I used my laptop to research everything I could find online about Edward Kiernan.

There wasn't a whole lot out there I didn't already know. He had briefly taught high school English Lit, while acting on the side. But his hobby attracted the attention of a New York drama coach who encouraged him to pursue it more seriously. Over the decades, Ed had taken various types of roles in regional and Off-Off-Broadway theaters, racking up good reviews and making a modest living, until he'd decided to try L.A. Even there, he'd paid his dues in commercials and bit parts before finally landing his more substantial role in *Boulevard Blues*.

Though Ed never got as much press coverage as the bigger names in the series—such as the veteran TV star who played the precinct captain—a line in a gossip column mentioned his involvement with one of his co-stars, Daphne Harrow. A photo showed them together at an awards show, and from what I could see, she fit the stereotype of the wholesomely sexy California blonde. Only a year later, though, tabloids announced their breakup, and implied that she'd been sneaking around with a star pitcher for the Dodgers. In one of the few interviews I could find that focused just on Ed, the columnist seemed to probe for juicy stories about his love life. Kiernan avoided specifics, though, and only quipped that he had "sworn off actresses."

Asked if it was true that he'd been engaged once, Ed still sounded reluctant to give any details. "That was very long ago," he told the interviewer, and wouldn't elaborate further.

Interesting. He must have been talking about Janet, I thought. But I had no idea how to find out any more information about what had happened between them. I never even knew her last name.

Aramis hopped down onto my keyboard, demanding my attention, and opened his beak in an elaborate yawn. I had to laugh. "You're right, buddy. This is probably all a waste of energy, and anyhow it's past our bedtime."

* * *

The Roseville jardinière, which I normally kept just inside my patio slider, consisted of two parts. The eight-inch-deep planter rested on top of a fourteen-inch-tall pedestal. Assembled, it weighed about forty pounds.

As I've mentioned, I'm not exactly musclebound, but at least I could manage each twenty-pound section separately. I didn't want them rolling around in the hatch of my medium-sized SUV, so the following morning I carefully nestled them in the floor wells in front of my back seats. Partly due to its sheer size, the jardinière was one of my most valuable pieces. As long as it didn't suffer any damage during the run of *Murder Most Noir*, I hoped to get it back and sell it another day.

A little after ten a.m., I pulled up at the curb by the rear entrance of the antiques center, where a grilled outer gate again protected the barn-sized door of the freight elevator. This time, the gate was secured with an old-school padlock on a thick chain. I remembered Fred telling us he'd be arriving late that day, and Kaye would open up. I'd never mentioned to her that I was bringing in a large piece, though, so she wouldn't have known to leave the back entrance open for me.

A pearly white Lexus sedan nestled beneath overhanging, leafy branches, close to the looming brick building. That looked like something Kaye would drive, so she must be here already. Much as I dreaded it, I'd have to face her one-on-one.

The front door remained locked, too. Maybe once inside, she had locked it behind her? It had an electronic keypad, but I'd never been given the code. I rang the bell and then knocked, with no answer. I did see a few lights on inside, but I knew Fred kept some on timers, so the place would never be totally dark.

Could Kaye have gone back out again, on foot, not expecting anyone else to come in so early?

I didn't have her cell number, so I could only call the center's landline. From the front stoop, I heard it ring on the sales desk inside. Then Fred responded…in a recorded message, giving the hours of operation.

Almost ten-thirty, and not a soul here!

That didn't last long, though. While I still held my phone, a little deep-blue Mercedes coupe swung into the parking lot. Adrian Marcus hopped out, in an impressive show of energy for a guy over fifty and not much taller than me. At first, he frowned to find me there—maybe he thought I'd cooked up some new scheme to steal away his customers? But I quickly explained that I needed to unload a large piece, and Fred had asked Kaye to open up that day, but neither of them seemed to be around.

"I can get us in," he assured me.

It figured that Fred would trust him, as another mature, longtime tenant, with the entry code.

Marcus joined me on the front stoop, punched a few numbers on the keypad, then paused to listen. "No beep. Funny...whoever closed up didn't set the alarm last night."

Too many odd circumstances, I thought, with a growing sense of unease. But it could have just been carelessness. *Fred was going for a checkup today...was he preoccupied with some health problem?*

Marcus and I entered with cautious steps, but nothing around the front sales counter seemed amiss. He found Kaye's cell number in a Rolodex and phoned her. After four rings, he apparently got her voicemail.

With a shrug, Marcus pocketed his phone again. "Guess we might as well just go to our stations," he said to me. "Fred didn't expect his appointment to run very late, so he should be here at least by noon."

"I was hoping to get in the back way." I told Marcus about the weighty jardinière. "I wanted to bring it up on the freight elevator, but the gate's padlocked."

He accompanied me back out to my car and peered inside at the two hefty-but-fragile Roseville pieces. "No problem, we'll just bring it up the front stairs. You carry the top, I'll carry the base."

I guessed coping with that morning's small mystery had turned us temporarily from rivals into comrades. When we split the weight of the garden planter, I could manage twenty pounds, and Adrian carried an equal load more easily, even up the long flight of stairs. He helped me set up the jardinière toward the rear of my booth, where it could stay half-hidden until Richardson came to check it out.

Natty, silver-haired Adrian then glanced toward the second-floor landing of the pulley elevator. "I still want to get this lift back in action, though. When the theater folks do return, they'll need it to take out my sofa and coffee table."

An idea struck me. "Do you think Fred could have stashed the padlock key inside somewhere? Maybe on this level?"

"I didn't see it anywhere in his office." Marcus stalked down the aisle and slid back the door that covered the entrance to the shaft. And that's all we saw—bare brick walls. The lift had to be far below us, in the basement.

"Funny, it would be parked down there," I said. "Is much stored in the basement?"

"I don't think so, because that level tends to be damp. Anything left down there too long could get moldy." Marcus peered over a low, fence-like barrier into the shaft. By the dim light, we could see through the gaps between the old boards.

"It does look like there's something inside the car, though," I said.

"You're right, something dark green. Probably just an old tarp."

That sounded logical, but this whole scenario—Fred being off the premises, and Kaye also missing and unreachable—set me on edge.

Adrian must also have been spooked, because he pulled out his phone again and re-dialed one of the numbers. A ringtone, some classical piece, echoed up from the depths of the soot-stained shaft.

I felt dizzy, not just from the vertigo, and stepped back from the threshold. "How do we bring the elevator to this level?"

Some color also drained from Marcus' normally rosy face. He stepped through the open door, onto a narrow platform equipped with the old pulley. The brake must have been off, because he grabbed one of the vertical ropes and, without even exerting much force, began to raise the elevator.

Once its interior came into view, we could see that Marcus had been wrong about the green fabric he'd glimpsed through the slats. Not a bulky, discarded tarp, but a long, flowy jacket of some kind.

Still draped over the sprawled body of a woman.

"Oh, no!" I breathed.

At least we'd solved part of that morning's mystery. We had found Kaye Burrell.

Chapter Six

When two Addamsville cops arrived, one stayed with us while the other checked on Kaye, probably to be sure she was beyond help. I heard him on the phone after that, no doubt calling for the crime-scene team.

Meanwhile, Officer James Gorey, a balding guy with a small, neat mustache and a low-key demeanor, separated me and Adrian. After all, if we had cooperated to murder Kaye, no sense in giving us a chance to synchronize our stories. At least we were allowed to retreat to our own booths, which were fairly private.

I explained to Gorey that, as far as I knew, Kaye was supposed to open the building at ten that day in Fred's absence. Who else would have known this? Anyone who'd been there the previous afternoon, I said, because Fred had spread the word before he left.

"When I got here today, the place was still locked up, and I didn't have the access code." So Gorey wouldn't think that our landlord didn't trust me with it, I added, "I've only been working here a few days, and I think Fred only gives it to certain people."

"But when Mr. Marcus arrived, he was able to let you in?" The officer jotted something in a small notepad.

"Yes. Adrian's a long-time tenant, so he knew the code."

Marcus had helped me bring up a large piece of pottery, I explained, and it was maybe fifteen minutes before he tried Kaye's cell phone a second time to see why she'd been delayed. "When it rang in the elevator shaft, we both looked down there, saw something odd, and brought up Kaye's body. Adrian

47

did try to revive her, but...I guess she'd been dead a while. Not overnight, though.'

My last statement caught Gorey's attention. "Why do you say that?"

"She had on a different outfit from what she was wearing yesterday." I did not mention that I'd noticed her clothing while she'd been accusing me of having stolen a valuable vase from her display.

"So she may have arrived this morning at ten, on schedule." Gorey made another notation. "What do *you* think happened to her?"

"I can't imagine. Fred and I both noticed her head was tilted at a strange angle, and wondered if she'd fallen into the shaft. But she was used to the way the lift operated, and from what I saw, she wasn't a clumsy person. Unless she had a dizzy spell, or lost her balance for some other reason..."

The officer nodded, his eyes sympathetic. "It must have been quite a shock for you, Ms. Joyce, to find her like that. Did you get along with Ms. Burrell?"

Uh-oh, this could be treacherous territory. "As I said, I just started here, so I barely knew her. I came to the center fairly often in the past as a customer, and maybe I saw and said hello to her then. But I never had a real conversation with her until yesterday, and that was only for a few minutes. Still, it *is* a shock to find anyone you know...like that."

"I'm sure it is." Gorey's relaxed demeanor suggested that he was satisfied with my answers. "That should be all for now, Ms. Joyce. I just need your address and phone number, in case we need to get in touch with you again."

"Of course." I provided them.

On my way out, I could see more uniformed cops taping off a wide area around the shaft. None of the other vendors had opened for business, and when I left by the front door, I saw why—about a dozen of them milled around on the sidewalk, held at bay by a couple more cops. Fred stood among them, his gray head rising a few inches above most others and his mouth, below his full mustache, gaping in outrage. I hoped he didn't have high blood pressure, because this morning's news could give any business owner a heart attack

As soon as he spotted me on the front steps, he called out, "Vivian, what's going on? They're saying we can't open today. They won't even let us into the parking lot!"

I pushed through the crowd until I got close enough to speak quietly to Fred, then told him what had happened inside. Marcus emerged from the front door next and joined us. He looked grave, but at least he'd also been set free...for the moment, anyway.

Cindy, of the Shabby Chic booth, showed up, too. She sidled nearer and whispered, "When they took the body away, just now, one of the EMTs said something about head trauma."

Fred's shocked expression returned. "So...what? She fell and got knocked out?"

None of us knew the answer, of course. I felt sure all of our speculations would be in vain until the Addamsville cops released an actual statement. But after all, we did have a stake in getting some answers. Even if Kaye might not have been the most popular vendor in the place, she'd been apparently healthy, alert, and nobody's fool. If someone could get the drop on her, when she was alone in the building, it probably could happen to any of us!

A familiar voice carried over the buzz of the crowd to distract me. By the front stoop, Mona shouted questions to one of the police officers. Funny—I rarely ran into my sister while she was on the job, but suddenly my new place of business had become a crime scene. She probably was trying to talk her way into the building, but a sturdy female officer blocked her, barking something about "...an official statement later today."

As Mona backed off with a discouraged frown, I waved an arm at her. She knew an inside source when she spotted one and hurried over.

"Viv, you know anything about this?" she asked.

"Probably as much as any civilian," I said. "Mr. Marcus here and I found the body."

My sister's eyes bugged out. "Shut up!"

"It's true." Adrian introduced himself to Mona and proceeded to tell her about our failed attempts to reach either Fred or Kaye, and all that had followed.

"We couldn't tell what killed her," I added, "but I'm sure the cops are in the process of figuring that out."

Mona got all this on her handheld digital recorder and asked, "Can I quote you both?"

Marcus shrugged. "Don't see why not. Those are just the facts, same as I told the cop, and we have nothing to hide."

By now, the police had taken a quick look around the center, and no doubt realized how challenging it would be to search that jam-packed environment for clues. They told Fred it would have to be shut down for the rest of the day. That was our first confirmation that they didn't believe Kaye had died from natural or even accidental causes.

None of us could get any information from them beyond that, though Mona was told if she called the police station at the end of the day, they might have more details for her.

We vendors who had shown up for work hung out on the sidewalk a while longer, then began to disperse. After my car and Adrian's had been thoroughly checked over—possibly for a murder weapon?—we got permission to remove them. In the lot, I muttered, half to myself, about the jardinière in the back of my vehicle that Richardson was supposed to pick up that day.

"Call him," Marcus advised. "Maybe you can head him off before he makes the trip out here. He'll need to come another day, anyhow, to pick up my things."

I realized I still had Tom's card in my purse and fished it out. To make the call, I edged away from the street noise and nearer to my car. Richardson's phone rang only a couple of times before he picked up. Probably not recognizing my number, he sounded wary at first. "Hello?"

"Hi, it's Vivian Joyce. From the antiques center? You told me you might be dropping by today to pick up that Roseville jardinière from me, but we've got a bit of a situation here..."

He let out an R-rated word when I told him one of the vendors had been found dead, and did not sound surprised that the place would be shut down for at least the rest of the day. "Thanks for calling me, Vivian. I *was* going to try to get back there today, but things are a little chaotic here, too. At least nobody's expired," he added, with dark humor, "but we're so far behind schedule that we're still painting flats *and* starting to block scenes at the same time, which doesn't work so well."

My gaze drifted, through the rear window of my small SUV, to the vivid green pieces of pottery that still rested on the rear floor. I had a brainstorm. "Listen, it sounds like you're super-busy, while I've got nothing to do for the rest of the day. The jardinière's already in my car. How about I drive over to the theater and drop it off? I'll just need someone to help unload it and take it wherever it needs to go."

"Well, I don't want to put you to any trouble..."

"I'm literally locked out of my workplace!" I reminded him. "Might as well do something useful."

"You're an angel, Viv! Okay, have you ever been here before?"

When I told him I had, though only as an audience member, Tom directed me to drive around to the rear of the theater. "You'll see a loading dock right behind the scene shop. Press the door buzzer and ask for Josie. You might have to try a couple of times, because she's also running around like mad today, but she'll be able to help you."

I told him I should be there in half an hour, if not sooner. After letting Marcus, Jeff, and Mona know where I was headed, I got behind the wheel and carefully guided my vehicle around the patrol cars and rubberneckers. Relieved to put the whole sad situation of Kaye's death out of my mind for a while, I also looked forward to getting a glimpse behind the scenes of the storied Addamsville Playhouse.

* * *

The building itself dated from the early 1800s, when it had served as a grist mill along the banks of the Delaware River. The playhouse moved into it around 1940, starting as a humble operation, a centerpiece for a rustic community of artists. But over the decades, Addamsville had evolved into more of a vacation and tourist destination, and big-name acts traveled from both New York and Philadelphia to appear there.

During my lifetime, the boom in electronic entertainment had taken some gloss off live theater productions. I still enjoyed them, though, and lately more people—even in my age group—seemed willing to actually leave their houses and go see a show performed (gasp!) in person.

I drove around the big, barnlike structure, which sported an updated burgundy paint job and fresh landscaping since I'd last been there. Gleaming brass hardware brightened the row of four white front doors. I knew the steeper center roofline, which originally housed the mill wheel, now accommodated the flies and rigging for the stage. More vehicles occupied the rear lot than the front one, and I drove back there, too.

I had no trouble finding the loading platform just outside the scene shop, and the door even stood propped open. I parked as close as possible. Even if I couldn't find Josie (whom I'd never met) right away, by making two trips, I could get the jardinière up the low ramp myself. Then I'd just have to locate someone to certify that I had delivered it, and to put it in a safe place until it was needed.

Once inside, I glanced around the scene shop, much larger and more professional than the one at my college. The warehouse atmosphere was offset by whimsical remnants of sets from past productions—a mock-stone archway over here, a two-dimensional, painted palm tree over there. The center of the space held three long work tables, and at one, a middle-aged guy in a T-shirt used a noisy jigsaw to shape some plywood into a zigzag. Shelves held industrial-sized tanks of spray paint, and hazy right angles of various colors overlapped on the cement floor.

I hung nearby, hesitating to interrupt the busy carpenter, when an athletic-looking woman about my age entered the shop, walking at a fast clip. I stepped into her line of vision and spoke up. "Excuse me…are you Josie?"

She halted, with a bob of her blonde ponytail. "That's me."

I explained I was from Addamsville Antiques and was dropping off a piece Tom Richardson wanted to borrow.

She glanced over her shoulder. "Oh, okay. He's working onstage right now…"

"He said he might be busy, but that maybe you could help me? My car's just outside."

I sensed Josie had a lot on her plate, too, but once I invoked Tom's authority, she accompanied me out to the parking lot. She carried the tall base of the jardinière up the ramp to the back door, while I brought in the slightly wider, bowl-shaped top.

As we assembled the piece in the well-lit scene shop, she had to admit, "That's pretty amazing—I don't think I've ever seen anything like it! And it's from the 1940s?"

I explained that the two-part planter would have been used in a garden or on a covered porch, probably to hold a fern or some other large, trailing species.

"Hey, that's a great idea," Josie said. "If we use it in the show, we should put something like that in it. A fake plant, of course."

Listening to the din of set construction around us, I started to worry whether the jardinière might get damaged accidentally during its stay at the theater. "I think Tom wanted me to find some safe place for it, until…"

"Oh, sure. We've got a storage closet back here for any valuable or fragile things." She led the way to a black-painted door, half hidden behind some old stage flats. It opened onto a surprisingly deep space, bulk items lined up along one side and ceiling-height shelving on the other. Once Josie had shifted a few things, we were able to tuck the jardinière stand safely into a corner and set its bowl on a shelf right above it.

On our way out, Josie stopped by a small, adjoining office to pick up a printed form. "This is the rental agreement. We'll need your contact information and the value of the piece. *If* anything should happen, the theater will reimburse you in full. But I promise we'll take good care of it."

"Thanks, I appreciate that." I leaned on the desk to fill out a form, and wondered if anyone at the theater would gasp over the value. Probably not, though, if they also planned to borrow Marcus's Art Deco sofa and coffee table.

"I'll go see if I can find Tom, so he can sign, too." Josie headed out the door that led to the stage.

Left alone in the scene shop, I traveled back in my mind to those college days when I had spent much of my leisure time in backstage locales. From sophomore year on, I'd played various supporting roles—painting flats, wrangling props, stitching up curtains and sofa throws. By senior year, I'd even had some design input on the bigger productions. Our unpaid crew was never very regimented, and when the costume department needed an extra pair of hands, I was also happy to take in a dress or hem a pair of trousers. Far too self-conscious to ever perform onstage, I still enjoyed the excitement of toiling on a tight deadline for a show, and overcoming the inevitable obstacles to make the production as dazzling as possible.

Sometimes when the curtain went up, the audience would actually applaud the set! That made all of us backstage folks feel like stars in our own right.

Through the open door, I heard voices across the hall. It sounded like the cast had already started some early rehearsals. Possibly just read-throughs, with the set still under construction. The Green Room might be nearby.

Time passed, and Josie did not return; maybe she was having more trouble than she'd expected locating Tom. Above the general murmur rose a woman's commanding, theatrical voice. No doubt that of Agnes Winthrop, the director—another person I had yet to meet. She must have said something clever, because three or four other voices, male and female, chuckled in response.

My curiosity got the better of me, and I stole nearer the stage door.

From there, I heard Agnes say, "Okay, let's break for lunch. Meet back here in an hour, and we'll go through Scene Three."

Folding chairs scraped on a bare wood floor, which told me the cast must be dispersing. I backed away from the door and almost collided with Tom Richardson, who came striding down the hall.

"Oh, Ms. Joyce. Just the person I was looking for."

"Please, call me Vivian," I said, "I was looking for you, too."

He held out the rental agreement with his signature. "Josie passed this along to me. She tells me the jardinière is fabulous and is tucked away in the storeroom, so I'll check it out when I have time. I guess that's the only piece we can get today? With the antiques center being shut down..."

"Yes, I'm afraid so. With any luck, we'll be open as usual tomorrow." I hoped!

"The reason I ask…if we use anything else of yours, we can just add it to this sheet, and you can total up the value. I think I remember which other items I wanted to try. If you can hang around a minute, I'll make a list, okay?"

"No problem," I assured him. Again, I had nothing else to do for the rest of the day…and certainly nothing more important than getting even more of my merchandise onstage!

As the tall man headed off again, probably to his office, I noticed another figure loitering in the hall behind him. Ed Kiernan held a stapled script and appeared to be reviewing notes from his rehearsal session. Or was he just stalling until Richardson left? Because now he glanced up with a bright smile and pointed at me. "Hello…Vivian, right? Didn't expect to see you again so soon. What brings you to this drafty old barn?"

Battling my self-consciousness, I explained about my delivery, but not in the same detail as with Tom. Maybe Fred, and even the police, would not want word getting around that we'd had a mysterious death at the antiques center.

On the other hand, it was sure to end up in the news tomorrow. "We had an…incident at work. It's still not clear what happened, so they've shut the place down to investigate."

Meanwhile, at closer range than before, I took stock of the ways in which Ed had changed, or not, since our college days. Boyish in his build then, at forty, he'd matured nicely—his V-necked, olive-green T-shirt stretched a little over his chest and shoulders. But he still stood just a few inches taller than me, which I kind of liked. (Steve's height used to intimidate me in an unpleasant way.) Ed wore his wavy auburn hair a bit shorter than in the old days, but until recently, he *had* made his living playing a police detective. The light scattering of youthful freckles had grown a little denser, maybe from all those years in the California sun.

One of the most notable changes since our college days, and even since I'd seen Ed at the antiques center—he was wearing glasses! Probably from some top designer, they were round with tortoiseshell frames, nerdy and hip at the same time. They suited him, though, as did the fine lines that fanned from the outer corners of his hazel eyes.

Those eyes twinkled now as he asked me, "No foul play involved, I hope?" I was too dazzled to catch his meaning right away.

"At the antiques center, I mean." He frowned. "Sorry, bad joke."

The comment made me wonder if Tom had told the actors about Kaye's death, but that seemed unlikely. "You've been playing detective too long."

"I'm sure I have, and now I'm at it again." He jerked his head in the direction of the theater door and the stage. "So, you brought us some kind of special prop today?"

Since Ed was actually showing some interest in me, this time around, I gladly played along. "Very special, and it's stashed in a secret place. I don't know if even you'll be allowed to see it, until…"

As if I'd invoked him, Richardson reappeared at my side. With a quick "Excuse me" to Ed, he passed me a handwritten list.

"This is from memory," he said, "but I tried to describe everything in some detail. Let me know if anything's confusing."

He requested about a dozen items, which made me giddy. I reminded myself that there probably would be rejects, because some would work better with his set design than others.

"Great," I told him. "I'll get these to you as soon as…as I can."

"Yes, a shame about the center being closed down. Hope that doesn't last too long."

I sensed Ed wanted to ask more about this, but a tone from my pocket told me I had a text message. Checking my phone, I saw Fred's name and number.

"Hang on," I told Richardson. "This might be an update."

It was, but not the kind I'd expected.

Get back here ASAP. Cops want statements from you and Marcus.

That shook me, but I still tried to play it cool. "Sorry, the boss wants me back there. Guess there's still some stuff to sort out."

With a jaunty salute, Tom turned on his heel and headed down the hall. "Just keep me posted, and good luck."

Lingering, Ed also looked disappointed. "Too bad, I was going to ask you to stay around for lunch. The theater restaurant hasn't opened yet for the season, but they do put out some sandwiches for us. Mostly baloney and cheese on white bread…though there's also a chickpea spread on rye, for the vegetarians." He shrugged in apology. "The perks of stardom!"

Damn the Addamsville PD. "Wish I could, but this call sounded important. Maybe a rain check?"

He smiled again. "Absolutely."

That invitation put a spring in my step as I hurried out to my car. Tom's list reassured me that I should have at least one more excuse to visit the theater again during off-hours.

Before pulling out of the parking lot, I phoned Fred to find out what the cops considered so urgent.

He groaned in answer. "It's a mess here, honey. The police say it was a homicide. Kaye was struck on the head with something hard, and they've even narrowed down a few possible murder weapons. They want to talk to anyone who might have had access to the building that morning, and especially anybody who had a beef with Kate."

I wondered, but didn't ask, *Couldn't that include at least half of her fellow vendors?*

"Unfortunately," Fred added, "based on our arguments with her this week, they're looking real close at me, Adrian…and you."

Chapter Seven

The Addamsville Police and Fire Department had recently moved into a spanking-new home on the edge of town. Its brick exterior and limestone trim gave a nod to local tradition, though the lines were clean and contemporary. The fire trucks occupied bays at the rear of the building, but I came in by the square-pillared front entrance.

I had no idea whether Fred and Adrian had given their statements and gone, or if one of them might already be under arrest. It all felt unreal to me. A couple of days ago, I had barely known these men; now we were all potential suspects in a murder case! Before coming here today, I'd considered asking Mona if I needed a lawyer. Perhaps foolishly, though, I still felt confident this would all blow over. I had done nothing that should connect me with Kaye's death. At the time when that probably had occurred, I wasn't even able to get into the building!

Once again, I met with unflappable Officer Gorey. I thought he still seemed to size me up as an unlikely murderess, which helped me relax a little. He read back the basic facts from the statement I'd given him earlier.

"You told me you were new to the antiques center, Ms. Joyce. Exactly how long have you been working there?" he asked.

"This would have been my third full day."

"And how did you come to rent the space?"

I explained that I'd visited the retail business over the years, and though Fred warned me that booths for new vendors rarely opened up, I'd asked him to keep me in mind. "I was already selling my vintage décor online, and at outdoor and pop-up events, but felt I could do better if I had a physical location besides my home."

Gorey consulted his notes. "You also said that when you visited before, you'd occasionally spoken with the deceased, Ms. Burrell, but that you never had a real conversation with her until yesterday. It was a rather heated conversation, though, wasn't it?"

I felt the blood drain from my face. Who had been mean enough to tell them about that? *Probably not Fred—after all, he took my side!*

"It was mostly 'heated' on her part." I explained that she'd accused me of moving a valuable piece of merchandise from her booth to mine. "I was as surprised to see it there as she was, and told her so, but she didn't seem to believe me. Fred Palasinski finally stepped in to mediate. He pointed out that a shopper could have picked up the vase, wandered around with it for a while, and then put it back in the wrong place."

"Did Ms. Burrell accept that explanation?"

"Grudgingly, I'd say. Our pieces are supposed to be marked, so if a buyer takes something to the sales desk, no matter where they picked up an item, the sale would go to the correct vendor. Kaye accused me of removing the label, but Fred found one crumpled on the floor near her booth. That finally calmed her down, but she still seemed to feel like I'd tried to put something over on her."

Gorey jotted something on his pad, then stroked his short 'stache. "Were you aware, before that, of how the sales were handled?"

"Absolutely. Fred explained that to me when I signed my lease, so I'd remember to tag all my merchandise with my booth number. Since I was new, it was fresh in my mind."

I sensed Gorey moving me a few rungs lower on his list of suspects. "Did it upset you to be accused of something like that, your first day on the job?"

Don't step into that trap, I warned myself. "I didn't take it personally. Someone told me afterward that Kaye was going through a messy divorce and had been on edge lately. And I figured in any marketplace, with so many salespeople competing for customers, there must be clashes now and then. But I did resolve to check my booth every morning, from then on, for any merchandise that didn't belong to me!"

I sensed Officer Gorey not only listened to my words but that his sharp gray eyes also took in every detail of my demeanor. So I wouldn't give the impression of being nervous or evasive, I reminded myself that I was being totally honest and had nothing to hide.

"You said you couldn't get into the building until Mr. Marcus arrived. Did you notice anything strange about that?"

I wondered what he was getting at. "Adrian did mention that, even though the door was locked, the alarm was off. He thought that was unusually careless of Fred."

A hint of a smile lifted Gorey's lips, and he told me I could go wait outside. He skipped any further warning about discussing the case with others, so I supposed I was no longer a suspect. Except...

"On your way out, Ms. Joyce, would you mind stopping next door to give us your fingerprints? Strictly for elimination purposes."

Since I hadn't been arrested, I could legally refuse, but what would be the point? I was pretty sure I hadn't touched anything at the antique center that could have been used to clobber Kaye, and probably the cops wanted the prints of everyone being questioned. At any rate, the modern process was clean and quick, just an electronic scan.

Back out in the hall, I found Fred sitting at one end of a long, blond-wood bench and texting on his cell phone. He might surround himself with artifacts of the past and use very low-tech methods to keep his books, but even he needed a way to handle his business when he couldn't be at the cash register.

"Everything okay?" I asked him.

"Vendors are asking when we're going to reopen, but I don't know yet," he said.

"Someone here questioned you already, I guess?"

Fred nodded. "Officer Bharani. He heard from somebody that I reprimanded Kaye the night before she died. I pointed out that I had nothing to gain by bumping off a longtime vendor, who not only leased forty square feet and always paid on time, but attracted some of our higher-end customers."

"Did he accept that?"

"I think so. He also wanted to know if the individual vendors could get into the building any time they wanted. I said I'd only given the entry code to a few longtime, trusted tenants, but I couldn't be sure they'd never told any of the others. He asked if that wasn't a security risk, but I explained we've mostly been concerned with theft, and each vendor is legally responsible for securing their own stock. Frankly, a mugging or other violent attack never even crossed my mind. In almost thirty years, the center never had anything like that...until now."

I could see that being called to the police station had badly shaken the older man. "Do you think you're in the clear now, at least?"

"I guess—he said I was free to go. But I heard the cops went through our whole building, looking for a murder weapon, and Bharani wouldn't say whether or not they found one. That's probably going to determine when, and if, we can get back to business." Fred glanced down the hall. "They brought Adrian here in a patrol car. He's still parked at the center, of course, so I'm going to wait a few minutes and see if he needs a ride back there."

Meanwhile, I called Mona and left her a message. I needed reassurance from someone who understood how these things worked and was solidly on my side.

As I hung up, Adrian Marcus emerged from one of the interrogation rooms...in handcuffs. He looked green around the gills, as my father used to say; even his hair, normally trained straight back from his forehead, was rumpled.

Fred sprang up from the bench. "Hey, what's this?" he asked the dark-eyed, youthful police officer. "You can't be arresting him!"

"Sir, I need you to step back," Bharani told him sternly, one hand stealing toward his duty belt.

"Marcus left the building last night *before* Kaye—before the victim. And he didn't come back until eleven this morning!"

I caught Fred's arm. "Don't make a scene here, you'll just get into trouble. We'll find Adrian a lawyer and get to the bottom of this."

I also wanted to get to the bottom of another mystery. Seemed like we three had been the only ones grilled about the crime so far. Which of our dear comrades had so helpfully told the police that Fred and I argued with

Kaye, the afternoon before she died?

* * *

At home that evening, I looked forward to putting the whole mess behind me. I fed Aramis, made an easy dinner for myself, and decided to catch up on some work that required little brainpower.

With my fine-feathered friend again riding on my shoulder, I started work on a pillow a customer had requested, my first day at the center. She and I had discussed various options for the edging—none (a plain seam), a flange, cording, or fringe—and I'd shown her examples of each on my phone. She'd opted for cording, which was lucky; I had a few colors on hand that would coordinate nicely with her pattern.

Barkcloth fabrics, with their large, exotic motifs, lent themselves well to throw pillows. Any one or two of those images could dominate a sixteen- or eighteen-inch square or circle, and if the design flowed off the edges, that just added to the drama.

My guest room doubled as my crafts and sewing studio, and I left the square folding table up and the sewing machine uncovered, because they see frequent use. The ceiling fixture and large window kept things pretty bright, but I also had task lights where I needed them.

A corner stand held my vintage-style LP turntable—a modern design that also plays CDs and MP3s—and I put on an old Brasil '66 album from my mother's collection. To a calming background of bossa nova, I sorted through my fabrics and trims.

My customer, Lucille Denby, wanted one high-impact pillow for the middle of her front porch loveseat and had chosen a remnant with a light sage-green background. I spread this flat on my cutting board and measured out two squares. Each "good" side highlighted a pair of oversized white orchids with bright-pink centers, framed by wavy bronze and teal-green leaves. A dark green cording around the edges, I decided, would frame it all nicely.

Aramis got tired of coping with my erratic moves and flitted to the top of my deco-style torchiere lamp, a reproduction that actually dated from the *Miami Vice* '80s. For a while my cockatiel buddy warbled sweetly along with the Latin music, until the tinkling strains of "Everything Old is New Again" interrupted both of us.

As I expected, the call was from Mona. I switched off the record player.

"How are you doing?" she asked. "I guess you still couldn't go to work today."

"I couldn't, but I had my share of excitement, anyway." I told her only that Fred, Marcus, and I had been re-interviewed at the police station. "But Mona, can you keep it under your hat for now? The cops probably don't want word to get out until they release an official statement."

With an edgy laugh, she asked, "They aren't arresting you, are they?"

"No, I'm fairly certain it won't be me! But I wouldn't like to cast suspicion on anyone else until...there's something definite."

"I wouldn't, either. But just a warning, Viv—when Dad reads tomorrow's story, he's going to freak. As far as he's aware, the police are still treating the death as an accident, but if they decide it's murder...you know how little it takes to set Dad off. He's going to think you're working in a dangerous environment."

"I'll keep that in mind." I knew she was not exaggerating. "Now, can we change to a more pleasant subject?" I recounted my trip to the theater and off-the-cuff chat with Ed Kiernan.

"So you took my advice? Good girl! How did that go?"

"Well, we had a longer, more private conversation today than we ever did in college," I said. "And guess what—he wears glasses now! Still looks damn good, though."

"People change, in almost twenty years. If you've gotten a little cooler, maybe he's a bit nerdier. Could be that the playing field's more level now."

Encouraging thought. "Funny...when he saw me for the first time at the antiques center, he acted like he hardly recognized me. But today he gave me a big hello, and even asked if I wanted to stay around for lunch. Unfortunately, that's when I got called to the police station. So now who knows what he thinks of me!"

"Let's hope he likes bad girls," Mona joked. "Well, you may get another chance."

I remembered several attractive females I'd spotted hanging around the playhouse, and my hopes dimmed. "If it's anything like college, by next week he'll have hooked up with somebody nearer at hand, in the cast or crew."

"Maybe not. He could still be a little wary, after getting burned by that actress on his TV series." A beep on Mona's line interrupted us. "Oops, the night editor's trying to get me—probably some question about my story. Have a nice, quiet evening, Sis, and try not to worry."

Attempting to follow this advice, I turned the stereo back on and returned to my sewing project. While I pinned the two right sides of the fabric together, with the cording basted inside along the edges, I listened to "Night and Day" sung to a salsa beat. The sultry lyrics nudged my thoughts back to Kiernan, and the fact that he'd actually invited me to eat lunch with him, even if off-the-cuff. He certainly must have had other options among the play's cast and crew, but maybe he really had decided not to date people he worked with anymore.

Could that possibly tip the scales in my favor?

I machine-stitched the two squares of barkcloth together except for an eight-inch gap on the bottom. From my supply closet, I fetched a twenty-inch-square pillow form, because for a snug fit, it needed to be one commercial size larger than the cover. I turned the pillow cover right side out, which also exposed the cording. Then I sat in my favorite rattan "peacock" chair to carefully stuff the piece, massaging the polyester-filled insert through the fabric gap a little at a time and then working it well into the corners.

Once the pillow stood up plump and proud, its central flowers framed by the dark edging, I admired the effect. I spent a few more minutes hand-stitching the lower gap closed, as invisibly as possible. Tomorrow I'd give the customer a call and ask if she wanted me to ship the pillow or if she would come to downtown Addamsville to pick it up herself.

Providing, of course, the antiques center does reopen by tomorrow. Fred seemed to think it would, and so far, I haven't gotten any calls or texts to the contrary.

Though it was only a little past nine, I'd had a busy day and felt exhausted. Too early to go to bed, but I couldn't think of anything I wanted to watch on TV. Maybe I could find a decent sitcom or a funny old movie. No crime shows, though, of any kind!

Weird to think I never watched *Boulevard Blues*, while it was on. I don't read much showbiz gossip, so I never even realized there was an actor in the cast named Edward Kiernan! I still don't get that cable station, but there are usually other ways, these days… Maybe another night, when I don't have so much on my mind, I can track down the reruns somewhere.

My ringtone sounded. I thought Mona might be calling back, but Fred's name showed up on the screen. "Hope I'm not disturbing you too late, Viv."

"Not at all, what's up?"

He sighed on the line. "Good news and bad news. We got permission to reopen the center tomorrow, though we'll need to come early and do some straightening up. I guess the forensics guys left a bit of a mess behind."

"Even more than our usual?" I quipped, trying to relieve the tension. "Well, at least we'll have a full Saturday of business, to make up for lost time. What's the bad news?"

"They think they've found the murder weapon, which is why they arrested Marcus. They found traces of blood, matching Kaye's type, on one of his lead-crystal candlesticks."

"You're kidding!" I clearly remembered the twin set. About eighteen inches tall, with sharp, geometric facets, they looked very sturdy. "Anything else? Fingerprints?"

"The cops did take Adrian's prints, but at this point, that's all he knows. Viv, those candlesticks were at the very front of his booth, on top of that big mahogany sideboard."

"You're right," I recalled. "Anyone passing by could have grabbed one and hit Kaye." Then the killer must have put the candlestick back in its place—pretty cold-blooded.

"Sounds like some other vendors told the police Adrian and Kaye didn't get on very well," he went on. "Yeah, they sniped at each other now and then, but it was nothing serious! They've both been tenants for many years, and I never saw any sign—"

"The cops are grasping at straws, Fred. They can't make a solid case against Marcus… unless they do find his fingerprints."

I'd just realized the foolishness of my comment before Fred responded. "But they probably will, won't they? Because it was his candlestick!" He groaned in frustration. "Anyhow, I'll see you tomorrow, if you're not too spooked at this point to come in."

"Don't worry, I'll be there," I promised.

Hanging up, I felt more determined than ever to find out who really had killed Kaye Burrell, and why. Sure, she had a prickly personality, but the other vendors seemed to recognize that and to shrug it off. Did she harass someone for so long that they had finally exploded?

And who were the unnamed colleagues who seemed to be throwing suspicion on everyone but themselves?

Chapter Eight

Addamsville Antiques reopened for business the next day. A few of us admitted to each other that we felt strange coming back to work in a building that had seen the violent death of a colleague. Word also had gotten out, via Mona's story in the *Herald* and other news sources, that Kaye Burrell's death was now being investigated as a homicide.

Even though Saturdays were normally our busiest, several booths remained unstaffed that morning. On my floor, the missing vendors included both Gerry and Ronnie. Well, supposedly they were a couple. Maybe they'd thought the center would stay closed all weekend, and had gone off someplace together.

The suspicious death on the premises did not seem to deter many customers, presuming they'd even heard about it. I've noticed that fewer people read their local news, these days. I started to do the kind of steady business I'd been hoping for, though mostly less-expensive stuff—a pair of "artworks" I'd made by framing two compatible barkcloth remnants, a 'forties tablecloth with a colorful fruity border, and a small cornucopia-shaped Roseville vase.

During a lull, I called the number of the Kramers' pawn shop to find out how Al was doing. I got only a message that gave the shop's usual hours. From Betty's cheerful tone, I suspect she had made the recording long before the robbery, and the shop probably remained closed until further notice. I just expressed my sympathies for their trouble and my hopes that both of them were all right.

Next, I phoned Lucille Denby to say her orchid pillow was ready. But when I suggested she come pick up her purchase, she turned evasive.

"Oh, gee…I don't know if I'll be free anytime soon. Anyway, I heard the center was closed…"

She'd already paid me for the pillow, so it didn't seem likely that she'd decided she couldn't afford my price. I figured she was just antsy about visiting a crime scene. "I could mail it to you, of course, but I'd have to charge extra. Do you live nearby?"

A pause on the line. *Really, Lucille, I'm not a murderer!*

When she did give me her address, I recognized it as being only about a mile away. I told her, "I'd be happy to drop the pillow off for you, no charge."

"Really, would you? Thanks so much," she said. "I wouldn't be so nervous, except…you know about that jewelry robbery a couple of weeks ago in Delaware? My son works at an electronics store in the same mall, and I've been thanking God ever since that they didn't also hit his place. We used to feel pretty safe, living around here, but lately—"

"I understand completely." Conscious of more prospective customers browsing through my wares, I told Lucille I could probably make the delivery by late afternoon.

"That would be fine. My front porch is screened, so even if I happen to be out, you can just leave it on the loveseat. Thanks again, Vivian, I appreciate it!"

After hanging up, I answered a couple of questions for a browser, who took my business card. Left on my own again, I pulled out Tom Richardson's list and gathered up the stuff he wanted to evaluate for *Murder, Most Noir*. As long as I was going out anyway, maybe I could run that errand, too. Into four large tote bags went three sets of draperies, half a dozen throw pillows, and two tropical-themed Turner prints in their original etched frames.

I'll need the freight elevator for this load—do I have the nerve? And speaking of scary, this almost cleans me out! I'm sure Tom will be returning some stuff, but how long will he take to decide?

Trying to imagine the décor of the fictional star's Hollywood apartment pulled my thoughts back to a TV show I'd watched the night before. With a little effort, I had managed to track down the pilot episode of *Boulevard Blues*, in which Ed had played police detective Patrick Harrigan—ethnically, not much of a stretch. And as Mona had mentioned, the series was an ensemble show dealing with several members of the L.A. police department, their families, and their significant others. What struck me most, though, was that Ed's character came across as fairly serious and intense. This marked a departure from our college days, when he mainly took on lighter roles, either satire or outright comedy. If he played a romantic lead, it usually was in a musical, because even at twenty, he'd had a strong singing voice.

But P.D. Harrigan brought out a whole different side of Ed—broody, hot-tempered, even dangerous. When he pulled a gun on a "scumbag" who already had escaped capture far too many times, you believed that frustrated "Pat" just might shoot the creep in cold blood.

Not at all the same guy who kidded around with the costume folks when he came here, or reminisced with me about our college days when I visited the Playhouse. But I guess that's acting!

A couple of hours later, I heard a cheerful commotion across the aisle from me. Adrian Marcus had returned to his booth, and Cindy and Fred welcomed him back. I joined them.

Marcus admitted he still wasn't totally off the suspect list. "But even though they found traces of Kaye's blood on the candlestick, there were no fingerprints at all. The killer either wore gloves or wiped off his prints." Adrian must have seen me glance toward the top of the mahogany buffet, because he added, "You'll notice that I've stashed its mate out of sight."

Cindy chimed in. "While the cops were so busy dusting for prints, did they think of checking the keypad for the front door, or the button to call the freight elevator?"

"I'm pretty sure they checked all of those." Marcus frowned. "Why do you think they also interrogated Vivian and Fred?"

Yes, that made sense, I thought. If the killer also wiped down those areas before he left—or had worn gloves for the whole operation—the only prints to show up would have been ours.

"Someone must have gotten into the building before us that morning," I concluded. "Maybe they surprised Kaye as she was opening up, and forced her to let them in."

Marcus leaned on his elbows against the buffet and frowned in concentration. "A couple of other possibilities—she could have known and trusted the person, or thought they were a customer. Though none of those explanations narrows the field very much."

"And try looking for clues in *this* place..." Cindy rolled her mascara-rimmed blue eyes.

"I know," I said. "It's so jammed with stuff, and not even particularly organized. Maybe someone saw a chance to pull off the perfect crime."

"Once they'd checked to see if anyone had a serious grudge against Kaye, the police apparently also tried to determine if anything had been stolen," Marcus told us. "That might explain the motive—Kaye caught a thief in the act and tried to stop him. But all they could do was question the vendors, and no one here claimed to be missing anything of value."

The killer could have struck her out of impulse, I thought, not expecting the blow to be fatal. Then, in a panic, he or she tried to keep the crime hidden for as long as possible. They had dragged or carried the body—depending on how strong they were—over to the elevator. If the car was already on the basement level, they must have just pushed her into the shaft.

Again, pretty damn ruthless. If the blow on the head didn't kill her outright, the fall might have sealed her fate.

I remembered something else. "Fred told me Kaye was going through a nasty divorce. Have the police looked into that? If her husband followed her here that morning, maybe they argued and he got violent."

Cindy shrugged. "Let's hope they *are* looking into her personal life. Just because she was found here doesn't necessarily mean one of us did the deed!"

Silently, I wondered if Kaye's husband stood to inherit her business assets. Judging from the age, condition, and rarity of her merchandise, that could amount to quite a haul. Worth killing for?

My gaze returned to Adrian Marcus' booth and came to rest on the dusty-rose mohair sofa and its coordinating coffee table. "I see the theater folks haven't stopped by for your things yet. I still have more stuff for them, too."

"Hope they won't think, now, that it's in poor taste," Marcus sniffed.

"Decorating the set of a murder mystery with pieces from a place that's had an actual murder on the premises!"

I could see his point. "Well, I was at the theater yesterday, and Richardson was totally sympathetic. He didn't seem put off by, or superstitious about, Kaye's death. Of course, I made it sound as if the cops still thought her fall might have been an accident."

As a well-dressed young couple hovered near his booth, Marcus squared his shoulders. Before heading off in their direction, he whispered to me, "Meanwhile, as they would say at the theater…the show must go on."

His words prodded me into action, too. I packed all the furnishings for the playhouse into my car, then stopped back at the cashier's window to let Fred know where I was going and why.

"Oh, glad you reminded me…" He searched his cluttered desk and retrieved a quart-sized resealable bag that held a few pieces of jewelry. "Lauren, from their costume shop, asked Ronnie to send her some more things on spec. As long as you're going there anyway…"

"Sure, no problem," I told him.

* * *

When I climbed the front steps to Lucille Denby's house and rang the bell, the slim, forty-something strawberry blond she greeted me more warmly than she had on the phone. And when I pulled the orchid pillow out of my tote bag, she positively gushed. "Oh my, that's wonderful! Even nicer than I expected. I love the colors!"

As she'd said, her house featured a full, screened front porch, which she'd furnished with wicker seating pieces topped by grass-green cushions. She popped the new, tropical pillow in the center of a loveseat, and it looked right at home. She thanked me again, but I reminded her, "You picked out the fabric—you've got a good eye!"

The slanting afternoon sunlight gilded the suburban streets as I slid back behind the wheel and drove on to the theater. I pushed down nagging fears that I was chasing after a youthful fantasy and making a fool of myself. I reasoned, instead, that I was helping out both the backstage folks and my fellow vendors by running this errand. And I shouldn't lose any business by being away from my booth for an hour or so. After all, any customer who wanted one of my pieces could still purchase it at the sales desk, and Fred would reimburse me at the end of the day.

Come off it, Viv. You're just hoping to bump into Ed Kiernan again.

I parked once more near the ramp to the scene shop. By now, I knew my way around the space and recognized Josie when she emerged from the storage room.

"As promised," I told her, "I brought the three sets of drapes, and I have the pillows right outside in my car."

Josie hadn't seen any of these items before, and her eyes popped. "Oh, these are *insane*—no offense."

"None taken. Tom said he wanted a really extravagant 'Hollywood' look."

"They're just what we need! The big plumes are my favorite, but he'll have to judge what works best with the set. It's still evolving."

I ran out to my car and brought in a couple of large-sized, clear plastic garbage bags that held the pillows. Checking out the various designs, Josie said, "These look great, too. Very flashy—they'll 'read' well from the stage."

"And Lauren asked one of our other vendors for some jewelry…" I held out the sandwich-sized bag with the latest baubles from Ronnie.

Someone across the studio shouted Josie's name, and she called out that she'd be right with them. "Vivian, would you mind dropping the jewelry off at the costume shop? Go all the way down the hall, make a right, and you'll see it on the left. Sorry to put you to extra trouble, but…"

"No trouble at all. I know you're busy, that's why I offered to bring everything here."

I didn't confess that I actually relished the chance to spend some more time poking around backstage. Listening to flats being drilled and hammered together, and bits of dialogue being rehearsed, took me back to a pivotal period of my life. In college, I might not have been a social butterfly, but I'd finally realized that design was my calling and I was good at it. More than straight interior decor, which I'd tried for a few years, I really enjoyed the challenge of creating something original, quirky—a setting that captured a particular era, embodied a certain character, or told a story. Maybe that's why I was happier now to re-sell offbeat pieces that represented an earlier, more romantic period.

The costume department still attracted me, too, with its three state-of-the-art sewing machines, cubbies filled with rolled-up fabric, and dressmaker's dummies that wore unfinished bits and pieces of garments. One at the far end of the room modeled a full-length, rose-colored gown with a fitted waist, plunging neckline, and padded shoulders. The epitome of old-Hollywood glamour, no doubt designed for the leading lady…who unfortunately got killed halfway through the play. Well, maybe not unfortunately, as far as the other characters were concerned; she'd been such a witch that the detective had far too many suspects to choose from. That dilemma, I gathered, inspired much of the show's dark humor.

Then I sobered. *A little too much like our real-life situation with Kaye Burrell!*

By asking around, I tracked down Lauren Murdock and delivered the costume jewelry. She enthused about the selections and tried a few, on the spot, with the rose evening gown. She seemed to be leaning toward a three-strand choker that mixed pink beads with faux pearls, but wondered aloud if it distracted from the dress. On impulse, Lauren grabbed the large, feather-shaped brooch, studded with rhinestones, which she had taken on her first visit to Ronnie's table. When she pinned that just beneath one padded shoulder, the effect was perfect, enhancing the plunge of the decolletage.

"This, I still like best," she decided, "and I can just see it on Marsha!"

Marsha Fuller was another member of the cast I didn't know except by name, from the show's poster. I assumed she was the leading lady with the glamorous red pageboy hairdo.

"Well, Ronnie said you're welcome to hold onto all of these pieces for the run of the show, in case you find other uses for them. I don't know if she really cares about getting a rental form…"

"I'll send one back with you, anyway," Lauren insisted. "We like to keep all these loans on the up-and-up."

A knock on the open door made her turn, and a male voice asked, "You wanted to see me, Lauren? Something about the jacket?"

"Oh yes, Ed, thanks. I'm not taking you away from rehearsal, I hope?"

"They don't need me right now, so Agnes said I could go." He stepped into the shop, and when he spotted me, his eyebrows did a little jump. "Vivian, again! Did you decide to join our crew?"

I felt embarrassed now, as if he could see right through my flimsy ploy. "Call me Viv, please. I'm just running another errand. Now that we can get back into the antiques center, I was able to bring Tom a few more things and Lauren some jewelry she wanted."

She gave my story credibility by cooing, "Ed, what do you think of this brooch? Perfect, no?"

"It's a dazzler, all right. Are we insured for all those diamonds?"

She swatted in his direction. "They're rhinestones, and you know it. But from the audience, they'll look like a million bucks."

"That's a relief," he said. "Didn't a jewelry store get robbed a couple days ago, right in the next town? We wouldn't want the theater to be receiving stolen goods."

"You're still in character," I noted.

It took him just a second to catch my meaning and laugh. "Thinking like a detective again, right!"

"I'll get that jacket." Lauren walked over to a rear costume rack.

Meanwhile, Ed held my gaze in a way that made even those tortoiseshell-framed glasses seem sexy. "I still owe you that lunch."

"A baloney-and-cheese sandwich?"

"I can do better than that. Tomorrow's Sunday, the one day they let us off this rehearsal treadmill. Maybe you and I could meet at an actual restaurant? Lord knows, there are enough of them in town these days."

I wasn't about to blow this opportunity. "That would be great, if you're sure you're not too busy."

"I'll be studying my lines, but I can take a couple of hours off from that."

"You still have my business card?"

"I do." He smiled again. "Be nice to reminisce with somebody about the good ol' days in college. I'll be in touch!"

Lauren returned then with a tan pinstriped suit jacket, which Ed slipped on over his T-shirt. It covered him almost to mid-thigh, and while trying to make a subtle exit, I heard the two of them banter about the length.

"Don't I look like I'm standing in a pothole?" he complained.

"That was the style, back then," Lauren insisted.

"I dunno. Maybe on a tall guy, like Cary Grant…"

* * *

From the parking lot of the playhouse, I called Fred to confirm that I'd dropped off both Ronnie's jewelry and my own pieces.

He told me another of my Roseville vases had sold in my absence. "The buyer sounded like he knew his stuff and might be back for more."

"Fantastic!" I said.

"Yeah, maybe things are looking up. Judging from my receipts, you had a pretty good day today, didn't you?"

"I did, thanks." I wanted to add, *You don't know the half of it!*

Maybe things *were* turning around, I thought happily. Not just for the Addamsville Antiques Center, but for me, too.

Chapter Nine

I said nothing to any of my work colleagues about the upcoming lunch date with Ed. For one thing, it would be too humiliating if it somehow fell through. But mainly, I didn't want to be the subject of gossip among my co-workers…at least, not this early in the game.

I would confide in only one person, and waited until I got home, fed Aramis and myself, and unwound a little. Then I called Mona.

Even though it was after seven, I got only her voicemail. She was probably still at work, hustling to make her reputation as an investigative reporter. "Call me when you get a chance," I told her. "I have some news…pleasant, for a change!"

Meanwhile, I busied myself with a totally frivolous activity—deciding what to wear to my lunch date the next day. I considered a sundress with a retro cherry print, but if we ended up at a casual place, that might be overkill. I could always wear a cardigan to dress it down (most restaurants were over-air conditioned for my taste, anyway). Still, I should also pick an option with pants, and not the same old capris Ed had seen me in twice so far.

I'd assembled a few combinations by eight o'clock, when my sister finally returned my call. She sounded tired but rallied to match my cheerful message. "You're right, I would be happy to hear some good news, for a change. Spill!"

When I told her Ed had asked me to lunch in town, her tone brightened even more. "See, I told you to give it a shot."

"All I did was find a couple of excuses, which were totally legit, to bring stuff over to the theater…and hung around a little longer than I really needed to."

"Sometimes that's all it takes. I'm so happy for you. Finally going out with your college crush!"

"Better late than never, right? Now I'm here, going through the classic airhead routine of trying to decide what to wear. Anything new with you?"

"You'll read most of it in tomorrow's paper. The old guy from the pawn shop, Al Kramer, is out of the hospital, at least. He and his wife were able to give the cops a few more details about the robbers, though they wore masks, same as at the mall jewelry store. And again, the hit seemed targeted—they just went for the flashiest stuff, the 'estate jewelry.' They forced the wife, Betty, to open up those cases for them."

That made me remember the few pieces of very pricey silverware and crystal that Kaye Burrell kept at the back of her booth, in sturdy, locked display cases. Our thief could easily have intended to target those. Maybe he had demanded she open the cases, and Kaye refused. Or maybe she just caught him trying to break into one.

If he'd been out to steal crystal, though, wouldn't he have taken Adrian's candlesticks? Instead of leaving one behind with traces of Kaye's blood still on it?

"I doubt they'll be able to sell the pawn shop's stuff on the street as easily as the watches, though," Mona added. "They might fence it out of state."

"If they do that, at least maybe we'll be rid of them." I was glad to hear that the Kramers were both okay and reunited. Whether they would ever have the courage to re-open their business might be different question.

"But your day was at least as exciting as mine," my sister decided. "Are you going to tell Dad about your date? He might stop trying to fix you up with the boring sons of his golfing buddies."

"I'll wait to see how things go tomorrow," I told her. "I'm still feeling as if it's a little too good to be true."

"Don't think like that. This Kiernan guy has had some tough breaks lately, and you've had some lucky ones. No reason why he shouldn't be interested in a smart, happening lady like you."

"Thanks for the ego boost, Sis. You've almost got me believing it!"

After we hung up, I took care of some after-hours business on my laptop.

I checked for new feedback on my most recent blog post, a history of the Turner prints. Some readers responded that they had seen these commercial artworks in their parents' or grandparents' homes and found them quaint but intriguing. One guy from South Florida said his collection of flamingo memorabilia included a sixteen-by-twenty Turner scene, on canvas, of several rosy birds flocking together in a lagoon.

Speaking of birds…Aramis, sick of being ignored, landed on my knee next to my keyboard and fixed me with a hard stare. I tried to make amends by whistling "Everything Old is New Again," and pretty soon it became a duet. He'd gotten very good at whistling that tune—the chorus, anyway. Maybe I should video him and add that to my web page?

In a surreal twist, I suddenly heard the nostalgic ditty coming from a third source, my cell phone. I glanced at the time on my laptop. Almost nine! Ed had promised to call, though, confirming our plans for lunch. When I grabbed the phone, I found a text, close enough.

Sorry 2b so late, got hung up at the theater. So, noon tomorrow? Want to meet at The Station?

Great, I answered. *CU there!*

Hmm, I thought, that was a pretty nice place. Definitely worthy of the sundress.

* * *

One of Addamsville's most popular and picturesque restaurants, the former train station retained most of its original turn-of-the-century features, including a tall, conical turret at one end and a huge clock above the main entrance. The moderately priced fare and casual atmosphere appealed to the locals as well as tourists.

Ed and I had arranged to meet under the clock. Not terribly original, but hard to miss. It had one drawback, though, that I hadn't foreseen—it also made *him* highly visible. By the time I arrived, he was already signing scraps of paper for two attractive women a few years younger than either of us. Their delighted giggles caused other passers-by to glance his way.

There you have it, Viv. Would you be up to dealing with this every time you're out in public with him? I hadn't expected Ed to be mobbed by fans, since he hadn't even been the star on his cable TV show. But he had excelled in his role, so I guessed he'd still acquired a following.

To his credit, as soon as he spotted me approaching, he thanked his admirers for their kind words but declined to pose with them for selfies. "I only do that at the theater," he told them lightly. "So get your tickets, and I'll see you there!" Then, with eloquent body language, he swung away from them in my direction.

He wore the glasses again today. For some reason, that soothed the butterflies in my stomach. So did his big, welcoming smile.

"Drumming up sales for the show?" I teased.

"Any chance I get. Glad you could make it, Viv!"

It felt odd to suddenly be on such a chummy basis with someone I'd grown resigned to admiring from afar. I almost had the feeling he would have given me a friendly hug, but hesitated because it might be too forward. Or might it stir up gossip among any onlookers who recognized him?

"I'm glad, too," I told him. "Like the playhouse, I guess, the antique center has a weird schedule. It's closed Sunday and Monday, but Saturday is our busiest."

Ed had made a reservation, so despite the weekend crowd, we got seated right away. I didn't know if his modest celebrity had greased the wheels there, too, but the middle-aged female server who brought our menus did seem especially attentive. Then again, by any standards, Ed was a nice-looking guy, his natural charisma bolstered, I'm sure, by his stage training. If he had worn the glasses to keep from drawing attention, he'd underestimated these other assets.

Once again, the college wimp in the rearview mirror of my brain asked, *What the heck is he doing with you?* I told her to shut up and reminded her that, as Mona had said, I "had it going on" these days. Especially in my ladylike-but-flirty sundress.

While scanning his menu, Ed asked, "Do you staff your booth full-time?"

"We're only required to be there three days a week, and some vendors stick to that. But since I'm just getting established, I like to put in more time. From selling at different events in the past, I've found I always do better if I'm there to talk up the merchandise. The average person doesn't know how old, unusual, or valuable something is without a little background."

"Very true. I saw some of the stuff you left with Tom for the main set, 'Gloria's' apartment." He glanced up slyly. "That's going to be quite a living room! Where do you find all of those wild draperies and pillows?"

I explained how I shopped at yard sales, estate sales, and flea markets, which usually had bargain prices. "I've even been known to pick up something left at the curb on trash day, if it's the right period and in good condition. That's how I spend a lot of my 'free' time, and I expect so do most folks in the antiques business. I also sell through my website, The Vintage Vixen."

"Hey, I like that title!" Ed grinned. "Kind of your personal style, too, isn't it?"

He gave me an appreciative once-over, as if he'd not only noticed but liked the retro sundress…and maybe also found the rest of me attractive. This from a guy who had last dated a gorgeous actress from his TV show! Maybe she had soured him forever on tall, leggy blondes? If so, I wouldn't question my luck.

The curly-haired waitress came back for our orders. Although prices at The Station remained reasonable, with the increased tourism in recent years, its menu had grown more adventurous. I ordered a fish taco with a side of spicy black beans, while Ed played it a little safer with a sandwich of sliced turkey and brie on a panini.

"I never heard of that combination before," he confided, after our server had gone, "but I got used to eating a lot of crazy things in L.A."

"You grew up not far from here, didn't you?" I asked.

"Doylestown, a little to the west. But we always kept a summer cottage on this side of the river, and I'm staying there for the run of the show. My dad and his wife live there now." I must have looked confused. "Second wife…he and mom divorced about six years ago."

"That does sound convenient, to have a family place so nearby," I said.

"Weren't you ever out to the cottage? We hosted a couple of cast parties, back in college. You must have been! If you were with the theater crew…"

Avoiding his eyes, I shook my head. "No, I don't think so."

If the theater kids had sometimes partied at Ed's house, no one ever told me. And even if I'd heard rumors, I would never have crashed without an actual invitation. *Besides, back then, he was dating Janet…*

This cast a brief pall on our conversation, and he took a long drink of his iced tea before continuing. "Listen, Viv, I wanted to apologize for not recognizing you, right off, when I came to the antiques center the other day. It just took me a minute to connect you with the person who did all of that backstage work in college. It *was* a long time ago…"

I was gratified, but also embarrassed, that he felt the need to explain. "Please, don't worry about it. I completely understand. Besides, you were two years ahead of me!"

"Still…I guess when people are in school, they tend to break off into cliques. You make friends with folks who have the same major and activities, and soon you've all got your inside jokes, and you hardly even notice anybody outside the gang. But looking back now, I can see that I might've missed a lot that way."

His analysis was so spot-on that I grew even more self-conscious and just waved a hand. "You're right, though. At that age, we all do it."

Our lunches arrived. The server set the plates and drinks in front of us and asked if she could bring anything else. Even when we said no, she lingered, eyes on my date.

She asked in a hushed tone, "You're Edward Kiernan, aren't you?"

With a small, wry smile, he whispered back, "Guilty as charged."

"I don't want to disturb you—I won't ask for an autograph or anything. I just wanted to say that my husband and I were big fans of *Boulevard Blues*, and we're *so* disappointed that there won't be another season. You did such a terrific job as Detective Harrigan!"

"Thanks," Ed said. "I appreciate that."

"So, you're in a show at the playhouse this summer?"

He looked happier to discuss that topic. "Yes, indeed, *Murder Most Noir*. I play a bumbling private detective who, I'm afraid, is almost the total opposite of Patrick Harrigan."

"Oh, dear." She laughed. "But we'll get tickets, anyway. I'm just glad you're still working, and I'm sure you'll land another big TV series in no time."

"Thanks again for your support...you and your husband."

I could tell the woman's comments flustered him. Once she had moved on, I sympathized. "It must be weird to have strangers come up and try to analyze your career moves."

Ed shook his head. "Y'know what's funny, though? My coming back here was really a crazy coincidence. Joel Kaplowitz, the managing director at the playhouse, already had another actor in mind for Harrison. A guy who did one of their spring shows. But he got scouted for a part Off-Broadway, so they let him out of his contract. Luckily, they still had my resumé on file."

"That *was* lucky," I agreed. "Unless you would have preferred the Off-Broadway gig..."

"Not really. This job has its pluses."

The waitress stopped back to ask if we needed anything else, which, for the moment, we didn't."

After she left, Ed cast a quick glance after her, then lowered his voice confidentially. "Y'know what's funny? From what she said earlier, I'm our waitress thinks I'm in a blue funk since the series ended, and just took this play to mark time until my agent finds me another TV show. But the truth is, I'm having a blast doing live theater again! It's less pressure, the playhouse folks are great to work with, and after a decade or so, I'm back here on my home turf. I made decent money from *Boulevard*, and invested a lot of it, so I'm in no big hurry to go back to that grind."

"Really?" All of that sounded encouraging to me.

"Yeah." He swallowed another bite of his sandwich thoughtfully. "Working here reminds me of those days back in college, and of why I first decided I wanted to act for a living. When there's big money riding on your performance, though—and too many sponsors to please—that takes some of the fun out of it."

"Sounds like the kind of thing that made me give up on a conventional interior design career and go into a funkier sideline," I said.

After we'd both made some headway on our lunches, Ed shifted the subject. "Hey, I almost forgot…on the local news, they said someone died recently at your antique center. Like, the day after Lauren and Tom and I were there. Is that why it was closed?"

Maybe because he'd been playing a detective for a couple of years, Kiernan did have a knack for putting clues together. "I actually…found the body. Me and Adrian Marcus, one of the other vendors."

Ed's hazel eyes widened behind the stylishly nerdy glasses. "You did? Wow, I had no idea…the paper didn't give many details. That must have been a helluva shock!"

"It was." I explained how Marcus had brought up the old elevator and checked Kaye, in vain, for any sign of life.

"Was it an accident?"

"We still don't know. The cops questioned quite a few of us vendors, because frankly, Kaye rubbed a lot of people the wrong way. There was no evidence that anyone had stayed in the building overnight, but still, three of us had to go down to the police station to be interrogated. Believe me, that's not as entertaining as it looks on TV."

He winced in sympathy. "No, it's not. Doesn't the antiques center have any security cameras?"

"A few old ones, but I gather they don't all work. And in such a cluttered place, they're pretty useless, anyway."

Ed leaned forward on his elbows, still riveted. "Gee, that's a real-life mystery. Sorry, I know you've still got to work in the place. Guess I have been 'playing detective' too long!"

"I'm pretty curious, myself. I don't like feeling suspicious of my colleagues, especially since I'm the new kid on the block."

We finished our lunches, and Ed ordered coffee for us both. As we talked on, I had the magical feeling that he didn't want our date to end any more than I did. Finally, though, he checked his watch and sighed. "I guess I should get back to the house. I've been promising to help my dad get his boat in shape for the summer, and I've *got* to make good on that this afternoon."

I'd heard rumors, back in the day, that Ed's family was pretty well-off, but no further details. "You have a boat? That must be nice."

"It's really Dad's boat, a thirty-foot Catalina. He used to work on it all by himself, but he had a mild heart attack this past winter and is still taking it easy. My stepmother Trish would help, but she's a Realtor and works a lot of weekends. My younger brother Ken lives in Philly and is kind of a workaholic, too." Ed's expression took on a nostalgic haziness. "In the old days, when we all lived together, the family did more sailing, but now that we've gone our separate ways, it's mostly Dad and Trish. I haven't been home enough, lately, to join them."

"Maybe while you're back here working on the play, you will," I suggested.

"Maybe so!" Ed brightened. "Anyway, Viv, I've really enjoyed getting to know you better. Sorry it took so long for us to actually connect."

I didn't remind him that in our college days, he'd had a steady girlfriend. In case Ed's relationship with Janet had tanked as badly as the one with the Hollywood blonde, why end our date on a downbeat note?

All I said was, "I've really enjoyed this, too."

Ed insisted on picking up the tab, and after only a mild protest, I let him. After all, he was a bona fide TV star.

"I don't suppose you have any more props to bring by the theater?" he hinted. "Ah, but I may have another excuse, soon, to visit your workplace! Y'know that guy who's got the booth with all the old police and military gear? He's loaning me a holster for my gun."

My nerves went on high alert. "Your what?"

"Don't worry, it's a dummy—doesn't even fire. The props department found a sweet replica of a 38. Colt Revolver, also known as a Police Special back in the day. Standard issue for any cop or P.I. in the 1940s. This may be a comedy, but we still want everything as authentic to the period as possible." Ed shifted into a deliberately cheesy Bogart impression. "Besides, Addamsville's not the sleepy little burg it used to be, right? With murderous jewel thieves on the loose, and antique vendors dropping dead in elevators, a guy just might need to pack some heat!"

I couldn't argue with that.

Chapter Ten

Sunday evenings, I usually post a new entry on my blog. Each week I focused on a particular aspect of vintage décor, and with spring in the air I decided to highlight chenille bedspreads. Being lightweight and often featuring floral designs and pastel colors, they tended to be popular for the warmer months.

I wrote:

The technique, embellishing cotton cloth with raised, tufted designs, originated in France—"chenille" is French for "caterpillar." At first, women working in their homes would embroider a white sheet with the same cotton thread used to make candle wicks. They pulled the threads through from underneath, a process called candlewicking. The style caught on in Colonial America, where the artisans created mainly formal, symmetrical, monotone patterns.

Catherine Evans Whitener of Georgia popularized the technique further in the 1890s, and by the 1930s, home crafters could buy sheets already stamped with many creative motifs. Before use the spreads were washed in hot water, which shrank them and locked in the yarn tufts. The designs became more multicolored and whimsical over the years, and homemade chenille spreads brightened up many a bedroom during the Great Depression. Large, multicolored peacocks were all the rage in the 1950s! By that time, more of these bedspreads were mass-produced, and they remained popular through the 1960s.

I illustrated my entry with file photos of some spreads I still owned and a few striking examples I had sold in the past. I embedded a link "for more information" that would take readers to a selection of chenille spreads I currently offered for sale.

As I posted the blog, I couldn't help flashing back on the first time Steve saw my bedroom, in my walk-up apartment in downtown Addamsville. He had found my vintage clothes amusing, at first, but snubbed his nose at my pristine 1940s chenille bedspread.

"Really, Viv," he'd complained, "that's so grandma!"

Toward the end of the evening I'd developed a bad headache, to spare him the discomfort of spending the night in "grandma's" bed. After that, I switched to a newer spread, but I probably waited too long to also start looking for a new boyfriend.

Also on Sunday evenings, I generally checked in with my father, but that night he called me first.

Dad had retired three years ago from his post-*Herald* job, to do public relations and marketing for a nationwide insurance company. He still golfed regularly with some buddies from that firm. He could have remained in the 1950s colonial house where we'd all lived for twenty-five years, but with Mom gone, I guess the rooms echoed with too many memories. Dad had signed the place over to Mona and Artie and moved to an active-adult community a few miles away.

There, he forced himself to socialize with the other over-55 residents, but he still pried into my life and Mona's more than he used to when our mother was alive.

Tonight he immediately got down to the real meat of his call. "I heard on the news that someone died at Addamsville Antiques! Fell into an elevator shaft, or something?"

I was getting better by now at downplaying the incident. "Nobody's sure yet just what happened. The cops questioned most of us vendors, just in case."

"In case...? They think somebody might have killed her?"

"Probably not, but she was kind of a paranoid, unpleasant person. I guess they figure she might have argued with somebody who gave her too hard a shove, then panicked and ran off. The center was shut up tight when I arrived that morning, and another dealer had to unlock the door for me. So…it's still a mystery."

Dad's mind then jumped to lawsuits, and when he asked some questions along that line, I had to admit the antiques center didn't have the tightest security measures. "That's all covered in our contracts, though," I explained. "We vendors agree to accept responsibility for our own booths. Of course, that applies mainly to our merchandise…"

"Not to being attacked by your co-workers, I'm sure." A hint of black humor crept into his voice.

My father started at the *Herald* as a reporter, worked his way up to News Editor, and helped Mona get an internship at the paper right out of college, so he and she shared the same sardonic view of human nature. I think Dad had loved journalism, too, but sensed that even in a key position he would never earn very much in that field. In those days, Mom taught history at the same high school that Mona and I attended—another respectable but low-paying gig. With a second daughter also headed for college, Dad had ditched the newspaper for something more lucrative. He claimed at the time that he'd also had enough of the late hours and deadline pressures. But I could see now that, unintentionally, I had been responsible for pulling him away from his chosen career.

He asked now about my hours at the antiques center. I told him they were very flexible, but I intended to be on site more often than not. "We get decent traffic during the week, but it builds closer to the weekend. Oh, and guess what? I'm loaning some things to a show at the Addamsville Playhouse!"

That did impress him, especially when I said the theater was paying me for the privilege. I wondered how much to confide in Dad, then decided to go for broke. "In fact, an old friend of mine from college is starring in the show—Ed Kiernan."

Dad didn't recognize the name, no surprise. He and Mom came to a couple of the college plays that I'd worked on, but I didn't expect him to remember, after almost twenty years, which students had appeared in the shows. "Oh?

I never heard you talk about him."

"Well, he was two years ahead of me. More of an acquaintance back then, really. But when I stopped over at the playhouse to drop off the drapes and the planter, we reconnected. We even had lunch in town today."

See? You can stop worrying that maybe your artsy, hard-to-please daughter got so disillusioned by her last boyfriend that she gave up on men entirely. I still have a life!

"Well, that's nice." Dad seemed to defer judgment on any guy he hadn't picked out for me himself. "This fellow is in a show at the playhouse? What does he do otherwise? I mean, for a living?"

Good old Dad doubted anyone could support themselves decently in a creative field, which was why he always fretted about me. "Ed doesn't need another job; he's a professional actor. A very successful one, in fact. He was in a TV series last year, *Boulevard Blues*."

A brief silence, I guess, while Dad searched his memory. "Never heard of that."

"It was on cable. Mona and Artie saw it, so they can vouch for him," I half-joked. "The waitress at the restaurant even recognized him! Anyway, don't get all agitated. Ed and I just had lunch, reminisced about college, that kind of thing. I don't even know if he's involved with anyone else."

Dad snorted. "You know he probably is! Those actor guys get around. Don't let someone like that string you along..."

"Please, I'm too old for a lecture. Do I cross-examine you about who you dance with, at those weekly mixers at your community? Ed and I are just friends."

"Um-hm," he commented, skeptically. "Now that I think about it, I do remember the name 'Kiernan' from some context, back in my newspaper days. Is his father in local politics? Maybe a councilman?"

I had not been in the gossip loop, back then, even to the point of hearing that much information. "No idea. I can ask, if I see him again. Would that make him more honorable in your eyes?"

Dad reacted to my snarky tone. "Honey, I just want to see you with someone solid and reliable. A guy who can support you if this business of yours doesn't make much money, or goes under completely. What if somebody does sue the antiques center because of the woman who died there? She must have had some family..."

"She's got a husband, but I don't think he's in any position to sue us. Last I heard, the police are looking at him as a possible suspect."

A beat of silence on the line, then my father spoke again, quietly. "You see, this is the kind of stuff that worries me. If you didn't need the money so much, you wouldn't have to work in such an unsafe place."

No, maybe I could get a nice, steady position at a big jewelry store in a shopping mall—with thieves pulling guns on me, breaking into the display cases, and shooting security guards on their way out.

"I'm not a quitter, Dad. I appreciate your concern, but I've been taking care of myself for nearly twenty years now, and I think I've done okay."

"It's true, you have. Just promise me..."

"I *will* be extra careful at work, at least until this case is solved."

Hanging up, I just wished there was something I could do to help solve it more quickly.

* * *

The next morning, I mailed some items to online customers—a set of draperies in a large, sturdy bag, and a vase well-padded in a strong box marked FRAGILE. Back home, I took advantage of the clear May morning to stroll around my leafy community for half an hour.

Built in the late '80s, Hunterdon Village consisted of about a hundred condos, including more expensive two-story units and the very reasonable semi-detached ranches, like mine. Here, as in many instances, I'd benefited from my taste for vintage. Someone else might have held out for a unit in a sleeker, more modern enclave, and for maybe fifty thousand bucks more, they could have purchased one nearby. But with my old-fashioned tastes, I found our suburban-colonial architecture and pastel exterior color schemes homey. And though we weren't permitted to grow vegetables, the otherwise lush landscaping reminded me I lived in The Garden State. People could think what they wanted about Jersey, but on strolls around my 'hood I inhaled no pollution, only fresh air with assorted floral scents and a nice, green tang of chlorophyll.

Settled back inside, I turned Aramis loose to flit around my home office and bedroom. I'd outfitted his tall cage with all kinds of safe but entertaining gadgets, such as a swinging perch, bells on strings, and chewy rope and cuttlebone toys that would naturally wear down his beak and claws. Still, fish gotta swim, and sooner or later birds gotta fly!

I'd never had his wings clipped, so I guarded against Aramis escaping into the wild, where I'm sure he wouldn't have lasted long among the suburb's cats and hawks. He did seem satisfied with his short flights around the condo, and alighted wherever he wanted to watch the human or animal action outside its many windows.

I had trained him to climb onto my finger when I needed to lure him back into his cage; putting some new food inside also would do the trick. He did insist on quality time with me every day, and if I had to be away from home for longer than that, I brought in a bird-friendly pet sitter to feed and socialize with him.

My choice of animal companion might have been influenced not only by that pet-hating former landlady, but by the birds that showed up so frequently in the vintage artworks and ceramics I collected. I'd briefly considered a full-sized cockatoo, but a little research told me they could be tough to deal with and needed more wing room than I could provide. So I opted for a smaller variety of parrot with better manners. Aramis had become such a good pal over the last few years that I never regretted that decision.

He rode on my shoulder as usual that evening while I moderated my blog and checked my emails. Most came from customers or other vintage fans with questions about collecting, easy enough to answer. Occasionally, one sent me a thank-you and even a photo, to show me how well the draperies, throw pillows, pottery, or artwork they had purchased looked in their home.

One message from Fred Palasinski stood out from the pack. When I had signed on at the antiques center, I had given my email address on my registration file card. Still, I didn't really expect Fred or anyone else from the business to contact me that way, except in an emergency.

As I began reading, though, I wondered if this message fell into that category.

Thought you should know…the cops found footage on one of our cameras that caught a guy poking around the second-floor booths early Thursday morning, when nobody should have been in the building. This might clear both of us—Adrian, too! Call me when you can.

The fans of my blog could wait. I grabbed my phone and punched Fred's personal number.

"Hi, Vivian," he said. "Sorry to bother you on your day off…"

"No bother, especially if it's good news. What's the story?"

"I don't even know if I'm supposed to discuss this with anyone else, but the cops didn't come right out and tell me not to…One upstairs camera that was actually working got footage of somebody prowling around that morning between nine-thirty and ten, before even Kaye was scheduled to arrive. The camera was mounted on a high beam, where the guy probably didn't see it, but it also didn't show his face, mostly the back of his head. He had short dark hair, wore a sweatshirt, and was pretty tall, so that rules out you, me, and Marcus."

"Could it have been another of the vendors?" I asked.

"Most of our longer-term guys are gray-haired, like Adrian and me, or balding. The few younger ones, I'd probably still recognize from their build or their walk. This fella didn't look familiar."

"But there was no sign of a break-in, right? So he'd have to know the door code."

"Exactly. I think there are some high-tech devices that can crack the code…but it's also possible someone *told* this guy the code. In other words, he had an accomplice inside."

My spirits sank again. "Which means any of us could still be suspects."

"Yeah, nobody's totally in the clear…yet," Fred admitted. "The guy was searching around the booths with a flashlight, as if looking for something to steal, and had a small knapsack with him. Funny thing is, the booths in that area weren't stocked with anything really valuable. At one point, around ten o'clock on the video, he looks over his shoulder like something spooked him. You can glimpse his face, but not clearly, and then he slips out of range of the camera."

"Ten o'clock," I repeated. "He might've heard Kaye downstairs."

"That's what the cops think, too. He must have known that the center doesn't officially open until eleven, but didn't realize that one of us usually comes in ahead of time. Could be she heard him or saw the flashlight, came upstairs to check, and blocked his only exit."

"If he didn't know how to use the elevator," I put in.

"Or couldn't reach it in time. If he was trying to get to it, he would have passed Adrian's booth…"

"But Kaye got in the way. So he grabbed the candlestick and knocked her out, or so he thought."

The rest of the scenario was easy to put together. Even if Kaye was just out cold, when she revived, she might be able to identify him. At any rate, the intruder wanted to hide the body until he could escape. He opened the door to the lift, saw it was all the way down at the basement level, and shoved Kaye into the void.

Still, it took a damned cold-hearted character to do that. If his blow to the back of her head didn't kill her outright, the two-story fall could well have finished her off.

"So the good news is, it doesn't seem like anyone currently working at the center murdered Kaye Burrell," Fred concluded. "The bad news is, the killer knew our hours of operation, possibly our door code, and enough about our layout that he came looking for something specific."

＊ ＊ ＊

Fred's phone call left me with a moral quandary, in more ways than one. I now had information that could provide a major scoop for my sister, the reporter. Maybe the police had not cautioned Fred against telling anyone, but I could see how it might hinder their solving the case if the intruder/killer found out they had him on videotape. He might even leave the area, or at least go into hiding. If he still felt confident that no one could identify him, he would go about his daily routine. That way, it might be more likely a cop would spot him...or that he would make a careless mistake.

Maybe that's for Mona and her editor to decide? They'll probably check with the police first anyway, to verify the information. But if the cops told Fred in confidence, I could get him in trouble by leaking the details to anyone else.

I decided, for the time being, to keep it to myself. Mona would be following up with the police, and if they wanted those details in print, they'd share with her. If they didn't, they might have their reasons.

That evening, with time on my hands, I got my mind off Kaye's murder and the surveillance video by investigating another mystery.

Online, I tracked down a second episode of *Boulevard Blues* and devoted an hour to watching the show. I fast-forwarded through the commercial breaks and any parts that got a little too slow and talky. As Mona and Cindy both had said, it was much like any other ensemble cop show, but not bad. Again, what surprised me most was to see Ed playing a very serious, intense character. In this episode, his detective became personally invested in solving a string of grisly murders and got into a shouting match with the police captain over how best to trap the killer. Ed became a totally different person from the happy-go-lucky guy I remembered from our college years, or even from our lunch the previous Sunday.

But that's his job, I reminded myself. *Guess he's good at it—very good.*

Daphne, the blonde he'd gotten involved with for a year or so, played a rookie cop at the same precinct. She stood out mainly for her looks, a stereotypical tall, tanned, and toothy California girl. She certainly bore no resemblance to me or, for that matter, to Ed's college girlfriend, Janet.

The showbiz gossip source said they broke up because Daphne cheated on him. Guess some women are never satisfied!

I remembered Dad asking me if Ed was related to some councilman. He hadn't mentioned a particular town, but it probably wouldn't be in Jersey, since the Kiernans came from Doylestown, Pa. That might be worth researching, if only to reassure Dad that Ed came from a respectable background, and wasn't likely to end up destitute if this acting thing didn't pan out.

I searched under *Councilman Kiernan, Pennsylvania*. And almost instantly wished I hadn't. The news story, admittedly, dated back about fifteen years. Still, the headline came as a nasty shock:

Councilman's Son Questioned in Drowning Death of Fiancée.

Chapter Eleven

I recalled something from my lunch date with Ed. When I'd commented that being interrogated by the police about a murder "wasn't as entertaining as it looks on TV," he had replied seriously, "No, it's not." Did he speak from personal experience?

The news story was brief, but it did name Ed and the deceased woman, Janet Lawler. Had to be the same "Janet" he'd been dating when I knew him. Interesting that he had stuck with her for years after graduation, and had even gotten engaged to her!

On an August evening, her remains had been found in his submerged car, a silver hardtop Corvette, which apparently had gone off the road about half a mile from the Kiernans' cottage. After identifying the owner from the license plate, the police had brought Ed in for questioning.

One factor worked in his favor, though—he had reported the vehicle missing two nights earlier, along with his car keys. Ed told police that he and Janet attended a party at another riverfront home, and after what he thought was a minor argument, she had disappeared. He had intended to go looking for her, but found the keys missing from his jacket and the car itself also gone. The hosts of the party backed up his story and said he was stranded at their place until someone else could take him home. Although Janet's parents wanted to press charges against Ed, the police had no choice but to release him.

A follow-up story, dated a week later, gave more details. Closer examination of the car showed the young woman had not been wearing a seat belt; the front windows had been rolled partly down, which let the water flood in quickly; and both alcohol and prescription sedatives had been found in her system. She also had gone off the road in a lonely spot with light traffic and no guardrail. A medical examiner concluded her death must have been either a DUI or suicide.

Gooseflesh rose on my arms. Even assuming Ed had told the truth, that must have been a horrible burden to live with. I wondered if it could have motivated him to leave the area, just a few months later, to seek acting jobs in Manhattan.

Though suspicious people, like the Lawlers, might think that just made him look guiltier.

I believed in Ed, anyway. If the evidence had been good enough for the police, it was good enough for me. But no wonder he'd had so little to say since then, to the press or to me, about his former fiancée Janet!

I tried to put the whole story out of my mind for the rest of the evening, but in my dreams the cast of *Boulevard Blues* gathered near a river to investigate a suspicious drowning. At one point I became the one sinking, without even the will to struggle, beneath the current of dark, fast-moving water.

* * *

I got to the antiques center a bit before eleven on Tuesday. First, I pulled the throws off my displays and, as usual, checked to make sure everything still looked okay. *Nothing missing that ought to be here, and nothing here that shouldn't be. Check.*

Then I hunted around for the second-floor surveillance camera that had caught our intruder, a week ago. I suspected it was the small, dingy-white dome with the black lens mounted high on an old crossbeam, near the middle of the vast room; that seemed the only one not blocked by any tall cabinets or dividers. It was aimed away from my booth, and more towards Cindy's Shabby Chic display, Ronnie's costume jewelry, and Gerry's pop-culture and rock-and-roll collectibles.

As Fred had mentioned, none of these folks sold anything terribly expensive. I couldn't imagine that a thief would break in just to make off with a gaudy Spider-Man lunchbox or a quilt patterned with faded roses.

Cindy Metcalf also began opening up, and when she caught my eye, the plump blonde woman hailed me. "Oh, hi, Vivian. Glad you came in today. I have a proposition—how do you feel about estate sales?"

This piqued my interest, and I hung nearby while she primped her display. "I've been to a couple," I told her. "They take a lot of energy, and you usually have to go early to get the good stuff. It's only worth it to me if they have the kind of older pieces I carry."

Framed as usual by black liner and mascara, Cindy's blue eyes twinkled. "I've got a lead on one this weekend, just a town away, that could be really promising. The photos online look great. Old trunks, quirky furniture from the 'forties and 'fifties, flowered tablecloths, landscape paintings. I spotted some things that could be good for you, too—some framed bird paintings and Hull pottery."

I appreciated her thinking of me. "You're right, that might be worth a trip. I haven't been shopping lately, because at first my booth was already crammed. But now that I've made some good sales and loaned so many pieces to the theater, it might be smart to restock."

"Then you're interested? We could go together. At these things, two sets of eyes are always better than one. You know I'm strictly Shabby Chic, so we won't be hunting for exactly the same type of merch. If I see something that's more your style, I can give you a heads-up, and vice versa. Plus, my Suburban can hold a lot."

She pulled up the web page for the sale on her phone, and as she scrolled through the photos, I saw the potential. The event ran all weekend, but I agreed that as professionals we needed to get there right at the start.

"Great!" Cindy said. "We'll head out first thing on Friday. You need to sign in as a buyer an hour in advance, and I'm sure there'll be a line forming long before that."

Having gone through this routine a couple of times, I gave her a crooked smile. "I know, that's the downside. But I'm an early riser, anyway."

We made tentative plans to be firmed up on Thursday. As we chatted for a few more minutes, I considered telling Cindy what I'd found out about the intruder on the surveillance video, but decided to keep it to myself. If Fred thought she needed to know, he'd share that information with her.

I was about to head back to my post when Cindy glanced past my shoulder and murmured, "Check out what's going on over there!"

I turned and saw a tall, square-jawed man, his dark hair lightening at the temples, at Kaye's booth. Well-tailored in a tie, sports jacket, and gray trousers, he began pulling the sheets off her merchandise. A second, shorter guy, balding and with glasses, followed a few steps behind. Now and then, they conferred, and the second man paused to tap on what looked like an electronic notepad.

"That's Kaye's husband, Peter," Cindy whispered.

"The taller one?"

She nodded. "He's an investment banker. Never cared much for her working as a vendor, from what she told me. Complained that she spent more time and money hunting for the stuff than she did selling it, and called it a silly hobby."

I felt a rare pang of sympathy for the deceased. "But Kaye had great taste and knew her field, didn't she? She probably preserved a lot of wonderful Craftsman oak pieces that someone else might have trashed, if they didn't know any better."

"Very true." Cindy's gaze followed the two men as they prowled around the shelves and cabinets. "I wonder where it all will end up now. That guy with the glasses has to be an assessor. I'm sure Peter wants to know what everything is worth, so he can sell it off and invest the cash."

"That's too bad," I commented, staying deliberately neutral.

She elbowed me. "Like to get your hands on some of that early Roseville, wouldn't you?"

"Only if he'd give me a big break on it, and I have a feeling he doesn't intend to do that."

"No, if anything, he'll probably jack up the prices from what Kaye charged. She also mentioned having a storage unit somewhere, and you can bet she stashed plenty more in there. Peter will probably send it all to some upscale auction house." Facing her own booth again, Cindy sniffed. "He might have criticized her 'hobby' when she was alive, but he's inherited a windfall now. I just hope while the cops were questioning all of us, they also took a close look at him!"

I hoped so, too. Especially since Peter Burrell was the first man I'd seen on the premises lately who fit the general profile of the guy on the grainy videotape—tall, slim, and with a full head of dark hair. And, as Kaye's spouse, he could easily have known the building's entry code, or persuaded her to let him in.

But really, would Kaye's husband have risked killing her at her workplace? Couldn't he have found a more private locale, or even hired a hit man? Unless he was trying to direct suspicion away from himself, and onto one of us...

Even after I went back to tending my own booth, I kept glancing in the direction of Kaye's. Finally, Peter pulled the sheets back over the merchandise, and he and the assessor retreated downstairs together.

Around noon, Adrian Marcus also strolled across the aisle to chat with me about Burrell's visit. "Would've been nice if he gave some of us first crack at her wares, but I never expected that."

"Probably just as well," I pointed out. "Then the cops would really be able to say that you or I had motives to kill Kaye."

"Fred, too," he added lightly. "After all, Kaye rented that forty-foot space for eight years. Once her inventory is cleared out, he can either rent out the whole thing again, or as two twenty-footers. He's always got a waiting list for new vendors. And over the years, I don't think Fred ever increased Kaye's rent, so he can probably ask quite a bit more."

"Sounds like we've all got motives galore." Again, I made no mention of the surveillance video, because I could not be sure if Fred had discussed that with Marcus, either.

That day, I had a fair number of browsers at *Vintage by Vivian*. I could always spot the people on their lunch hours, who either scanned things idly or made quick, efficient purchases, having done their comparison shopping the previous weekend. Usually, the impulse buys were less expensive items, such as smaller pieces of pottery or framed artworks. Still, one lady, who either did not need to work or maybe ran her own business, had the time and the means to look over a few of my chenille bedspreads. She sprang for a pricey "wedding ring" design in mint condition, and confided that she would be giving it to a friend as an engagement present.

Around five o'clock, riding on a high from a successful day, I got a phone call from Tom Richardson at the theater. He'd decided which draperies, throw pillows, and other décor to use for the set of *Murder Most Noir*, so he could return the pieces that didn't make the cut to me.

"Rather than make you drive back here, though," he said, "we can deliver them to you. Will you be around tomorrow?"

"I certainly can be," I told him, secretly disappointed not to have another excuse to visit the playhouse.

"Terrific. Lauren also needs to return a few things, so our props assistant Lenny is going to drive her over. He's got a truck that can accommodate everything and everyone. They'll probably get there a little early, like last time, to avoid your regular customers."

"Thanks for the heads-up," I said. "I'll be here by ten."

"Great. Oh, and our marketing director is talking with Fred about program ads for you and Adrian and Ronnie...any of the vendors who are lending stuff for the show. If you have a logo or slogan for your business that you want to use, send that material to her." He gave me the woman's email address, and I scribbled it on the back of one of my business cards.

The thought of a prominent ad in the show's program got my adrenaline pumping again. That could mean many more days like this one, with brisk traffic. Plus, maybe a boost to my online sales, for out-of-towners who might take home their programs from the show. I no longer nurtured any desire to become a famous set designer or an interior decorator with celebrity clients. To build my current business into a solid success would satisfy me just fine.

Well, that and...

With the show coming together, and rehearsals no doubt stretching longer and growing more intense, I wondered when and if I'd ever get to see Ed again.

* * *

It was my usual night to dine with Mona, and before I left work, she gave me a call. "Unfortunately, our kitchen is torn up right now, because we're replacing the countertops. They're being fabricated, and in the meantime, all we've got for a work surface is plywood."

"Come to my place, then," I invited her. "But you can bring dinner."

"You got it. How about something from Spiro's?"

"I'll never say no to that!" I'd eaten before, with her, at the local Mediterranean restaurant. We both called up the takeout menu on our phones, and I made my selections. I gave Mona my ETA and figured she would get to my condo about half an hour after I did. That should give me time to whip my own kitchen into good enough shape to play hostess.

When I first moved to my current nest in Hunterdon Village, I hesitated to invite even a family member to eat there. We vintage aficionados have our own prejudices, and I'd hated the 1980s flat-panel, cream-colored cabinets framed in strips of dark wood. The sterile style offended me, as did the lack of any cabinet knobs or pulls. But after some online research, I bought paint that adhered well to the laminate cabinet material. I'd painted them a uniform off white, drilled some holes, and added chrome hardware worthy of a retro diner. The "bisque" stove, overhead microwave, and dishwasher coordinated well enough, so I accepted them as more welcome modern conveniences.

At home, I straightened up any clutter I'd left behind that morning and fed and apologized in advance to Aramis. I usually let him out as soon as I arrived, but my sister, for some reason, got edgy if the bird flew around while she was present. I think she imagined that he'd poop on her shoulder, get tangled in her hair or shed feathers into her food. He never did any of those things, even with me, but Mona wouldn't be reassured.

For someone who's always been single, I can claim to have two full sets of dinnerware—one I inherited and one I bought for myself. For special occasions, I'd scavenged a set of eight Franciscan Coronado dishes, in assorted earthy pastels. On another antiquing jaunt, I'd found a set of tall drinking glasses, each with a leaping gazelle in a different pastel color, that coordinated perfectly.

For tonight's casual dinner with my sister, though, I again pulled out Nana's hardworking "Starburst" plates, saucers, and coffee cups. They came with a chip here or there, but that never discouraged me. All the pieces bore a design of stylized "atomic" explosions in aqua, green, and yellow. On a different antiquing jaunt, I had found a set of Mid-Century "highball glasses" with a similar starburst design.

Mona showed up with paper sacks that gave off enticing fragrances of garlic, feta cheese, and assorted tangy herbs. She looked none the worse for wear after her long day chasing down news stories, prying information from reluctant interviewees, and then knocking out the articles on deadline. With the warmer weather, she'd switched to khaki trousers and a lightweight navy blazer, which she shed to reveal a short-sleeved, sky-blue knit top.

"I am starved!" she declared, as I began to open the aromatic cartons. "I usually grab an afternoon snack, but I was so busy today I never got the chance."

No wonder she stayed so slim, I thought. "Well, now you can relax."

Mona pulled out one of the chairs from my white-painted, cottage-style dining set, authentically 1940s. With its enameled green tabletop, we needed no cloth. I knew Mona liked a light beer at the end of the day, so I opened a chilled can and poured the contents into one of the tall, retro glasses.

"Ah, I need this, too," she said.

My sister always burned calories more efficiently than me, and for herself she spooned out a helping of rich *moussaka*—lasagna-like layers of eggplant and ground beef topped with a creamy bechamel sauce. More weight-conscious, I happily tucked into my grilled chicken-and-vegetable kebab on a bed of savory rice.

Meanwhile, my plates revived memories for Mona. "When Nana died, Mom was ready to junk this set because it was too old-fashioned. She couldn't believe you actually wanted it. You were still in college, but I remember you stowed the box it in a corner of your room, and kept saying you'd use the dishes in your first apartment."

"Which I did," I pointed out. "Mom never shared my mania for vintage, but even she had to admit it was more practical than throwing them out or even donating the set to charity. And it's a nice reminder of Nana."

Once my sister had satisfied the worst of her hunger, she moved on to fresher topics. "Guess what? Today, we found somebody to give us a sketch of one of the jewel robbers! Well, the Delaware cops did. A bystander spotted the two guys running away and got a pretty good look."

I paused for a sip from my water glass. "I thought they were wearing masks."

"They were, but I guess when they got close to their getaway car, one of them pulled his mask down." She tapped her temple. "Brilliant, right? Got a partial on the license plate, too."

"That is progress! Hope they never find out who IDed them, though, considering they shot a security guard during that job."

"Maybe, after that boneheaded move, they realize they're in even deeper trouble now," Mona reasoned. "They've already made a pretty big haul, so let's hope they lie low for a while."

I started on the second of my two kebabs, using my fork to ease the grilled chunks of lamb and vegetables from the skewer and onto my dwindling bed of rice. Meanwhile, I told Mona that I had not heard back from Betty Kramer about the status of her husband's health or of their pawn shop business. I speculated, "Wouldn't that stolen 'estate' jewelry be marked in some way that will make it hard to fence?"

Mona shrugged. "It probably is, but thieves can work around that. They can take those pieces out of state to less reputable pawn shops. The proprietors are supposed to ask sellers for ID, and keep it on file, but a license is easy to fake. The most valuable jewelry, they might fence through a middleman on the black market. Find one unscrupulous customer with deep pockets, and that stuff will disappear forever."

Oh well, I thought, it's not as if those pieces still belonged to somebody who would miss them for sentimental, or even financial, reasons. "If the mall jewelry store was insured for this kind of thing, maybe the pawn shop is, too."

"They are, which is why the cops might have slacked off on their investigation...except that the guard at the mall got shot. Now the thieves are wanted for not only grand larceny but assault with a weapon, causing bodily harm. If that shooter is smart, he's already far away by now."

I couldn't resist a smirk. "But we've already established that he *isn't* smart, right?"

"True. So maybe he'll slip up again and the cops will finally nail him." With a grin, my sister suddenly veered onto a new subject. "Meanwhile, Viv, I think you've been keeping secrets from me."

That brought me up short. I'd been debating whether to tell her about the surveillance video of the antiques center intruder. If the police hadn't released that information to the papers yet, they might wonder how Mona found out...and I could get in trouble.

I must have looked guilty, because she needled me further. "Dad ratted you out!"

"Dad—?"

"He told me you had lunch on Sunday with that Kiernan guy."

Though this topic came complete with a whole different set of secrets, it was still easier to deal with. "Well, if you know that, you know everything. We had a nice, innocent conversation about our college days, about how show biz isn't all it's cracked up to be, and even about the murder at the antiques center."

"Was Detective Harrigan able to solve that for you?"

I rolled my eyes. "Poor Ed, he only did that show for one season, but the character may dog him for the rest of his life." I told Mona how the restaurant server had over-sympathized with Ed about the series' cancellation until he was embarrassed.

"Just shows he made an impression on a lot of viewers," Mona pointed out. "I agree with her—he'll get another big TV role, soon enough. Though you probably wish he'd hang around here."

"Not sure how long he will, after the run of the play. Plus, you might have gathered that Dad's not too thrilled I even had lunch with Ed. I think he's still hoping to fix me up with some nice, boring insurance wonk with a steady income."

"Oh, bull. Steve seemed like a pretty solid citizen, at first, and look how he turned out! You've hardly dated at all since then, and speaking as your older sibling, forty's just around the corner. I say take advantage of any opportunity, even if it's just for fun."

"You're probably right." I ate in silence for a minute before confiding a more serious concern. "The last time I talked to Dad, on the phone, he said he remembered hearing of a councilman in the area named Kiernan. I got curious enough to check online, and I think I figured out why it stuck in his mind."

Glad we were in the privacy of my kitchen, and not some crowded restaurant, I shared what I had discovered about Ed's past.

By the time I finished, Mona's dark eyes were practically bulging. "Holy crap, that's some story! At least it sounds like the police were satisfied that he wasn't driving the car and couldn't be held responsible. Maybe this Janet was just a wild party girl?"

I shook my head. "Not as far as I remember. Just the opposite, in fact—she was mousy and quiet. About my height, but thinner, with long, boringly straight hair, a pale complexion, big eyes, and always dressed very nondescript. Hardly the type you'd expect to get stoned at a party, steal her boyfriend's 'Vette and drive into a river!"

"He said they had a fight at the party," Mona reminded me. "Maybe that set her off."

"I guess. The whole thing does make me wonder about their relationship. I always sort-of admired Ed for sticking with Janet, when she was nowhere near as attractive as some of the student actresses he played opposite in our college shows. Of course, I only knew what I heard through the gossip mill, which was probably watered-down and second-hand. After all, I wasn't a cast member—just backstage crew." *You never even knew about the parties at his family's lake house,* I reminded myself, *so you probably missed out on a lot of inside information.*

Mona thoughtfully chewed the last mouthful of her *moussaka* before she popped the key question. "Gonna ask him about it?"

"I really hate to," I admitted, with a grimace. "It's got to be a painful memory. Besides, I wouldn't want him to think I went snooping into his past."

"Tell him the truth. Say your father's an old newspaper guy and remembered hearing the story. That's only a slight exaggeration. Let Ed take it from there."

I dropped my gaze to my plate, where the last few chunks of meat and peppers had lost their appeal for me. "What if I don't like his answer? I've sort of put him on a pedestal, all of these years. Now I might find out things about him I don't really want to know."

"Better now, Viv, than after you get even more involved." Mona's eyes sought mine. "Am I right?"

As usual, she was.

Chapter Twelve

When I got to the antiques center just before ten the next day, I found it already open. Of course—Tom Richardson probably had alerted Fred that he would be coming by to return a few things and pick up a couple more.

I closed the umbrella I'd brought to ward off the light drizzle and stashed it in a corner of my booth. After I uncovered my display, I filled my time by scrolling through the local headlines on my phone. I came across the police sketch Mona had told me about, of the robber who had fled from the Delaware robbery. The black-and-white drawing showed a guy with a broad face, blocky chin, full lips, and heavy-lidded eyes. I marveled that an eyewitness who just saw him running towards the getaway car could have remembered such details. The rest of the article said he was about six feet tall with an athletic build, probably in his thirties, with dark hair.

The surveillance camera at the antiques center had not caught our intruder's face, but the build, hair color, and age range sounded similar. If the same two guys had robbed both the mall jewelry store and the Jonesburg pawn shop, one of them could easily have still been in our area the morning Kaye was killed. In today's story, Mona quoted Betty Kramer as saying that, from what she'd seen of his face above the mask, the man in the mall sketch could have been one of the pair who'd robbed her and her husband.

That still didn't mean, though, that he was the same guy in the antiques center's grainy video. If someone was out to steal high-priced items, why poke around our place? The locked cases where Kaye kept her most valuable pottery and silver, and which some other vendors also used for their more fragile, pricey antiques, had not been tampered with at all!

Maybe he didn't anticipate those problems; he thought he'd pick up some small valuables and get in and out fast. But when Kaye surprised him, he still couldn't risk her identifying him. Or maybe it had been some other, less experienced thief, and the superficial resemblance to the Delaware-mall robber was just a coincidence.

The front buzzer, sounding while the center was officially closed to the public, announced the return of the Addamsville Playhouse folks. They checked in with Fred downstairs, then made the climb to the second floor. Tom's tread sounded heavy, probably because he was carrying a few things to return to me.

With a smile, he handed over a set of draperies patterned with oversized ferns and leaves, in shades of teal green and magenta on black. "These read a little *too* strong from the stage—they might steal the scene from the actors!" he said, with a note of regret. "But I do like this design, so I held onto the version with the light gray background. That one's just dramatic enough."

I agreed, "Probably a better choice."

"And we kept the jardinière, of course." From a large tote bag, he removed a carefully wrapped Turner print of egrets in an etched, mirrored frame. "You can have these guys back, because we decided on the flamingos—more 'Hollywood.' If you don't mind, we'll keep all four throw pillows, just in case we need something to punch up a side chair."

"No problem," I said, "just as long as nobody actually punches any of them, during a fight scene! Those old fabrics can be fragile."

Tom chuckled. "We do have a fair amount of onstage mayhem, but I'll tell everyone to go easy on the props. Is Adrian around this morning?" He craned over his shoulder towards Marcus' booth. "I'm returning a bookcase to him."

"Haven't seen him so far." I heard a rumbling from about twenty feet away and felt the familiar vibration of the freight elevator.

So did Tom. "That's probably the bookcase, now. It has glass doors, so we figured that was the safest way to bring it up."

The gatelike barrier rose, and two slim men in jeans and hooded sweatshirts stepped out. With care, they rolled out a dolly bearing a square piece of furniture that had been wrapped and tied in old blankets. One of the guys pushed back his rain-dampened hood, revealing spiky hair dyed green at the ends, and asked, "Where does this go?"

"Over here, Lenny, thanks." Richardson directed him to Marcus's area.

The second hooded man kept pace with him, holding their cargo steady as the dolly rolled over the aged wooden floors. Tom pointed to the spot where the bookcase originally had stood and helped them lift it off the crude platform.

"It's okay, boss, we got this," Lenny's partner wisecracked, getting my attention.

"Wouldn't want you to strain anything, Kiernan," Tom tossed back. "We need you onstage, not doing the grunt work."

"It's good exercise." Ed brushed back his hood, too, and my heart did a little skip when I glimpsed those short auburn waves. He scanned his surroundings for a minute, caught me staring, and gave me a cheery salute.

As I smiled back, I suffered an irrational pang of guilt. How would Ed feel if he knew I'd been checking up on the circumstances of Janet's death, and even analyzing them with my reporter sister? Suddenly, that felt disloyal, somehow.

"Go down and see if the army dudes are here, so you can pick up your holster," Tom told him. "You might pass Lauren on the way—she wanted to get something more from the jewelry lady."

I had not seen Ronnie so far that morning, and wondered if Lauren would need any help choosing what she wanted. Okay, that excuse also would let me keep Ed in view, and see if he actually had brought along a realistic-looking 1940s police revolver on his visit today.

Near the head of the main staircase, I found Lauren hovering in limbo, probably because the display tables of *Bauble and Bangles* were still blanketed. "I don't like to go poking around without Ronnie present," she told me, "but last time I was here, she said she'd be happy to lend me anything else she had. Do you think..."

I folded back the big blanket so Lauren could scan the stock on the main table. "If there's anything you really want, I'm sure Fred can call and ask her about it. He might even be able to tell you the value for your release form."

With this in mind, Lauren combed through the assortment of gaudy costume pieces. This time, she mostly ignored the brooches and earrings and seemed to concentrate on short necklaces, but at first, nothing impressed her. She worked her way towards some older pieces arranged on a small, antique dresser, muttering half to herself, "I want something to fill the neckline of a low-cut gown. It's very simple, but it's green satin, so it needs... What's in here?" Lauren zeroed in on a large tabletop jewelry chest with four drawers. She pulled them out one by one and rifled through more strings of beads and paste gemstones. "No, I don't see anything here that's quite... Oooh, wait a minute!"

Lauren fished something from the back of the last drawer and held it up to the light. Even from several feet away, I could see it gleam.

"This is perfect!" the costume designer crowed. "Vivian, what do you think?"

Of course, I was no expert on either jewelry or costuming, and hadn't even seen the special gown. But the necklace was spectacular, for a fake. Almost a choker, it featured a double strand of pearls from which hung a center medallion—mixed seed pearls and rhinestones surrounding a large, square, green gem.

"They'll be able to see that even from the back rows!" Lauren gushed again, then inspected the piece more closely. "I can't find a price on it, though, or any other markings."

I also checked the back of the medallion, but the filigreed metalwork was so textured that it would have been hard for Ronnie to write anything on it. "Maybe there was a tag that fell off." I remembered the incident with Kaye Burrell's vase. "Or maybe Ronnie just added the piece recently and hasn't had a chance to tag it yet."

To save time, I phoned Fred at the front desk and explained the situation. He was busy helping a customer, but he gave me Ronnie's cell number so I could check directly with her. She didn't answer, and I left her a brief message. Before hanging up, I snapped a close-up photo of the necklace and sent that to her phone, too.

Lauren waited for a few more minutes to see if I got any response, then checked the time on her own phone and winced. "Oh, man, I really want to take this back to the theater with me today. Do you think Fred…"

I nodded. "Sure, talk to him about it. He probably can give you some kind of paperwork and get the details from Ronnie later."

"I'll go do that right now. Thanks for your help, Vivian!" She trotted briskly down the main stairs with her faux treasure.

Meanwhile, I heard rather than saw activity from the big, army-green corner booth on the first level. Heck, I had nothing important to take care of at the moment—why not yield to temptation, and go down to spy on Ed?

I found him discussing the merits of a compact, shiny revolver—probably the one the theater had provided for him—with Carl Randolph. The taller, heavier man grasped the weapon like an expert, testing its grip and balance.

"Real nice replica," Carl said. "And I've seen the real thing. This is a .38 Detective Special, single-action and with a short barrel, which would be realistic for your character. The Police Special was double-action and had a longer barrel, but plainclothes detectives and PIs preferred these 'cause they were easier to conceal. Unless you want it to be bigger…"

"I personally don't have any problem with the size," Ed told him dryly, "as long as it's visible to the audience. This is so shiny, it ought to be."

"Solid nickel. Like I said, a real good facsimile." Carl checked the weapon's chamber to make sure it was empty. "Does it fire at all?"

"As far as I know, not even blanks."

Carl pointed the gun at an empty patch of brick wall, and I heard a soft click…but nothing else. "Interesting. It does cock, though."

"Yeah, that's what the prop guy told me. I guess they made it like that to add a little drama."

The vendor nodded again. "Okay, we got the holsters over here. A belt holster hid the gun better and allowed for a faster draw. A shoulder holster would show more, when you reached inside your coat."

Ed mulled this decision. "Which actually might be better, for our purposes."

While the two men debated these fine points, I scanned the other offerings of the Randolphs' large, green-tented booth. Carl and his brother Morty kept much of their merchandise locked in acrylic cases, similar to the ones used by Kaye and Adrian.

Because these items are very collectible, or very dangerous?

I peered in fascination at the gas masks, canteens, flat-brimmed helmets and peaked officers' caps, swastika armbands and Red Cross insignias. The various medals could have been worth a lot, but they were well secured, as were the weapons. The Randolphs might not carry any firearms, but I shuddered to think how some of those cleaver-sized knives and long daggers would have been used in combat.

Finally, Lauren stopped by and offered her opinion. Ed left the Randolphs' booth with both the leather shoulder holster and the faux revolver, in a generic brown paper sack, and met up with me in the aisle.

"Told you I'd be back," he said lightly, but in a low tone that felt intimate. "This place intrigues me, I can't stay away."

"You did a good job earlier, masquerading as a humble crew member, when you helped bring up that bookcase. Very brave of you both, to ride up in the Lift of Doom."

Ed's eyes widened behind his glasses. "Y'know, I was halfway up before it even occurred to me. Is *that* where the woman's body—?"

"It is. Though the cops have gone over it so thoroughly, since then, I'm sure they left it pretty clean."

He shuddered. "Still! In L.A., they probably would have saged it—that New Age stuff—to get rid of the bad energy."

Lauren met up with us again at the foot of the stairs and told Ed, "We should get going, now. It's almost eleven."

"Ah, yes." He rolled his eyes, for my benefit. "We'd better scram before the more respectable customers show up."

I walked toward Fred's front office with them. Nodding toward the bag Ed carried, I warned, "Better not run any red lights with that in the car!"

"No problem," Lauren assured me. "The theater holds a permit for this gun as a stage weapon. And even though New Jersey has strict firearms regulations, you're allowed to carry a fake gun as long as you don't use it to try to commit a crime."

"Really! So I guess you don't need to have someone official on the set to make sure the gun is handled safely, and all that?"

"Fortunately, no," she said. "Not for something like this."

"We had to do that on the set of *Blues*," Ed told me, "and it always made me kind of nervous. Even when you're only shooting blanks, accidents can happen and people can get hurt. But I don't even pretend to fire this thing in our show."

I smiled in relief. "Glad to hear it."

He let Lauren get a few steps ahead of us to say her goodbyes to Fred, and faced me again. "Listen, Viv, things are getting pretty intense now at the theater, with only a couple of weeks 'til we open. But let's keep in touch, okay? If you want, we can at least grab another lunch, or even dinner."

"I'd like that a lot," I said.

With another megawatt smile, he gave my upper arm a quick squeeze. "Then we'll make it happen. Meanwhile, don't go finding any more dead bodies!"

I wandered back to my booth in a happy fog, but gusts of self-protective skepticism soon cleared my head. Did Ed have any serious interest in me, or was he just leading me on, as someone to kill time with while he was in town for the play?

At this point, I decided, he still thought of me mainly as a friend, a pleasant reminder of his younger days. Even back then, he'd always had a knack for charming people, and flirted lightly with the girls in the cast and crew. If Ed and I did remain "just friends," could I be satisfied with that?

Why not? Heck, it would still be more of a relationship than we ever had before!

For the time being, I pushed all thoughts about his ill-fated engagement with Janet to the basement level of my mind. I almost felt relieved that, so far, we'd never had enough time or privacy for me to ask him about the almost-literal skeleton from his past.

Chapter Thirteen

Traffic at my booth was sparse that afternoon, and while lounging on my rattan loveseat and checking (hoping?) for responses to my latest blog, I almost dozed off. Around three o'clock, the sprightly notes of my ringtone snapped me back to attention. So did Ronnie's number on the screen.

"Viv, thanks for calling me." She sounded a little drowsy herself. "Guess I should have come in today, but I woke up with a migraine."

"Ouch," I sympathized.

"Yeah, I get them once in a while, often enough that I have prescription meds. I took one of those this morning, and I'm just starting to feel like myself again." She paused, as if to remember why she'd called me. "Anyhow, I'm kind of puzzled by the picture you sent. Are you sure Lauren found that necklace in my booth?"

"Positive, I was with her at the time. She said you told her if she ever needed anything else from your stock, she could just help herself."

"Yes, I did. It's just that I don't even remember this piece. Where did she find it?"

"She was rummaging through that jewelry box, like a little dresser, at the rear corner of your table. It was at the back of a drawer. I can't give you any more information, because it wasn't tagged with a price or even your booth number."

"Sounds like I must have overlooked it completely!" Another beat of silence on the line. "Y'know what probably happened? About a month ago, I answered an ad by someone who was selling a big 'lot' of costume jewelry. I swear, this stuff must have belonged to a drag queen—very flamboyant. I brought it home, dumped it all on my kitchen table, and spent most of that night tagging the things. But if I let one slip by, it would be no surprise. I was bleary-eyed by the time I finished! Next morning, I just scooped it all into my suitcase and brought it into my booth."

Sounded plausible, I thought. Though even under those circumstances, I still wouldn't have expected her to forget the faux pearl-and-emerald choker. Of course, if it somehow got shuffled to the very back of a drawer...Out of sight, out of mind.

"Anyway," Ronnie said, "I'll get in touch with Lauren, give her a price, and when I come in tomorrow, I'll square everything with Fred. I know he likes to keep his books in order."

"He does!" I agreed, with a chuckle. "Feel better, and hope I'll see you tomorrow."

*　*　*

The days were getting longer and warmer, and that evening after dinner, I decided to unwind by the community pool. I figured it would be quiet, any kids still tied up with homework or after-school activities, and many commuting adults probably not yet home from their jobs. The water still would be too cool to swim in, at least for my taste. Nevertheless, I put on shorts and a T-shirt, loaded a new romantic suspense novel into my e-reader, and staked out a poolside lounge chair.

The community's outer fence and a long row of maple trees screened the pool area from the public road. I enjoyed just listening to the light breeze rippling through their vivid green leaves, combined with the lusty song of a robin perched somewhere in their midst. The management company took pains to always keep something in bloom from spring through fall, and now tulips, crocuses, and irises began to unfurl their bright heads in the various garden plots. Except for occasional passers-by, I had the place to myself, and for the moment, I imagined that Hunterdon Village was my private estate.

I used to think that when I "grew up," I'd move somewhere that stayed warm all year long, Florida or California. As an adult, I'd realized this was easier said than done, but I guess I still indulged my fantasy via the tropical flora and fauna of my vintage fabrics and Turner prints.

On the other hand, maybe California isn't all it's cracked up to be. Ed doesn't seem to miss it very much—he sounds happy to be back in New Jersey!

Letting the e-reader drop to my lap for a minute, I reflected that maturity also had changed my concept of the ideal man. I gravitated toward the kind of romantic suspense plots where a strong female character helps the male protagonist triumph over terrible odds and bring down the bad guys. But the typical hero in those stories tended to be brooding, cool, and tough, repressing his real feelings for his partner until the very end.

Had I been looking for someone like that when I'd ended up with Steve? It hadn't occurred to me that such a guy also might be rigid and out of touch with his own emotions. That once he felt sure his partner had committed to the relationship, he might turn judgmental, controlling, and arrogant.

Though I'd never dated Ed in school, I'd remembered him as much different from that type. As far as I could tell, since we'd reconnected, he still was. Ironically, for an actor, Kiernan seemed even less concerned than the average guy about maintaining an "image." Secure but also spontaneous; more apt to poke fun at himself than anyone else.

As the sun began to set behind the trees and the air cooled, I officially relinquished my girlish dreams of pairing up with a steely-eyed James Bond. I'd be much happier with—what was his name, again?—a "Danny McDougal."

Unless, of course, Ed came with a different set of character flaws. Such as turning a blind eye to his girlfriend's addiction to drugs and alcohol...with fatal results?

* * *

Thursday morning, as I came in the front door of Addamsville Antiques, I passed Ronnie by the cashier window. She and Fred seemed to be dealing with paperwork for the loan of the "pearl-and-emerald" choker to the playhouse, and I shamelessly paused to listen.

Ronnie told him she could only estimate how much it might be worth, based on her general experience with costume jewelry.

Fred squinted at her phone, which displayed the photo I'd sent her of the necklace. "If it's in good shape, I'd estimate a couple hundred dollars, right?"

"Even though I didn't look it over carefully, I'd say so, too." She wrote something on the theater's printed form.

"Seems to me, you're loaning them your best stuff," Fred needled her. "You also let 'em have that big rhinestone pin…Don't you want to keep things like that for your actual customers?"

Wisely, Ronnie just smiled. "First, not very many of my customers buy such extravagant pieces—they're still kind of costly, but too obviously fake. Second, the theater is paying me just to borrow them. And third, if I can tell customers that those pieces appeared onstage at the Addamsville Playhouse, more people probably will want them, for whatever price I ask!"

Fred jutted his lower lip in surrender. "Good points, all of them."

I let the two wind up their business and ascended to the second floor. Cindy Metcalf was arranging silk flowers in a white enamel chamber pot, on top of a pale-gray painted side table. When she saw me pass by, she asked if we were still on for the estate sale the next day.

I assured her I was, but hadn't yet checked out the offerings online.

"You will need to do that," she said, "so you won't waste time, and can head right for the merchandise you want. At least this isn't one of those really monster sales, where you have to get your name on the list a day in advance. But it's still first come, first served. If it starts at nine, we'd better be there at least by seven, to get a good place in line."

That sounded a little daunting, since I'd already gotten into the routine of later-to-bed and later-to-rise, but I knew she was right. The earlier you hit one of these events, the better crack you had at the quality pieces. "Should I meet you there?"

Cindy frowned in thought. "You've seen my SUV in the lot, right? The big old Suburban?"

I had noticed one such vehicle that took up more than its fair share of real estate. "The metallic bronze one?"

"That's my baby. It holds a lot, so unless we go completely nuts, we probably can get all our purchases there. If you decide to buy something extra bulky, like a large piece of furniture, I'm sure the showrunners will take a deposit until you come back for it."

I didn't plan to get that kind of thing, anyway, since right now my booth was near capacity. "Okay, so you want to travel together?"

We made plans to meet in the parking lot the next day, at about six-thirty, and take Cindy's bronze behemoth to the estate sale.

For the rest of the afternoon, during my spare time, I studied the event's web page, which included a lot of pictures. They weren't very professional, though, and a shot of many small knick-knacks spread out on a dining table didn't tell me if any would be worth my time. I did spot what looked like an early-midcentury wooden cabinet that intrigued me, though, and a stack of folded bedcovers that included flowered quilts and some chenille. Maybe I could strike a deal with Cindy—let her have dibs on the Shabby Chic florals while I plundered the second group?

I also knew from past experience that if I decided to target certain items, I should decide in advance how much I was willing to pay for them. Then I'd bring an ample amount of cash—which some sellers still preferred—but not so much that I'd be tempted to overspend.

Foot traffic stayed slow for the rest of the day, and since it was another beautiful, warm afternoon, I decided to leave work a little early. I passed Adrian, who relaxed in one of his deco armchairs, reading something on his phone, but I could see across the room that neither Ronnie nor Gerry were at their stations. Maybe they'd been tempted to play hooky by the beautiful spring weather, too.

I said goodnight to Fred and left by the front door. As I rounded the corner of the building, I thought I heard a harsh whisper from the direction of the rear lot. That made me slow my steps in caution. I realized it came from a figure hunched over what must be his cell phone, in the shadow of the building's old fire escape. A few steps closer, and I recognized Gerry by his voice and his mussed, dark-blond locks, though he faced away from me.

"How the hell was I supposed to know that would happen?" he hissed to whoever was on the other end of the line. "It was just a freak thing! I wasn't even around..." The normally laid-back vendor ran an agitated hand through his hair, rumpling it even more.

I felt a bit guilty for eavesdropping, but he stood between me and my car. And frankly, I was too curious to go back into the building, or kill time somewhere else, while he finished his call. I sensed it might take a while.

"No, she doesn't know," Gerry said. "I thought I could pull it off without telling her, but now...look, yelling at each other like this is wasting time! We've got a big problem, and we need to solve it. Gimme a few minutes to think, and I'll come up with a plan. I swear I will!"

When I saw Gerry thrust the phone back into his jeans, I retreated around the front of the building and waited in the recessed doorway. A minute later, the black Trans-Am with the golden Firebird on the hood sped out of the lot.

I exhaled and dared to get into my own car, then wondered why I felt so on edge. Even if Gerry had some kind of personal problem, it certainly had nothing to do with me! I guessed, after the recent traumatic events at my workplace, I worried about anything serious enough to rattle one of our vendors that much.

Had Gerry been arguing with Ronnie? Somehow, I doubted that, even though she apparently had left work early, too. Did she catch him with another woman? Had he gotten someone else pregnant—was that the unforeseen "problem"? Maybe.

He must really love Ronnie, though, if the thought of losing her frightened him that much.

Whatever, Viv, it's their relationship. Definitely none of your business!

* * *

On the phone that night, Mona sounded listless, because her streak of front-page stories had broken. Neither the Delaware nor the Addamsville police had uncovered any new leads on the jewelry store or pawn shop robberies.

"I get the impression they're moving on to more urgent matters," she told me. "The security guard and the pawn shop guy are both recovering from their injuries. And like I said before, the businesses were insured, and the pawn shop is using that money to install better security. So, at this point, I guess they're also prepared to write off their losses."

"How would the cops recognize the stolen pieces, anyway?" I thought of the way we labeled everything at the antique center. "Would they be etched in some way, or..."

"I've been researching that, and it varies. Top designers usually have their name or logo somewhere on a piece, but if it's small, it could be scratched off. The stores also keep photos on file of everything in their current inventory. But you're right—it wouldn't be easy to prove that a particular ring or watch came from a particular store."

"Well, even if the heat is off those robbers, you've still got our local murder mystery to pursue," I reminded her. "Do the Addamsville cops have any new ideas about the Kaye Burrell case?"

"Yes and no. They told me they have surveillance footage from your building that shows a guy prowling around there the morning she was killed. Apparently, it's not very good quality, but they've called a few people back in for questioning, including her husband."

So the police finally shared that information with *the Herald*—good.

"I suspect Pete Burrell, too," I told Mona. "A few days ago, he came to the center with an appraiser to evaluate all of Kaye's merchandise. Word is that he'll inherit everything, and since Pete has no desire to go into the antiques business himself, he'll probably turn it into cash as quickly as possible."

"Mmm. But my contact says Pete also has an alibi for that morning, a business meeting with some of his banker buddies. Pretty solid character witnesses." As if this looked like a dead end to her, my sister then changed the subject. "Speaking of seemingly solid characters, did you ever get a chance to ask Ed Kiernan about that...incident in his past?"

Did she have to keep bringing it up? "No, I didn't. He was actually at the antiques center again today, for a little while. But he was busy, and I certainly wasn't going to discuss it with so many other people around."

"No, of course not," she relented. "Sounds like he's finding excuses to drop in on you, Viv."

"He had a perfectly valid reason to be there." I told her about Ed's picking up a holster to fit a replica 1940s police revolver.

"Terrific." Mona gave the word a sarcastic twist. "As if we don't have enough civilians with guns running around town!"

"Hey, Sis, make up your mind." I was losing patience with her. "Just a few days ago, you were pushing me to go out with Ed. Now suddenly you're finding fault with everything about him, just like Dad. And neither of you have even met him!"

"I guess that's true," my sister admitted.

"I'm a decent judge of character, and I think he's a good guy. He doesn't put on airs like a celebrity. He says he's more comfortable being back in Jersey and working at the playhouse than he was in L.A. He's down to earth, he's smart, he's funny..."

"Okay, okay. All I'm saying is, if I were you, I wouldn't rush into anything until I heard his explanation for what happened with that girlfriend, fifteen years ago."

"I don't intend to 'rush into anything,' and I don't think Ed does, either. Even though he did talk about us getting together again, I think for now I'm parked strictly in the Friend Zone." I glanced at the clock and saw it was getting late. "Really, I can't argue about this all night. I've got to get out super-early tomorrow to an estate sale! But seriously, Mona, I can't imagine that Ed did anything to cause or contribute to Janet Lawler's accident. He didn't seem like that kind of guy when we were in college, and he still doesn't."

"Fine." She sounded more sincere this time. "You're absolutely right, Viv. Dad and I have never met him, while you went to school with him and have also spent time with him lately. It sounds like he's been a perfect gentleman and has charmed you all over again. Just keep in mind, Sis...the guy is an actor."

Chapter Fourteen

M y rare argument with my sister kept me tossing in bed for half the night. It felt like I'd just settled down for a decent sleep when my alarm woke me at five-thirty.

Fortunately, I'd prepared for the estate sale the evening before. Having tackled a few in the past, I knew the drill. I brought an envelope with lots of cash—especially small bills—a thermos of coffee, and a couple of energy bars. I wore comfy athletic shoes. I'd done my online research ahead of time, mentally mapping out what rooms I wanted to hit and what items I wanted to look for.

When I pulled into the antiques center parking lot, just after dawn, I found Cindy even better equipped. She had stocked the vast cargo space of her Suburban with tarps and blankets to cushion any large purchases, and with assorted hard-rubber storage containers for any smaller ones. Her cooler held not only turkey sandwiches for our lunch, whenever we got around to it, but enough bottles of water to take us across a small desert.

"We might want to go easy on the drinks, though," she warned. "At most of these sales in private homes, they don't let you use the bathrooms."

I cast a wistful, backward glance at our big converted factory, which housed two multi-stall bathrooms, one on each floor. But even if it had not been locked up tight, the idea of ever again venturing in before business hours unnerved me too much. Ed had warned me not to find any more dead bodies, and I intended to take that advice.

So, without further ado, Cindy and I set off on our drive to the next town. On the way, she explained that our target house dated back to the turn of the century, and the widow vacating it was in her nineties. She'd lived all of married life and raised two children there. Now that Mom was finally moving to a nursing home, the middle-aged "kids" had hired a professional company to organize and dispose of the contents.

"From what we saw online," Cindy said, "I suspect it's one of those cases where her children took whatever they felt was still usable but have no interest in the really old stuff."

"I love it when that happens." I smiled and rubbed my palms together, like a cartoon villain. "They leave all those treasures behind for the likes of us!"

Unfortunately, I would soon find out there were quite a few of "the likes of us" ready to compete for such prizes.

Estate Sale signs decorated the front lawn of the two-story, brown-brick home, its gracious, cream-colored porch matching the trim of the windows. I could just glimpse all of this over the heads of the twenty or more people who massed in front. So far, a low wrought-iron fence and a sweatshirt-clad official with a clipboard still held them at bay.

"Good," said Cindy, undaunted. "Not too many others here yet."

Yikes. She'd expected even more at not-quite-seven a.m.?

Curbside parking was almost gone, too, but by some miracle Cindy found a spot just a couple of blocks away, shoehorning her Suburban between two more modestly sized SUVs. Then we trekked back to the house, carrying three empty tote bags apiece. Besides no bathroom access, estate sales also did not usually provide shopping bags.

Cindy and I passed another fifteen minutes on the sidewalk in front of the place, while the showrunners handed out numbers. A sign warned that only a dozen shoppers would be admitted at a time, and I guessed even the holders of the lowest numbers wouldn't make it in before the official start at nine.

As the morning warmed up, I shrugged out of my nylon rain jacket, rolled it up, and slipped it into one of my totes. My companion smiled at the top I'd worn that day with my ankle-length pants—a loose white tee with a black-and-white photo of Katherine Hepburn and Spencer Tracy, exchanging suggestive smiles.

"That's cute. What movie, *Woman of the Year?*"

"Very good!" I commended her.

Cindy's own deep-blue tee, stretched across her considerable chest and midriff, read *Antiquing is my cardio.*

We agreed that if we got separated, we would meet at the rear of the house, by the garage, in two hours. Most of the time, though, Cindy and I gravitated toward the same rooms and the same general categories of merchandise. We both bypassed the newer, cheaper knick-knacks and any older stuff that was either too formal and elegant or too kitschy. The goodies we sought fell somewhere in between.

But while Cindy pounced on anything with a romantic, weathered, "country" appeal, my taste skewed more funky and exotic. Among the ceramics, she snatched up a fluted milk-glass vase, while I grabbed an eight-inch-long figurine of a stalking black panther. In the kitchen, she picked out a timeworn enameled colander, and I put a "sold" sticker on a set of six highball glasses, patterned with gold leaves and still in their original brass caddy. (I couldn't safely carry those around the crowded house with me, even in a tote.)

We diverged again in the bedroom, which we'd both seen online. Cindy bagged an old rose-patterned quilt and a multi-pastel afghan, while my radar went off full blast (if only in my head) when I glimpsed a vivid, oversized floral pattern. Rummaging through a stack of heavy, folded fabrics, I pulled out two drapery panels: one with burgundy heart-shaped leaves and arching turquoise ferns on a soft beige background, the other with bold, abstract stripes in mixed red-and-chartreuse on black. They had no mates in sight and a few moth holes, but no problem—they'd still make wonderful pillows.

Cindy noticed how eagerly I stuffed these into one of my totes and chuckled. "You made a score, too, I see! Don't look now, but the armoire has chenille bedspreads. We'll fight over those."

By the time we reached them, we had more competition than just each other, but she fell in love with a sweet pink spread with a pattern of burgundy bows, and I opted for an ivory one with a more geometric design. I mentally kept track of how much I'd be paying at checkout and knew I was nearing my limit. My colleague also remarked that we'd probably seen the best of the home's offerings, at least for our purposes.

While we took a breather to chug some water, Cindy told me about a friend of hers who was vintage-phobic. "I've known her since college, but she can't even come to visit me anymore. She's too sensitive to be around older houses, furniture, even knick-knacks."

I'd never heard of such a thing. "What do you mean? Is she allergic to the dust, or…"

"No, no. It's the 'vibes,' I guess. She's 'psychometric,' she says. If she walked into a house this old, she'd pick up all kinds of impressions from the people who lived here in the past, and could feel overwhelmed. Even if I gave her this bedspread, and it turned out the last owner died in that bed…Marilyn would know, and she wouldn't be able to keep it."

"That's crazy!" I burst out, then caught myself. "I don't mean I don't believe you, or her. But how hard must it be to go through life like that?"

"She can't wear anything from a thrift shop, because she picks up on emotional baggage from the first owner," Cindy went on. "And she doesn't even tour historic sites, especially not anyplace where there was some kind of a battle. I guess she'd re-experience it."

As a vintage lover, this horrified me. "Can you imagine if she ever visited you at work?"

My fellow vendor laughed out loud. "A World War II parachute factory, packed to the rafters with musty antiques? Poor Marilyn would have a seizure!"

I could only imagine such a person riding up in the building's scary freight elevator, or stopping by the Randolph brothers' tent filled with antique weapons. Although…her sensitivities might have come in handy when the cops were trying to isolate the weapon used on Kaye Burrell!

At a more leisurely pace, Cindy and I moved on to the attic's displays of discarded toys, which suggested both boys and girls had grown up in the home. When I spotted a slightly rusty Flintstones lunch box, I nudged my companion. "Think we should pick that up for Gerry?"

She glanced at the price; the showrunners obviously knew its value to collectors. "Hell, no. I mentioned this sale to him a couple of days ago, but he just shrugged. If he wants it, he can come get it himself."

I said nothing more, but couldn't help noticing other things that might be of interest to our fellow vendors. The attic also offered racks of old clothes, somewhat picked over, but a few of the hats, purses, and shoes possibly could work for the Ledermans. A mirrored tray on top of a beat-up dresser displayed Baubles and Bangles' kind of jewelry, such as a splashy peacock brooch with turquoise enameling and rhinestones in the tail.

I thought of calling Ronnie, but maybe she had decided to pass on this sale, too. Anyway, she'd been tending her booth even less than usual lately.

Cindy waited until we were almost done before claiming her bulkiest prize, a small red-maple side table with curvy legs and a single drawer. Pretty scratched up, it didn't look like much. She made me laugh by admitting, "My customers like things a little distressed, but this looks like it's had a nervous breakdown!" Still, it was priced to move, so she daydreamed aloud about painting it cream and replacing the drawer's knob with one in green glass.

I guessed all of us vintage buffs shared the urge to transform another person's old junk into something fresh and wonderful.

Around noon, we paid for our purchases and loaded everything into Cindy's roomy vehicle. With the hatch door still raised, we sat on the bumper to guard our purchases and gobble the turkey sandwiches. Between bites, I suggested again that maybe we really should tell some of our colleagues back at the antiques center about the sale, since it was scheduled to run another whole day.

Cindy only gestured toward the dense crowd milling around the front of the house, jostling for numbers. "By tomorrow, there won't be much left, anyway. Tell the Ledermans, if you want to, though I didn't see any really spectacular clothes that would be worth their while. But Ronnie and Gerry?" She shrugged. "Those kids need to learn to hustle for themselves."

I didn't think of them as "kids," exactly, since they were only about ten years younger than me. "Gerry does seem kind of blasé about manning his booth. Maybe he just doesn't need the money. Does his family have bucks?"

"Hmph, I doubt it. I got the impression he really scrimped to pay for that Firebird he drives. I've heard him gripe about shelling out too much for a stack of old comics, and joke that he needs to marry a rich woman... even though he seems to be involved with Ronnie, and I doubt she fits that description."

I didn't think so, either. "At least she spends a fair amount of time at her booth and has collected some beautiful pieces. The playhouse is using two in their upcoming show, for their leading lady to wear with her evening gowns."

"So I heard. Well, at least that should give Ronnie's business a boost." Cindy took a swig from her water bottle, then eyed me curiously. "The theater folks have been dropping by our humble establishment almost weekly, haven't they? I noticed you and Ed Kiernan chatting the other day, over by the Randolph brothers' area. Reminiscing about your college days?"

"We have been, a bit. He seems to have a new appreciation for his home turf, after the glitter of L.A. Or maybe he just missed live theater—he really seems into the playhouse production."

"Maybe he's also into you." Cindy lifted one penciled blonde eyebrow.

"I should be so lucky!" I dropped my empty bottle back into her cooler to be recycled later. "Anyhow, we ought to head back to the center and divvy up our loot."

"And use the restroom." Cindy closed the Suburban's hatch, and we took our seats up front.

She turned into the parking lot of our workplace around three-thirty. Unloading the maple side table and a few other heavy items, Cindy debated whether to use the elevator. "I'm being silly, of course, but after Kaye... Though you'd probably feel even more uncomfortable, wouldn't you, Viv?"

My flesh did creep a bit when I pictured the dingy gray shaft, but I'd have to get over that eventually. Besides, the set of 1950s highball glasses would travel more securely in the lift, too. "That's okay, I'll ride up with you."

At least a clean, new tarp now covered the spot where Kaye had fallen to her death. Cindy operated the pulley with an experienced hand that minimized the noise and shaking. Still, after only two stories, I breathed easier when the barn-sized door slid open at our floor.

My colleague carried her table across the aisle to her own booth, and I cleared a temporary space for the set of glasses on a bookcase at the rear of my space. I shuttled back and forth via the front entrance to bring up a few knick-knacks and folded linens that could go directly on my shelves. (The main stairs of my new workplace provided all the daily cardio I'd ever need, I figured, while carrying my merch added some upper-body work.) There would be time to tag everything I'd just bought with prices tomorrow; I always liked to put in a full shift on Saturday, anyhow. A few things that needed cleaning or mending went into my trusty flowered tote bag, to come home with me.

When I stopped at the front counter to say hi to Fred, he reported that I'd sold a small Turner print of hibiscus flowers that morning, which bolstered my already good spirits. I told him the estate sale had been worth the trip for both me and Cindy, and asked if the Ledermans were in that day. He said Sally was, so I stopped by there.

"Hi, Viv," she hailed me with a grin. "We just got some cute new cardigans that might interest you."

I wiped a hand across my perspiring forehead. "Great, but I'll check them out tomorrow. Right now, I'm a little sweaty from doing the estate sale on Elsey Avenue. If you can get away early, you or Ben really ought to hit that place. Some very cute hats from the fifties and sixties…pillboxes, and those feathered 'cocktail' headpieces. What're they called, fascinators?"

Sally's lips puckered with interest; she pulled out her phone, punched a number, and relayed this info to her husband. "Elsey Avenue, Viv says…Okay, good luck." Hanging up, she told me, "He's out making a delivery, but he'll jump right on it. Thanks for the tip! Not everybody here is generous enough to share their sources."

I laughed. "You should have seen Cindy and me storming through the place. We should be competition for each other, but our tastes are just far enough apart that we always homed in on different things."

After promising to check back tomorrow about the cardigans, I climbed the stairs to my own level. A quick glance showed that both Ronnie and Gerry were still AWOL, so I couldn't share any tips with them. Maybe Cindy was right, and they just didn't have much ambition for the business.

But Gerry, especially, talks like he's got big dreams, and those usually require big bucks. He's got "Money" as his ring tone, for God's sake! Doesn't he ever make the connection that maybe he should work a little harder? Or does he think someday, through sheer luck, he'll just strike gold?

* * *

After dinner that night, I took a shower and a short but refreshing nap, then sorted through the day's loot. I set aside anything dusty or dingy to be carefully hand-washed, and took stock of any drapery or tablecloth remnants that would make good pillows. Lucille Denby had passed along my business card to a friend who'd asked me to create two for her, so I needed to send that person some sample photos.

In between all of this, I wanted to post on my blog about my day at the sale. I knew I should also start on my next article for the quarterly magazine *Vintage Living*, which supplemented my income a bit. My column, inspired by my ringtone melody, was titled "Everything Old…" I also got a discount on any ads I ran in the magazine.

Which reminded me—I should update my standard ad to mention my new presence at Addamsville Antiques!

Just thinking about this to-do list tired me all over again, and the balmy evening outside the kitchen sliders held much more appeal. I decided to bring my laptop out to the patio so that, while getting some work done, I could also enjoy the sunset. Aramis had already retired to his cage to eat, so I simply shut the top of it and wheeled it outside, too. That excited him—he always liked to check out what the neighborhood's wild birds were up to.

I sighted my human neighbors less often, since the shrubbery tended to screen our patios from one another. In my couple of years in the condo, I'd had brief conversations with the older couple to my right, the Remicks, who often hosted their rather rambunctious grandchildren. (You didn't want to share the pool with that crowd!) The male couple in the attached unit to my left, Alex and Richard, were much quieter neighbors, luckily, because we shared a wall in common. I spoke to them mainly when one or the other walked their Bichon Frise, Emily, along the fenceline. Emily and Aramis found each other fascinating, while the Remicks' grandkids scared the tailfeathers off my poor boy.

From my comfy lounge chair beneath a trailing Boston fern, I emailed my prospective new pillow customer a few shots of my latest batch of fabrics. Then I pulled together a short blog entry, with bullet points, on how to get the most out of an estate sale. I made some notes for the longer magazine article, but since that wasn't due for a while, I'd finish it another night, when I wasn't so beat.

Lastly, I checked my email. Surprise, surprise, a message from Ed! He'd used my official work address, so I guess he'd gotten it off my business card.

Saw on the local news that cops have a surveillance photo of the guy who broke into the antiques center, but I'm sure you already know that. Anyone you recognize? I almost feel silly in our rehearsals, playing at solving a mystery, when you've had a real crime at your workplace. Stay safe, Viv, okay? If there's any trouble, go hide in Carl and Morty's booth—at least you'll be well-armed!

Got to get back to work now, and I'm sure we'll be slammed all day tomorrow, too. Are you free for dinner on Sunday? I've got an issue I'd like to discuss with someone **not** involved with the theater.

That sounded intriguing, and dinner was a step up from lunch.

If the setting was private enough, maybe I'd also get up the nerve to discuss a sensitive topic with Ed?

Chapter Fifteen

Saturday morning, workers began packing up the stately Craftsman oak furniture that formerly belonged to Kaye Burrell, while her widowed husband stood by to supervise. So many of her things needed careful handling that I expected the process to take half a day. It might put a crimp in our usual weekend foot traffic, but I doubted Peter Burrell cared about that. Spotting his head of dark hair and silver sideburns across the aisle, I reminded myself that he was one of the few men I'd seen around the place with the coloring and general build of the intruder caught by our surveillance camera.

But again, that made little sense. If he wanted to bump off his wife, why risk doing it at the antiques center, right before we opened for business? Even if he didn't want to leave any incriminating evidence at their home, he certainly could have found someplace more secluded!

Maybe, much as I liked solving mysteries, I just didn't think like a murderer...

Beyond Kaye's half-deconstructed booth, I also glimpsed Gerry Rubello setting up for business in his corner. He seemed to move stiffly today, and his cheek looked shadowed by more than his usual trace of beard. He also glanced toward all the activity in the middle of the room, and happened to lock eyes with me. But when I raised a hand to greet him, Gerry only frowned and sharply faced away.

What's that about?

Then I told myself not to take it personally. He might just be annoyed because Burrell had chosen noon on a Saturday to pack up his late wife's treasures.

Adrian Marcus, who occupied the space next to Kaye's, made no secret of his displeasure and wandered my way for a quiet gripe session. "He's sending all of her things to an auction house. Fred suggested that it might be considerate to let some of us have first pick, but he says Burrell almost sneered at him."

"From what I heard, Peter always treated Kaye's business here as some frivolous hobby, anyway," I recalled. "Well, much as I'd love some of her Roseville, I'm sure I couldn't afford what he would charge me." Across the room, I saw Gerry comb one hand back through his surfer hair and glimpsed a distinct bruise on his forehead. "Rubello's looking a little worse for wear today, isn't he?"

"I asked him about that. Said he borrowed his cousin's motorcycle and crashed it." Well-groomed as always, in pressed khakis and a dark green polo shirt, Adrian rolled his eyes. "Slight case of arrested development there, I'd say. Might also explain all the campy posters, gag toys, and cartoon lunch boxes."

I smiled at this bit of armchair psychoanalysis, but also remembered Gerry's agitated phone conversation in the parking lot a couple of days earlier. If my theory was right, and he'd been cheating on Ronnie, could she have been responsible for those bruises? The woman wasn't too brawny, but maybe she knew martial arts...or just pushed him down a flight of stairs! Gerry had sure sounded worried about the repercussions...

Rubello must have noticed the two of us watching him and whispering to each other, because he scowled again and paced in our direction. Marcus stiffened his spine, as if ready for battle if necessary, while I tried to defuse the situation.

"Sorry if we were staring," I said. "Adrian just told me you had a motorcycle accident. That's a shame. I hope you're okay!"

"Yeah, I'll just bet you do. You both probably wish I'd gotten messed up even worse, so my booth would be up for grabs, too."

I could tell this accusation shocked Marcus as much as me. "W-why would you say that?"

"I've heard the other vendors asking whether Kaye's stuff was for sale and how soon her space would be available. Adrian, you're probably just itching to expand, and you've been here so long that Fred would probably give you a nice break on the lease."

The older man shook his head. "If I asked any questions like that, it was just out of idle curiosity."

"And you, Miss Vi-vi-an…" Gerry drew out my name sarcastically, and this close up, I could smell beer on his breath. "You've had your eye on Kaye's stuff since the first day you moved in, haven't you? Trying to sneak one of her best pieces into your booth, then pretending you had no idea how it got there!"

Not that again. "It was a mistake. Why would I do that? Fred would have recognized it, and Kaye would have gotten the sale anyway."

"Maybe you didn't realize that, huh?"

Gerry's tirade had started to draw the attention of passers-by and, worse, of Peter Burrell.

Cindy Metcalf hurried over from her booth to intervene. "What's going on here, Gerry? You're upsetting the customers!"

Adrian gave her a tight smile. "I think Mr. Rubello drank his breakfast this morning, no doubt to kill the pain from his supposed motorcycle injuries."

For some reason, Gerry ignored him and went back to hammering me, maybe as an easier target. "Right from the first day, *you* were always chatting everyone up, asking questions about how they got into the business and how things worked around here…looking for an opportunity, I'm sure. And one day I saw you admiring Marcus's candlesticks, even touching them. So I figure *you* killed Kaye!"

"Gerry, for God's sake—" said Cindy.

"She's new here. We don't know anything about her," he persisted. "Maybe after Kaye made trouble for her, Viv decided to get even. She *did* find the body…well, her and Adrian. They might have done it together, to get their hands on her merchandise."

Struck dumb with fear and anger, I couldn't even respond. Meanwhile, I almost felt Burrell's stare boring through me, even from about thirty feet away. All of us had been questioned by the police and cleared of suspicion, but could Rubello's crazy rant stir all of that up again?

A shadow fell over us as Carl Randolph joined the group. The vendor of military collectibles stood well over six feet, with a build like a slightly paunchy wrestler. He would have cut an intimidating figure even without his Vietnam-vintage army cap, snug olive-drab T-shirt, and camo pants.

"What the—" Carl seemed to censor himself, for the sake of the nearby customers "—Sam Hill is going on over here? Fred said you guys need to pipe down!"

Our boss could hardly have sent a more effective messenger. The rest of us instantly ratted on Gerry, repeating his accusations, but Rubello himself clammed up. I guess he didn't want Carl to add any more bruises or sprains to his medical records. Chastened, we all promised to tend to our own booths and behave ourselves like good vendors for the rest of the day. Carl clumped down the stairs in his army field boots, to relay that information to our landlord.

An hour or so later, the moving crew had packed up and taken away the last of Kaye's things, and Gerry also cleared out shortly afterward. I was basking in a sense of relief when I got an email on my phone from Fred, which I could see also had been copied to Adrian and Cindy.

Before you leave today, meeting in my office.

Yow! I was grateful it wasn't just me, though. Surely he couldn't think all three of us had conspired to murder Kaye Burrell!

* * *

The Victorian arch that gave the cashier's window a genteel appearance did little to hide the internal clutter of Fred's office. Scratched and dented black metal filing cabinets secured papers he needed to keep under lock and key, and stacks of labeled shoeboxes held, I presumed, less important records and receipts. All of this suggested a laid-back management style, but at the moment, Fred's demeanor was anything but.

The three of us sat in folding chairs to face his wooden schoolteacher's desk, though personally, I didn't think Cindy belonged there at all. She'd done nothing but try to de-escalate the conflict!

"I just want to warn you," our landlord said, "that we could have a serious situation on our hands. Whatever set Gerry off, he's planted the idea in Peter Burrell's head that certain vendors here had motives to murder Kaye." When we started to scoff, he interrupted. "I reminded him that a surveillance camera caught a stranger prowling around the booths—a guy who doesn't resemble anyone on your floor—around the time Kaye arrived and almost an hour before Vivian and Adrian got there."

"What did he say to that?" I wanted to know.

"Oh, you could have been working with a boyfriend who found out the code, somehow, and broke in ahead of time. Then you arranged to show up with a witness who could 'find' Kaye's body along with you. Or else all of us, including me, were in on the conspiracy!" Fred shook his grizzled head. "Even Gerry can't decide how it happened, but he's determined to put the blame on someone here."

When I recalled Gerry's snide accusations earlier that day, it suddenly occurred to me that maybe *he* had suggested the cops consider me and Adrian as potential suspects in Kaye's murder. Who else had been near enough to hear her accuse me of trying to steal her vase? Rubello had acted friendly enough when I first moved in, helping me carry my storage bins and even flirting with me a bit. But maybe he was one of those unpredictable types who could turn on a person for very little reason.

Cindy told Fred, "You see why things spun out of control."

"Yes, we didn't start it!" Dignified Adrian sounded, for a second, like a petulant schoolboy.

"I understand," said Fred. "The point is, it can't happen again. We had not only Kaye's widower and his crew here today, but a floor full of prospective customers, and they all heard things they shouldn't have. I expect my tenants to respect each other, not start feuds or throw around wild accusations. Or, for that matter, to come to work half in the bag."

Cindy sniffed. "Yeah, that was a first, even for Gerry."

"I already spoke to him privately. I warned him that, by our contract, I have the right to evict anyone who creates a hostile atmosphere for the others, and he certainly did that today. I think he'll control himself from now on, but if he doesn't, I expect you to alert me."

We all agreed, and the informal meeting broke up. I hung back, though, feeling I might have the most to lose in this situation.

I reminded Fred that Gerry had tried his best to throw suspicion on me, in particular, and Peter Burrell seemed to be taking it all in. "You don't think, do you, that he'll go back to the cops and insist they interrogate me some more?"

"It's possible, but without any new evidence, they probably won't pay him much attention." My boss sighed. "Y'know what baffles me? This isn't really like Gerry. He's never had serious issues with the other vendors before, and why he would single out you—! It feels like kind of a desperation move."

"Could he have money problems?" I wondered aloud. "He does seem a bit obsessed with that subject."

"Yeah, that's kind of new for him, too. He always kidded around about hoping to get rich from his pop-culture memorabilia, but lately the jokes have a sharper edge to them." Fred scratched the thinning spot on top of his head. "Maybe he's got some debts building up?"

'Could be." The only other situation I could imagine Gerry getting desperate about might be his relationship with his girlfriend...or girlfriends? "Ronnie hasn't been in to work for a few days now. Think there could be any connection?"

"Not that I know of. She called yesterday and said she's out of town, taking care of a sick relative."

"Ah, that explains things."

Did it, though? I wondered, as I drove home. Her story could be true, or it could be one of those handy excuses that would be hard for any of us to check.

Kind of like Gerry's story about falling off a cousin's motorcycle.

＊＊＊

That evening I tried to forget about the nerve-wracking day by doing some more work on my magazine article. To illustrate it, I photographed some of my own finds from the estate sale. After that, I hand-washed the new-to-me barkcloth remnants (some old pieces can be too fragile to throw in a machine), and searched through my stock for any solid-colored fabrics and trims that might coordinate with them. One of the black-background panels, in particular, was so moth-eaten around the edges that I'd probably cut just a big square or round piece from the center, and back it with solid burgundy velveteen.

With Aramis's help, I even found some olive-green braiding that would echo the dashes of chartreuse throughout the pattern. (I got it away from him before he chewed it too much.) Not a glamorous way to spend a Saturday night, but at least productive.

I soon stopped feeling sorry for myself, though. My phone rang, and this time I recognized Ed's number. *Really? I thought he worked late on Saturdays!*

That turned out to be true, but he'd used a break in the action to give me a call, which I found even more flattering. "Gotta get back to rehearsal in a few minutes," he told me, quietly, "but would you be free for another lunch tomorrow?"

I pressed the phone to my left ear, letting Aramis remain on my right shoulder. Playing it just a bit coy, I said, "So far, I should be."

"Great! Like I said in my text, I need to spend time with someone who isn't working, in any way, on *Murder Most Noir!*"

"I guess I do fit that requirement." My feathered friend tugged hard on my hoop earring, and I giggled. "Aramis, you bad boy, stop it!"

Ed's tone cooled. "Oh…sorry. Am I interrupting something?"

"He's nibbling my ear." I let Ed worry for just a sec before explaining, "My bird. I usually let him out when I'm home and working on a project. He likes to sit on my shoulder and critique."

"Ah." The voice on the phone relaxed. "I saw his picture on your website. Very handsome!"

So he'd been checking up on me, too? Maybe that was a good sign. "You sound a little frazzled. How are things going?"

"They're going." He sighed. "We're at that midpoint where we've got the basics in place but still need to polish the diamond, you might say. We're all so tired, though, that we're either delivering our lines flat or over-emoting. Even though Agnes is a genius—and we all know it—we're starting to resent every change she suggests." Ed turned philosophical. "It's par for the course. By the end of next week, I'm sure we'll pull it all together."

"I'm sure you will, too. Still, I can sympathize," I said. "We also had some tension today at the antiques center, and I don't really know what it was all about. People who usually get along fine were at each other's throats."

"Gee, who would've thought, in a sedate place like that? I hope no priceless collectibles got broken!"

"No, but Big Carl from military memorabilia came over from his turf to get everybody under control."

"For real?" Ed laughed at the image. "We could have used him over here. Apparently, we even had a foiled break-in last night."

"At the theater?" That brought my flippant attitude back down to earth.

"Luckily, the place has an alarm system. I guess somebody smashed a locked window and then tried to open it, which alerted the security company. Their guard showed up in time to see this dude running back to the parking lot. Not in time to catch him, though. I guess as soon as he saw the guard's flashlight, he bolted. Hopped on a Harley and tore off."

"That's pretty crazy," I said. "Why break into a 'dark' theater? You folks don't even have a show on now, so there's probably nothing in the till, right?

"Exactly. It still might make some sense if he'd been trying to get into the box office, though that has even better security. But he broke a window all the way in back, where the props and costumes are. None of that stuff is really worth a lot, in terms of resale—it's not like priceless Broadway memorabilia. So unless he's a major theater buff, who's just *got* to have a memento from one of the playhouse's past shows, it makes no sense."

"Mmm...no more than someone prowling around Addamsville Antiques in the early hours, and then killing a woman who discovered him there."

I heard silence as Ed considered the similarity. "Jeez, you're right. I almost forgot about that! Probably no link, though, except in both cases the burglars were kind of stupid. I think even Danny McDougal could have outsmarted them."

It took me a second to remember that McDougal was the bumbling PI in *Murder Most Noir*, not the highly competent police detective Ed had played in his TV series. With his features and coloring, Kiernan might always have to struggle against being typecast as an Irish cop!

I heard a muffled voice call his name, and he shouted that he'd be right there. "Anyhow, Viv, we'll have to get into all this a little more tomorrow. Let's find someplace out of town where I won't run into anybody from the theater, okay? There's a nice little Mexican restaurant over our way...I mean, near my dad's place."

The small slip reminded me that Ed was currently crashing with his father and stepmother in the family's riverside cottage. "Sounds great. Now, get back to work—the show must go on." At the memory of Kaye's sprawled, lifeless body, I almost added, *But be careful!*

I hung up, reflecting that at least I'd matured over the past two decades. In college, I'd been so in awe of Ed that I'd barely had the nerve to speak to him. Now we were bantering about the stresses of regional showbiz and the local crime spree.

Nice to think that these days, when Ed needs a breather from the cast, crew, and conflicts at the theater, I'm the one he calls! I hope he doesn't feel differently after I ask him about Janet Lawler, and what really happened to her fifteen years ago.

Chapter Sixteen

A mong my many retro quirks, I actually subscribe to the Sunday edition of the *West Jersey Herald* in print form. Not just out of loyalty to Mona, but also because few things beat a good old-fashioned newspaper for lining a birdcage—especially now that most of them use non-toxic soy inks. It felt very old-school that Sunday morning to relax on my patio recliner, a potted Rose-of-Sharon shrub blooming on my left and Aramis whistling in his cage on my right, and to read a broadsheet paper, just as Nana Vivian might have done.

For a change, the front-page headlines did not spoil my peaceful mood too much—no dire national or international crises seemed to be looming. While working my way back towards the local news, entertainment, and home-themed sections, I did come across one minor headline that made me sit up straighter:

POLICE RELEASE SECURITY PHOTO OF JEWELRY-STORE ROBBER.

This came from the *Herald*'s sister paper in Delaware. It wasn't exactly a breaking story, of course, since the robbery had taken place early the previous week. Maybe the Delaware cops hadn't wanted to reveal, too soon, that they possessed a pretty clear image of one of the thieves. But perhaps because they'd had no luck tracking him down so far, they were now soliciting help from the general public. The article requested that anyone recognizing this individual contact Chief Antonelli at the nearest precinct.

I studied the photo, a bit blurry when enlarged for print. In what seemed a boneheaded move, the guy had glanced back over his shoulder so his face was caught on camera. The device could have been well disguised, I thought, or something might have startled him. A mask still covered his lower face, but you could make out a few distinctive traits, such as sharply angled eyebrows and a widow's peak. He also appeared to have short, dark hair…just like the intruder on the surveillance video from the antiques center.

His other features looked familiar, too. Not like someone I saw every day, and not much like the sketch of the man seen fleeing through the mall's parking lot. Still, I felt I *had* encountered this guy before…sometime, somewhere.

Be helpful if you could remember where and when, Viv. You might have some real info to share with the Delaware police.

A half-hour later, I was back in my bedroom choosing what to wear for my second Sunday lunch date with Ed. For a neighborhood Mexican restaurant—and possibly a difficult conversation—nothing too fancy. The weather had turned a bit cooler, so maybe my long-sleeved seventies T-shirt? Its chili-red, paisley design would liven up my flared jeans and wedge sandals.

My nostalgic ring tone interrupted that train of thought. I hoped Ed wasn't canceling, but the screen showed another number that I had added only recently.

"Viv, glad I caught you at home," Cindy said. "Do you have a few minutes?"

"Just a few," I warned her. "I've got lunch plans."

"I won't keep you too long. This is kind of gossip, but it could be bigger than that."

I sat on my bed, next to the top and jeans I planned to wear, and waited to hear more.

"I left a message for Ronnie on Friday, after the estate sale, and she just called me back. She thanked me for my tip about the costume jewelry, but said she couldn't have gone to the sale, anyway. She spent the weekend taking care of a sick relative."

"Oh," I said. "That's a shame."

Cindy frowned. "It's also kind of weird. That's the exact same thing she told Fred the other day. But think—who says 'relative' instead of 'my aunt' or 'my sister'? Maybe I have a suspicious mind, but it sounded like a shaky excuse."

Ordinarily, I would have thought this was splitting hairs, but… "Y'know, I felt the same way about Gerry's story, that he felt off a motorcycle. Do you think the two of them are having problems? Hard to believe Ronnie could beat him up—!"

"I never thought of Gerry as the violent type, either, but he sure went off the rails yesterday, didn't he? I mentioned that incident to Ronnie, and it seemed to throw her, too. She stammered and said Gerry's been stressed out with 'family problems,' but they should all be under control soon."

"Maybe that's the case," I allowed. "Or could that be some kind of code? Maybe Ronnie is…"

" 'In a family way,' as they used to say? Who knows. Gerry doesn't talk much about his own relatives, except for that cousin Mitch with the motorcycle. He sometimes brags about the crazy scrapes the two of them got into when they were growing up."

Something stirred at the back of my brain. "Did you ever meet Mitch?"

"He comes by the center, once in a blue moon. I think he works at an automotive-repair place in the area. Gerry mostly talks with him outside, in the parking lot."

My memory sparked. "I think I saw them together once, too, from a distance. My first day on the job, in fact. What does Mitch look like?"

"Hmm…his features are a little like Gerry's, but he has a narrower face. His last name is Rubello, too, and people used to take them for brothers. But Mitch is taller, with darker hair."

I decided to voice my suspicions. "Sort of like the guy on our surveillance-camera video?"

A startled silence on the line. "Oh, gee…I don't know about that! Why would Mitch break into our building when he could visit Gerry there any time? And why on earth would he attack Kaye Burrell?"

"Very good questions." I glanced at my classic Timex wristwatch. "Cindy, I do need to get going, but check out the *New Castle Herald* today. You should be able to find it online." I told her about the security-camera image from the Delaware store robbery. "It could be a very long shot, but see if that photo rings any bells."

"Seriously, Viv? From a robbery in Delaware?"

"But probably by the same guys who hit the pawn shop in Jonesburg a week ago. Just have a look at the picture." My pulse raced at the thought that I might have stumbled onto an important connection. "Could be that Mitch is still getting himself into some 'crazy scrapes,' with or without Gerry's help."

* * *

When I pulled into the lot of Pablo's Hacienda, Ed already had arrived. I found him leaning against a black PT Cruiser with wood-grain door panels. Since I knew Chrysler stopped making that model more than a decade ago, this intrigued me.

"Borrowed Detective McDougal's patrol car for the day, I see?"

I'd hoped to provoke his white grin and wasn't disappointed. "You caught me. I wanted an inexpensive used car, for just running back and forth to the theater, and when I saw this one on the lot, I couldn't pass it up. About as close to the old 1940s 'paddy wagon' as I could get."

I stroked the polished black front fender. "I looked at a second-hand Cruiser when I was starting my business. Unfortunately, even though it's got decent hatch space, I really need more for the times when I pick up or deliver furniture."

He eyed me up and down. "You must be stronger than you look!"

"Oh, I am. Remember, I did my time in college with the backstage crew."

As we strolled toward the adobe entrance archway of Pablo's, Ed rested one hand lightly on my shoulder, and the tingle spread through the rest of my nerve endings. Unlike our first getting-reacquainted meal at The Station, this felt more like an actual, if still casual, date.

"I hope you like this place," he said. "It's been here for decades, run by a local family, the Ayalas. I used to come here with my folks, so here they still think of me as 'Kiernan's kid.' They've probably never even heard of

Boulevard Blues, much less watched it, which suits me just fine."

"They won't bug you to autograph any napkins?"

With his free hand, Ed held open the carved wooden door for me. "Exactly. So this time we shouldn't be interrupted."

Sounded like ideal conditions if I wanted to bring up a difficult subject. *Might sabotage our date, but it's probably now or never.*

Inside, Pablo's was everything you'd expect in a family-owned, New Jersey version of South-of-the-Border décor. The center, open area, carpeted in a brown-and-orange abstract pattern, offered half a dozen round tables for larger groups; on this quiet Sunday, only one family had taken advantage of the extra elbow room. Along the wall, leatherette-upholstered booths nestled beneath more faux-stucco arches. Red clay tiles jutting out above suggested a roofline, and assorted, colorful sombreros hung on the pillars in between. Almost like a stage set, I thought.

A middle-aged server with piled black hair greeted us with a gap-toothed smile. The embroidery on her crisp white shirt identified her as "Felicia." She obviously knew Ed, and he introduced me as "my friend, Vivian." Felicia handed us laminated menus and we turned our attention to the lunch fare, which looked ample and varied.

"Everything here is good," he told me, "but it's pretty authentic. If you're not up for anything too hot, I can recommend some milder stuff."

Taking his advice, I went for a chicken enchilada platter. Ed asked for the Huevos Rancheros in what sounded like excellent Spanish pronunciation. Honed, I suspected, on the West Coast.

Once Felicia had taken our order and our menus, I commented to Ed, "I guess they must have a lot of Mexican restaurants in Los Angeles."

"They do...but some have gone too upscale and pretentious." He creased his long, slim nose. "It's funny...I listen to Ted, the set designer, carry on about giving our play a sense of 'old-school Hollywood glamour.' Sometimes I feel like telling him it's not all it's cracked up to be, especially these days."

I responded cautiously. "I guess you had some unfortunate experiences out there, with the show being canceled, even though it did have a good first season! And...I heard you dated one of the actresses for a while, but that ended, too."

"Let's just say, you can spend a big chunk of your life dreaming about a goal, imagining how great it's going to be...and once you achieve it, you realize it's kind of an illusion. There are so many Hollywood types who give you a big rush, but only until some new face comes along. Professionally and personally." He seemed to shrug off his gloom. "That's why, even if I complain sometimes about the stresses at the playhouse, I'm comfortable there. Those folks are more grounded and easier to deal with, and there's not as much back-stabbing." With a skewed smile, he added, "Some are a little high-strung and temperamental, of course, but so am I. That comes with the territory."

"Speaking of temperament," I said, "show biz folks don't have the market cornered..."

"That's right, on the phone you said there was some more excitement this week at your antiques emporium."

Without naming all the names, I told him one vendor had started wildly accusing others of killing the woman I'd found in the freight elevator, either to get their hands on her merchandise or just because they didn't like her.

Our meals arrived, and we spent a minute appreciating the colorful presentation and inhaling the various aromas. One bite of my enchilada told me that, while not overly spicy, this must be authentic family cooking from south of the border.

Ed cut into one of the two sunny-side eggs that topped his large tortilla, and also dipped the forkful into some salsa before popping it into his mouth. After savoring this, though, he returned to the thread of our conversation. "Wow, that guy Gerry does sound kind of unhinged. Maybe he's got a guilty conscience, himself!"

"Well, we can be pretty sure he wasn't the person on the surveillance-cam video, 'cause he's got lighter and longer hair. Anyway, Gerry has ready access to the place, so why would he have to sneak around?"

"He still might know something about the murder."

I smiled. "Is that Danny McDougal or Pat Harrigan talking?"

"I guess those roles could be rubbing off on me," Kiernan admitted. "Or maybe there's a reason I keep taking them. I've always liked mysteries."

"Me, too." I saw an opening to bring up the Janet Lawler incident, but just then, the brunette server seated a family with young kids at the table next to ours. I didn't want to discuss anything so potentially upsetting with strangers nearby.

Instead, I remembered the attempted break-in at the theater and asked Ed if he'd found out any more about that.

Cutting into his second egg, he shook his head. "There's another incident that doesn't make much sense. Hard to tell if the guy was hoping to corner a woman working late in one of the studios, or if he thought there might be something worth stealing. We do have tools in the scene shop, but they're locked up at night."

I enjoyed another mouthful of enchilada, topped by green chili sauce, before continuing my speculations. "Break-ins at both the antiques center and the theater, though...makes me wonder if there's some link."

Ed raised one eyebrow. "Maybe he's after that big planter you leant us! How much is that worth, anyway?"

"To a serious collector, high hundreds to maybe a thousand. But I doubt some bozo off the street would know that. Besides, it's in two heavy pieces, a pretty awkward thing to steal. Especially through a broken window."

"I can't see him making off with your draperies, either." Ed seemed to search his memory. "Anything smaller that he might know about? Some of that jewelry you gave Lauren?"

I shrugged. "Anyone who thinks that's worth stealing is deluded. Ronnie's merchandise is all low-rent stuff, pure paste or plastic. The big pieces will work great for the stage, but I'm sure anyone who really knew jewelry could tell the difference."

"I dunno...I was in the costume shop yesterday, and Lauren had one of those dress forms decked out in a long green gown and a necklace that looked pretty dramatic. Was that one of Ronnie's?"

"Was it mostly pearls, with a big green stone in the middle, like an emerald? Yes, that was hers." I explained how Lauren and I had discovered it at the back of a jewel-case drawer, and Ronnie said she hadn't even had time to price it yet.

"Even so, the guy might see something like that through the window, and what does he know?" Ed persisted. "He thinks it's real and tries to steal it."

I struggled to remember how the rear of the theater was laid out, in relation to the parking lot. "Is there a window where someone could see into the costume department?"

This made Ed pause, too. "From the side of the building, maybe. Not from the back, where the guy broke in—I think he would have ended up in the scene shop. But maybe he figured once he got inside, he could find his way around."

We didn't seem likely to solve the puzzle that afternoon. "Well, now that he knows you have good alarms and a crack security team, he probably won't be back." I shifted to what ought to be a lighter topic. "Did you and your father finish getting the boat in shape last Sunday?"

"Yeah, it wasn't too badly off, considering we've had it since I was a teenager. I did most of the refurbishing work, because I'm better at that—never could get the hang of sailing. Trish also tried to learn, but neither of us has been around enough to really practice. We'll have to wait until Ken gets some time off—he's a good sailor."

"I never realized before that you had a brother," I said. "Did he come around when we were in college?"

"Not much, since he went to Penn State. Now Ken's a successful patent lawyer, puts me to shame." Ed smiled, but I sensed some truth behind the quip. Maybe his father, like mine, had urged him to get a "real" career instead of pretending to be other people for a living. Although with the money Ed must have made from even one season of his series, which was still being re-run, he surely kept pace with his brother these days.

I remembered him saying Ken lived in Philadelphia. "It's nice that he's still in the area."

That provoked a slight frown. "Seems like he's always working, though. Especially since Dad's health isn't so good, I wish Ken would look in on him once in a while. That's one reason why I didn't mind coming back east—it lets me pop in on the old man more often."

When our check came, Ed grabbed it once again. I pointed that out and told him, "Sometime when your schedule calms down, you'll have to let me make dinner at my place."

Yikes, did I actually blurt that out?

"Sounds only fair," he agreed, a glint in his hazel eyes. "I do want to check out my rival, this Aramis guy."

"I dunno. We've been together for five years now, and even though he's just a featherweight, he *is* the jealous type."

Ed chuckled, and the warmth of his gaze made me suddenly self-conscious. "Too bad it took us almost twenty years to get to know each other, Viv. That was probably my fault."

I shrugged. "Back in college, you had a steady girlfriend, didn't you—Janet? That was the word among the theater crowd, anyway."

He sobered. "That's true, I did. You remind me of her, in some ways! She was smart and funny and creative, too. Janet had problems, though, more serious than I knew at the time."

The subject finally had been broached, but I waited until we'd paid the check and stepped outside before saying any more. Between the restaurant and the parking lot stood a pair of colorfully painted wooden benches, probably for the convenience of people waiting for their reservations on busy nights. I suggested to Ed that we share one of those seats for a minute.

"I may not have mentioned this before," I began, "but my father also used to work for the *West Jersey Herald,* as a reporter and then News Editor. When he heard your name, he asked me if you were related to Councilman Kiernan in Pennsylvania. I told him I didn't know, but out of curiosity, I looked online..."

Ed's jaw sagged a bit, and he obviously knew where this was leading. He glanced off across the parking lot and muttered, "Boy, I guess that story's never really going away."

"I'm afraid not, with today's electronic archives. Anyhow, I read about what happened with Janet. That you were completely cleared, which of course you should have been. But would you be comfortable telling me what really happened?"

He drew a long breath before diving into the backstory. "Janet always seemed different from most girls, but I liked that about her. She was very smart, with a dark sense of humor, and a good artist. She did these wild, surrealistic paintings, and was in some exhibits at her own college. She was never good in crowds of strangers, but I told myself she was just shy."

When he paused, I filled the silence. "I remember her a little, from our backstage parties in school. She did seem very quiet."

"That never bothered me much, but after a while, she started to show another side. In private, she'd sometimes turn on me for what seemed like no reason. She'd suddenly call me nasty names...once she even threw a book at my head! I guess she also started acting that way around her parents, because they took her to a doctor. He diagnosed her as bipolar and gave her some medication. Which seemed to help, for a while."

"But that night...you two were at a party?"

"We were wrapping a show I did at a community theater, something like the playhouse here. Kind of a big deal, though, because there were some off-off-Broadway scouts in the audience that night. The show had gotten great reviews, and we were all celebrating...except Janet. It seemed like the more success I had, the more it threatened her. She kept asking to leave the party, but hell...this one New York agent was talking to everyone in the cast, giving out his cards. When would I get a chance like that again?"

I could imagine Ed's dilemma. He wanted to stay to the end, and his antisocial girlfriend started to feel like a wet blanket, even a drag on his career.

A group of four middle-aged folks passed us, chatting and laughing, on their way into the restaurant. Maybe coworkers on a lunch break. Ed paused his downbeat story until they'd gone inside.

"I kept telling Janet, 'just a little while longer,' " he went on. "I even pushed her to go mingle until I was done, find some other people to talk to. But that wasn't Janet, she just... couldn't. In those situations, she always depended totally on me." The pain in Ed's eyes now made me wish I'd never raised the issue. "Finally, she shot me this cold, angry glare, as if I'd totally rejected her, and walked away. Maybe I should have gone after her, but at that point I was kind of mad, too. I figured I'd stay another half-hour, tops. Then whatever did or didn't happen with the agent, I'd find Janet and take her home."

"But by then she was gone?"

He seemed to relive the moment. "When I couldn't find her, I put on my jacket to go outside. I reached into the pocket—no car keys. And when I went outside, no car, either. I'd left the jacket at our table, over a chair. Only Janet would have known, for sure, which jacket and which car in the lot was mine." He shook his head. "If you read the news story, you know the rest."

"It said she had drugs in her system."

"The prescription stuff. She wasn't supposed to drink at all while she was taking it, and she usually didn't! But I guess that night she got so frustrated, she stopped caring about what happened. And of course, no one else at the party knew her situation. They figured I'd be driving her home...so they served her." His clasped hands hung between his knees, and now he twisted them tightly together. "So many times I've thought, if only I'd left when she asked me to..."

I touched his shoulder. "You couldn't have known. And it still might have happened at some later point, Ed. Sounds like Janet had a pretty serious illness."

He poked a quick finger under his glasses, but then his mood shifted; he sat up straighter against the back of the wooden bench. "I don't talk much about what happened, not just to protect my own reputation, but also Janet's. It's bad enough for people to think she got wasted at a party, borrowed my car, and drove it off the road. But I'll never know if taking the car was just a trick she played on me, thinking she'd leave me stranded at the party. It could have been deliberate suicide—even her doctor told us that was possible."

By now, we'd spent close to half an hour on the restaurant bench, and he'd certainly told me everything I needed to hear...maybe more. I started to feel guilty myself, and apologized for making him dredge up such painful memories.

"No," he insisted, "it's good that you asked about it. Smart of you, really, to make sure I wasn't hiding anything. Friends need to be able to trust each other, right? God knows, I've learned that lesson over the past few years."

More patrons came and went from the restaurant now, passing at close range. I think both Ed and I felt we should move along. We walked back to his car, where he faced me and said, "Thanks for being so patient, Viv, listening to my downer of a story. I hope it didn't spoil your afternoon too much."

I squeezed his arm. "Thank *you* for trusting me enough to tell me the details. The news article left a lot out, but I can see that they probably were shielding Janet's family and her memory."

"I haven't talked about her death in a long time, for the same reason. I especially never mentioned it to anybody when I was out on the Coast. Those gossip rags take any hint of scandal and run with it!" He raised his eyes to the heavens in relief. "It's good to be back in the real world…and able to confide in somebody again."

Ed saw me to my car and pecked me goodbye on the cheek. I thought of kissing him back on the lips, but after our somber conversation—and with yet another sedan pulling into the restaurant lot—the timing felt wrong.

After we went our separate ways, though, I reflected on what he'd said about youthful dreams often not living up to reality.

I guessed that over the past eighteen years—despite my time spent with Steve and in shorter, less-serious relationships with other guys—I'd never completely forgotten my college crush on Ed. He'd remained my elusive ideal, always just out of reach. Now, with very little effort on my part, he had suddenly come into my life again.

I was finally getting to know the real Ed Kiernan, and *he* was far from a disappointment. Even better, in fact, than I'd imagined.

Chapter Seventeen

I had turned my phone off during our lunch, and when I checked it, I found a couple of messages. The first was from my father, the second from Cindy Metcalf. I figured neither of those could be too urgent, so I waited to return the calls until I'd driven home, fed Aramis, and let him out of his cage.

I did usually talk to Dad on Sundays, but at the moment, I didn't feel like reporting to him that I'd been out with Ed. So I called Cindy back first.

Her brief message said she had taken my advice and checked out the photo of the jewelry-store robber in the online edition of the Delaware paper. She agreed that, allowing for his masked lower face, the man did somewhat resemble Mitch.

When I got her on the line, though, she had some valid questions. "But Viv, why would someone who was after high-priced merchandise also sneak into our building? Gerry would have told him that we don't carry much along that line."

"Gerry also could have given him the entry code, though," I pointed out. "And think about it…on our video, the guy was upstairs, hanging around Gerry's and Ronnie's booths."

"No one reported anything missing, and neither of them carry anything that valuable anyway. He passed up Kaye's pricier stuff…"

"Or maybe he was just checking out her area when she came upstairs and caught him, and that's why he killed her."

Cindy caught her breath a little. "I guess that's possible. But a few other vendors also keep expensive things under lock and key. Really good jewelry, even historic memorabilia. There was no sign any of those cases were even tampered with."

Even with the whole condo to explore, Aramis alighted on my head and began to nibble at my messy topknot. Hoping he didn't see it as a potential nest, I struggled to stay focused on my conversation with Cindy. "I think this guy wanted to get in and out quickly, before Fred showed up, so he wasn't going to hang around trying to open padlocks. Those cases are Plexiglas, too—it wouldn't be an easy smash-and-grab job, like in most jewelry stores."

"Still sounds odd to me. Maybe I just don't want to think one of us has been abetting a murderer." She fell silent for another beat. "It'll be interesting to see if Gerry has the nerve to come to work tomorrow, after the performance he put on yesterday."

"Or if Ronnie finally does," I reminded her. "I do wonder what's really going on with her!"

By the time we hung up, I felt talked out for the day, though something still nagged at me. I emailed Mona and passed along my theory that there might be a connection between the break-ins at the antiques center and the theater, though I couldn't figure out just what.

After all, the work of following up on those crimes belonged to Mona…and the cops. I should just leave it to them.

When I tried to call my father back on his landline, I got voicemail, so I left a message. Told him I'd been out to lunch with a friend, was kind of tired, and would try him again tomorrow. With any luck, Dad might be off somewhere bolstering his own social life. He recently joined a ballroom-dancing group in his community that met on Sunday afternoons.

I changed into loose yoga garb and settled down in my studio with my laptop. With my feather-headed supervisor keeping watch from the top of the torchière, I checked my website for any new orders. Just one—a guy in Pennsylvania wanted a pair of my barkcloth pillows, in one of the dark, exotic patterns, so I'd get to work on those tomorrow. I also responded to a few comments and questions pertaining to the estate-sale article on my blog.

After that, I turned to some nuts-and-bolts jobs. Close scrutiny of the two chenille bedspreads I'd picked up at the estate sale revealed just a few tiny moth holes in each, so I dug out my sewing box and got to work mending them. For background music, I searched through a couple dozen old LP records I had salvaged from Nana's vast collection. Her taste was very eclectic, so the albums ranged from symphonic to Sinatra and Streisand to classic rock. For a second, I considered the soundtrack for the 2001 stage musical of *The Producers*...then realized why it had tempted me. Ed co-starred in our college production of that show, singing and even dancing a bit as Leo Bloom, the Matthew Broderick role.

No need to wallow in any more of those memories. I've got my hands full these days, adjusting to the forty-year-old version of Ed!

I settled on an album by jazz flutist Herbie Mann.

Before turning in for the night, I decided to also deal with some other cool finds from the Friday sale, the old sheet music. This didn't take much effort, as I liked to tamper with them as little as possible. Some customers would only care about the covers, but others might want all the music intact. I'd found it best to use a very simple brown, black, or metal frame that did not compete with the cover artwork. Sometimes I added a plain white mat for extra drama, and to hide any worn edges. If the customer wanted to remove the music to actually play it, or to upgrade to a fancier frame, they could easily do so.

Just one downside, tonight. The romantic titles of the vintage tunes and deco images of male/female couples again kept reminding me of Ed.

Pull yourself together, Viv! Would Katherine Hepburn let some guy throw her totally off track? Just be his friend, for now, and take it one day at a time.

Besides, you may have more important things to worry about, if the break-in at the antiques center really is connected to the one at the theater...

* * *

The next day, Monday, promised to be cool and rainy, so I made the time to return my father's call.

He tended to panic if I was out of touch for too long, imagining that I'd met with some disaster. I knew he still remained badly shaken by my mother's out-of-nowhere cancer diagnosis and rapid decline, just a few years ago.

"Sorry to worry you," I told him. "I was out to lunch yesterday with a friend."

A short silence. "That actor guy again?"

"Yes, Ed Kiernan. He's so busy with rehearsals at the playhouse now that Sunday's about the only time he has free."

I could picture Dad's frowning face, complete with the wire-framed reading glasses and graying mustache. "Viv, why do you want to get mixed up with somebody like that? The play will run a few weeks, and then where will he be? Back to California, probably, or New York, for some other project."

"Maybe not." I tried to sound unconcerned. "As far as I know, he hasn't got anything else lined up in the near future."

Wrong answer, it just gave my father more ammo. "So he'll be unemployed? Ha, even better!"

Though Dad's negativity annoyed me, I still had to smile. "I'm sure Ed earned enough from his TV series to let him be choosy, these days, about what jobs he takes. You make him sound like a bum on the street! He's got roots here, family in the area. Heck, if I'd dated him in college, you would have seen nothing wrong with it."

"That was almost twenty years ago. He's a grown man now, he's been around that Hollywood scene..."

No doubt Dad imagined all kinds of drinking, drugging, and womanizing. "I'm sure he has, but frankly, Ed sounds pretty disenchanted with all that. He keeps talking about how good it feels to be back in live theater and on his home turf. Anyway, like I told you before, he's a friend. He's gone through some tough stuff and needs someone to talk to, someone who's not involved with the theater. That's all."

"Yeah, that's the way it *starts*." A weighty pause on the line. "Look, honey, it's not just about his line of work. There's something you should know about..."

"What happened with his fiancée fifteen years ago? I already do."

I heard Dad's sharp intake of breath. "You mean he told..."

"When you asked me if he was related to some councilman, I looked it up online. And after lunch yesterday, I asked him about it." I related Ed's explanation and added that his description of Janet's temperament jibed with what little I'd seen of her behavior in our college days.

"I dunno." My father snorted. "The guy must have done something to send her 'round the bend like that. And she had drugs in her system..."

"Meds for her emotional problems, mixed with too much booze. I totally believe him, Dad. He seemed very sad just discussing the whole incident, and feels guilty that he didn't pay more attention..."

"Maybe he's got more than that to feel guilty about."

"Enough!" I insisted. "I'm not discussing this with you anymore, so let's change the subject. Are you still going to meetings for that Singles' Club in your community? Don't they have some big picnic coming up for Memorial Day weekend?"

"Okay, don't listen to me. I just hope you're not sorry."

My strategy worked, and Dad ended our call himself. As I set my phone down, Aramis flitted onto my finger.

"I knew that would shut him up," I told the bird, with a wink. "He can dish out the relationship advice, but he can't take it!"

Still, I worried for the rest of the day if my father had a point. Was my attraction to Ed doomed from the start? Even if we did begin a relationship, would he constantly be moving on to new jobs? New roles that not only took him out of the area, but kept pairing him up with beautiful, sexy actresses? How could I ever hope to compete with that?

The picture jolted me back to my college days, when my bushy hair, twenty extra pounds, and conspicuous braces had made me fade into the scenery...at least as far as the more glamorous theater crowd was concerned.

* * *

Tuesday morning found me back in Booth 17, tweaking my display to accommodate the new acquisitions from the estate sale. I switched out a couple of sets of draperies I had hung over the garment rack and replaced

156

them with chenille bedspreads—those might appeal to more buyers during the warmer months. I had recently sold one of my large Turner floral prints, so in that space I mounted a pair of the framed sheet music covers, in deco-pastel color schemes.

While I was still using hooks to adjust these smaller pieces on the pegboard backing, I heard a soft voice behind me. "Vivian?"

I turned to see Ronnie, looking different from usual that day. Her big '80s hair had deflated a bit; she wore a baggy gray sweatshirt with her stretch pants, and her face seemed bare of makeup. Her spooked expression and edgy behavior made me wonder, again, if she'd been through some kind of physical illness or trauma. Well, she had said she was caring for someone who was ill...

"Hi, Ronnie," I said. "Good to see you back. Is your...relative doing better?"

She blinked, as if taking a second to comprehend the question. "Oh...yes. Yes, she is, thanks for asking. I've got...a different problem now, though, and I'm hoping you can help."

That got my attention. "Sure, anything."

"You remember the necklace that Lauren, from the theater, borrowed from me? I need to get it back."

My scalp prickled, but I tried not to jump to any melodramatic conclusions. "Oh, dear. Why?"

"When you asked about it and sent me the photo, I'd forgotten that I already promised it to another customer. I guess I was so distracted by my...aunt's health crisis, I didn't remember at the time. But now the customer insists on picking it up, because she's going to a big party and wants to wear that necklace."

"She paid for it already?"

Again, Ronnie took a split second to answer. "She put a deposit on it, but she's coming here with the balance. Tomorrow."

"I see." My fellow vendor seemed to be making up this story as she went along. "Have you contacted Lauren about getting it back?"

"I did, but she got snippy with me. She said they've practically designed a whole scene around it, in Act II, and she can't imagine finding anything else

157

at this point that would work so well."

Browsers began to hover at the next booth, so I sat on my loveseat and gestured for Ronnie to join me, for more privacy. "Did you explain to your customer that it's supposed to be in a show at the playhouse, starting next week? I would think she'd appreciate that. She might not have it in time for this particular party, but afterward she can tell people it was worn by the leading lady in *Murder Most Noir*. The run of the show is only three weeks…"

Ronnie frowned and grew more agitated. "She doesn't care about any of that. She's used to getting what she wants, when she wants it, and won't take 'no' for an answer. Please, Viv, you've got to help me!"

Great. "What do you think I can do?"

"I know you loaned the theater some pieces for Tom Richardson. Gloria says you're also friendly with Ed Kiernan, that you went to school with him."

"Yes, but—"

"Can you talk to Lauren for me and explain the situation? I don't think she's taking it…seriously enough."

All right, there definitely was more going on here than just the selfish whim of some temperamental customer. Whatever it was, I'd somehow landed in the middle. "I'll try, Ronnie. I'll call Lauren this afternoon and see if she'd be willing to substitute another necklace for that scene."

"Thank you so much!" A flicker of the old brightness finally crossed Ronnie's plain features. "You're a doll, Viv. A lifesaver!"

* * *

I gave Lauren a call, but was not surprised when it went to voicemail. I knew they were all into dress rehearsals that week, and she'd be busy with last-minute tweaks. I was also sure that she wouldn't want to deal with any additional, unnecessary changes. But I'd promised Ronnie, so I relayed her request, with my own apologies, to the costume designer.

As I was closing up for the day, Lauren got back to me, sounding testy. "I just can't *believe* this! Like I don't have enough to deal with, right now."

"I know, I know. It sounds crazy to me, too. But I guess this customer has

Ronnie pretty intimidated."

"She had that necklace stuffed at the back of a drawer. How much could she have cared about it then? I'll bet after you took the photo of it, Ronnie showed that to another customer who decided they *had* to have it. Maybe that person offered her a lot for it, more than our rental fee, so now Ronnie's gotten greedy."

Our jewelry vendor had struck me as more frightened than greedy, but I admitted, "That's possible."

"Well, tough nuts. She signed a contract with us, so we have dibs for the run of the show. There's no way I can return it now. That piece is a showstopper, it 'makes' that whole scene in the second act. Ronnie and her customer can damn well wait three weeks to get it back." I heard someone in the background shout Lauren's name. "Look, I don't have time for this now. Sorry to take it out on you, Viv. Ronnie shouldn't have put you in the middle."

"I fully understand, Lauren. I'll deal with her. You just go do your job."

I could have passed this news along to Ronnie immediately, but I knew she'd only pressure me some more, and I'd had enough drama for one day. Besides, while talking with Lauren, I'd gotten another call, from Betty Kramer of the Jonesburg pawn shop. In a message, she thanked me for asking how she and her husband were doing after the robbery.

"Al is home from the hospital, but we've closed up shop for the time being, and we're trying to decide whether to make it permanent," she said. "Maybe we've just been lucky, but this is the first time in twenty-five years that we've had this kind of violent robbery. Not sure we'd want to risk it again, at our ages."

Coming so soon after my conversation with Ronnie, this message from Betty Kramer felt like too big a coincidence to ignore. I had no customers hanging around my booth, so I called her right back.

Again, the older woman thanked me for being so thoughtful and assured me her husband was recovering medically from his shock. I tried to be tactful while drawing her out about a few details. "The police seem convinced that the men who robbed you were the same ones who robbed the mall in Delaware. But that's odd, isn't it, since you carry such different merchandise?"

"You would think so," Betty agreed. "But we do have some high-end estate pieces. When wealthy families fall on hard times, one of the first things they often do is hock the family jewels, especially the older stuff that has gone out of fashion. They might not want to wear it to a party anymore, but the individual gems are still valuable."

My theory started to take shape. "The paper did say the robbers concentrated on the estate jewelry."

"They made right for it, as if one of them had scouted out our place in advance. I once told Al we should keep that stuff in a safe, but of course, then people just visiting the shop wouldn't be able to appreciate it. Besides, these guys made me open the display case, at gunpoint. If they knew the estate jewelry was in a safe, they still could have done the same thing."

A shudder crept into the woman's voice as she relived her trauma, and I felt bad for bringing it up again. "Well, I hope after you and Al have gotten over this scare, you do reopen your business. Maybe with a high-tech security system? But I can understand why you might not."

"Yes, we'd like to live to see our grandkids grow up!" Betty Kramer chuckled darkly. "But thanks again for calling, Vivian."

Ending the call, I felt I could line up a few more pieces of the puzzle, but they still didn't form a complete, logical picture. I emailed one more person who might be able to help me…

* * *

In the soft glow from the table's candle lamp, my sister pondered her glass of white wine. "What if," she asked slowly, "the guy who broke into the antiques center didn't come to steal anything?"

When I'd contacted her at the paper an hour earlier, Mona had been finishing a story on deadline but suggested we meet at Applegarth's. I agreed that was best. In a booth at the pub, we could discuss some shady issues fairly privately.

This new theory of hers surprised me, though. "You think he went there deliberately to kill Kaye?"

"No, he probably only did that to avoid being seen and identified. But let's go over what we know. At the store in Delaware, the two guys stole watches. But at the pawn shop, they went for the estate jewelry—different types of things pawned by all different sellers who needed the cash."

Chewing on a mozzarella stick from our shared appetizer plate, I started to see where my sister was headed. "Nothing would be marked, so there'd be no way of knowing where it came from."

Always-logical Mona ticked off key points on the slim fingers of one hand. "Someone involved in the robberies got into your antiques center just before it opened. There was no violent break-in, so somehow he knew just when it would open and had the entry code."

I nodded. "He had an inside connection."

"But if he did know one of the vendors, he also would have known there was nothing terribly valuable to steal. At least nothing he could easily grab, right? So what if he *left* something there?"

That caught me off guard. "By accident?"

"On purpose. He and his partners had some high-end stuff in their possession, with the police hot on their trail. Ordinarily, since all of that jewelry was insured, there might not be a lot of pressure to recover it and arrest the thieves. But at the mall, they'd also wounded a security guard. That's a whole new ball game."

"They couldn't afford to be caught with the loot." I followed her logic. "Wherever they might have planned to hide it, maybe they decided not to keep it all in one place."

Mona turned up her palms, as if the solution were obvious. "So they disperse it. One of them has a connection with the antiques center, who tells him the jewelry lady there has a lot of flashy-but-fake pieces that could pass for the real thing."

"The thief sneaks in to plant some real treasures among Ronnie's stock," I reasoned. "But he doesn't want her selling them by mistake, so he stashes the best stuff in out-of-the-way places. Like the very back of a drawer, she probably doesn't open often."

"Bingo! Then your friend Lauren happens to spot this beautiful necklace, thinking it's really just paste and glass…"

"Holy crap." I recalled the huge green stone at the center of the piece, and slumped back in my seat. "That's a real emerald!"

"You said Lauren called it a showstopper."

I took a big swallow of wine to calm my nerves. "So even though the guy wasn't stealing anything, he still couldn't risk being caught. When Kaye Burrell surprised him, and probably made her usual fuss…"

"He grabbed the handiest weapon he could find and whacked her. Then he might not even check to see if she was dead or alive. He'd done what he came to do, so he dumped her down the elevator shaft and beat it out of there, as fast as possible."

It must have been Mitch, I thought, because Gerry would have given him the idea to stash the piece among Ronnie's things. She might have been genuinely unaware when I'd first asked her about lending the necklace to the theater. She honestly assumed that it had been part of some big "lot" she had purchased and signed it over in good faith.

But now someone wanted it back.

Someone higher up than Mitch, I thought. Someone who didn't do his own dirty work, but who scared the crap out of all three men.

Gerry's whimpering on the phone had nothing to do with anything as normal as Ronnie or some other girlfriend getting pregnant. Have must have told her about the hidden jewelry, and she freaked out over him involving her in the scheme. And his bruising "motorcycle accident"? Maybe Mitch, or the other partner in the two heists (pictured in the sketch of the Delaware mall thief), had demanded the necklace back. When Gerry couldn't produce it, someone had worked him over.

If there were any more stolen pieces stashed in Ronnie's booth, her boyfriend had probably returned them to Mitch by now. But the biggest prize still remained out of Gerry's reach.

In the costume department of the Addamsville Playhouse.

Chapter Eighteen

When we parted that evening, Mona suggested she might ask her editor if she could check for links between the incidents at the antiques center and the playhouse. She wasn't sure he would go for it, though, because on the surface the connection seemed flimsy.

Meanwhile, I thought of reaching out to Officer Gorey on the Addamsville force. When I remembered his gruff, no-nonsense demeanor, I also feared I wouldn't be taken seriously. Still, on my drive home, my mind continued to race.

I remembered how panicked Ronnie had acted when she feared she couldn't get the necklace back from Lauren—her concern that the person demanding its return "won't take 'no' for an answer." Would someone physically attack her? Maybe not, once they knew the piece was out of her hands.

But someone had attempted to get into the shop area of the playhouse. Most likely, they would try that again.

They won't find the theater so empty this time, though. Everybody's working late this week. If tonight's dress rehearsal includes the scene with the green gown, the necklace might not even be in the costume shop. Marsha Fuller, the actress who plays Gloria, could be wearing it!

That would complicate things for the robbers, but might not discourage them entirely. After all, one had shot a security guard during the Delaware job! I doubted either gunman would make an attempt onstage, where the cast and crew might overpower him. He could wait until the actors took a break, though, and try to grab Marsha.

Someone else could get hurt, too...even killed. Maybe Lauren, or—

I pulled into the parking space outside my condo, but stayed in the car to redial Lauren's number. Voice mail again. Tersely, I recorded my concerns. "Everyone there should be careful tonight. I think that pearl-and-emerald necklace is the real deal, and someone wants it back in the worst way. Literally—they might do anything! Just be on your toes."

Inside my condo, I suffered the outraged shrieks of Aramis, even though I'd fed him before going to meet Mona. He wanted company, and I lifted him out on my finger to stroke his feathers for a few minutes and calm him down.

I couldn't soothe my own nerves as easily.

What if Lauren never listened to my message? What if she saw my name on her phone and thought, *Why won't Viv leave me the heck alone? I'm not returning the necklace, and I don't have time for this drama!*

Little did she suspect that she could end up with far more drama than she'd signed up for, than any of them had. And Ed...he also knew nothing about any of this! Lauren probably hadn't even mentioned our conversation to him.

A gunman might figure he could intimidate a woman and get what he came for without any bloodshed. But if Ed interrupted them and gave the guy a hard time...

Things could go very, very wrong.

Tears of panic welling in my eyes, I eased Aramis back into his cage and tried Ed's phone. Got a recording there, too, and left him the same basic message I had for Lauren.

"Sorry, pal," I told Aramis, "but Mama's got to go out again."

I needed to see for myself that everything at the theater—and everyone—was still okay.

* * *

The evening fog thickened as I drove toward the river, and by eight o'clock, it hung heavily around the looming, barnlike Addamsville Playhouse.

164

Nevertheless, lights burned in most of the ground-floor windows, and maybe a dozen vehicles stood in the rear parking lot.

I pulled into a slot at a distance from the building and considered my approach. So far, I saw nothing amiss. If I barged in and started warning people of some threat that might or might not materialize, would they turn on me in irritation, thinking they had more urgent business to deal with? Should I just keep watch, myself, and call the cops if I did see something go wrong?

How long, all night? Maybe I should have picked up a Box O Joe to keep me awake!

Meanwhile, it looked like the cast and crew of *Murder Most Noir* were relying on takeout to get them through tonight's session. I heard a car door slam at the other end of the lot, and a tall, athletically built man emerged from beneath the trees. Wearing a blue polo shirt, matching pants, and a blue-and-red billed cap, he strode toward the rear door of the playhouse with a pizza delivery. A couple of full-sized pies, to judge from the big, black warming bag that he carried in his arms.

As he passed beneath one of the pole lights that edged the lot, something about his quick, determined step alerted me. The cap covered most of his hair, so I couldn't even see if it was light or dark, but there was a certain sharpness to his nose…

He'd also left his vehicle toward the back of the lot, which seemed odd if he wanted to get in and out quickly with his delivery. I didn't see anything as obvious as a van parked among the tree shadows. Pizza places also used sedans for smaller orders, but weren't they kind of flashy, too—bright red or white, with the company name?

Turning on my engine, I cruised slowly across the paved area, just near enough to get a better view of the far corner. Even so, I almost overlooked the only vehicle parked there, because it was low-slung and mostly black. Closer up, though, I could make out the golden firebird wings spread out across the hood.

I did not pull near enough to recognize the man who sat behind the wheel, but knew it must be Gerry. The getaway driver for tonight's job?

Damn, that's a good cover. Mitch can pass for a delivery guy, bringing pizza for some of the hungry crew, and who's going to question him? Even if Lauren and Ed got my messages, they could still be fooled.

He probably thinks he'll sneak into the costume shop and grab the necklace while everyone else is busy onstage.

This time I parked as close to the building as I could, drew a deep breath and stepped out into the fog. I hesitated for a second and pulled out my phone. Maybe before dashing in there, I ought to dial 9-1-1. Better to risk a false alarm than—

I barely heard the running steps behind me, or had time to react, before a strong hand grabbed my phone. "Don't do that, Viv!" Gerry hissed in my ear. "You don't wanna cause trouble."

I tried to snatch my phone back, but he held it out of reach and shoved me away.

Even though I could read the panic in his eyes, he insisted, "It'll be okay. While everybody's busy with the rehearsal, he'll get what we need and we'll be out of here."

"No, he won't," I warned Gerry. "He's after the necklace, right?"

"It's on a mannequin in the costume shop."

I shook my head. "Not tonight. Marsha's wearing it, onstage."

"Marsha—?" The name obviously meant nothing to Gerry.

"The lead actress. This is a dress rehearsal, and Lauren told me they'd be using that piece."

Gerry squinted in anger, and possibly pain, as if thinking harder than was normal for him. "Okay, then, *you* go in. They trust you. Check the costume shop, just in case. If it's there, you can sneak it out. No one needs to get hurt, and you'll save everybody a lot of trouble."

And abet a crime, I thought, but it still might be better than endangering any more lives. I agreed to this because I needed to see for myself that things hadn't already gotten out of hand. I hoped to hell that Ed was onstage, rehearsing, and had not crossed paths with Mitch Rubello, who was likely to be armed.

I told Gerry, "I'll do my best. I don't want anyone hurt, either."

I headed for the nearest entrance, the same one Mitch had used, next to the outdoor ramp. It brought me into a short hallway between a storage area and one of the dressing rooms. I heard nothing from the second of these spaces but looked in, anyway, on the chance that Marsha might be in there changing. Empty, and I saw neither the glamorous green gown nor the necklace anywhere in sight. I made a left down a longer corridor past the backstage restrooms. (I wasn't going to scout those out unless I absolutely had to.) A right turn at the end took me past the Green Room, also empty right now, and the "star" dressing room. I guessed that would have been Ed's, for this production, but the door was closed.

The costume shop stood open, and for the moment, I saw no one in there. Sewing tools, swaths of fabric, and spools of trims lay strewn about on the main table and other surfaces, but that could have been normal. Possibly Mitch had not checked out the backstage areas before tonight, and found them confusing, because I had somehow beaten him here.

Not by much, though. I heard an angry male voice out in the hall, arguing with Lauren.

My heart thudded, and instinct told me to hide. If Mitch did not realize I was here, I might have a better chance of saving both Lauren and myself.

I ducked behind a short wall that concealed the adjoining laundry room.

Though Mitch propelled the costume designer roughly into the studio by one arm, she seemed to keep her cool. "What is it with you people and that stupid necklace?" she huffed. "First, I had Ronnie from the antiques center driving me crazy all day with her calls, saying she promised it to some mysterious customer. Now you're after it. Is that who you're working for? Did her customer send you to get it from me?"

That question seemed to throw Mitch, but he rolled with this explanation. "That's right. It belongs to her, so hand it over."

"You're too late. I had someone drop it off at Ronnie's apartment about an hour ago. Figured it wasn't worth all this trouble. I'm sure she'll be happy to sell it to…whoever hired you."

I saw Mitch reach beneath the hem of his polo shirt and yank a small pistol from his jeans pocket. "You're lying."

"I'm not." Lauren's voice quavered, but she stuck to her story. "Why should I go through all of this abuse for a piece of junk that she probably picked up at a yard sale?"

The intruder narrowed his eyes beneath the sharply angled, dark brows. "I bet it's on that actress. Is she wearing it now? Or did you stash it somewhere else?"

"It's not here," Lauren still insisted.

Mitch worked his jaw in agitation. Things surely were not going the way he'd planned. He wasn't wearing his usual mask, because that would have looked odd for a pizza delivery guy, and he had to realize that the designer would be able to identify him. Luckily for Lauren, he couldn't shoot her before he found out what she had actually done with the necklace.

He leveled the gun with greater resolve. "Maybe we'll just hang out here until the rehearsal is over and the leading lady comes back to change. Bet *she'll* be willing to hand it over to me without a fight."

"I'm telling you, I gave it back to—"

"What's going on here?" a stern male voice demanded from the hallway. "Lauren, is this guy bothering you?"

A shock went through me, and despite the risk, I had to peer around the half-wall into the costume shop. Ed stood in the doorway, wearing his Danny McDougal gear. Pleated pants, white business shirt, suspenders, and leather shoulder holster...which held the brown-handled revolver.

Still, Lauren kept control. "Just a misunderstanding, officer. This guy seems under the impression that one of our props is some kind of priceless treasure, even though I've explained to him that it's not."

Ed faced Mitch with a stony expression. "And do you make a habit, young man, of breaking into places of business and threatening people with firearms?"

I nearly choked in panic. This was insane! *No, Ed, stop! Mitch has already shot one man, and he could shoot you, too. Don't joke around—you're not a real cop!*

The confrontation did seem to baffle our intruder for a second. He clearly didn't know what to make of this slightly older guy with the vintage getup and stilted lingo. He looked almost ready to laugh until Ed slid the revolver from its holster and leveled it, straight-armed, at Mitch.

"I'd suggest you step away from the lady," he said. "Now."

His obvious ease with the weapon, combined with his uncanny calm, suggested he meant business. Mitch raised his eyebrows, but still didn't totally buy the threat.

"Gimme a break," he said, though with a nervous edge. "You're not a cop. You're an actor, your picture's on the poster out front!"

"That may be, but *this* is a real 38 Colt police revolver that's already taken down its share of bad guys. It still works great and I know how to use it."

My brain screamed, even louder, that Ed was backing himself into a situation he might not survive, and I couldn't just stand by. I stole out of the laundry room, crouching low, and hid behind a dress form that was partly draped in fabric. Luckily, Mitch and Lauren both had their backs to me, and if Ed noticed my stealthy move, he gave no sign.

"That Dick Tracy piece of crap probably isn't even loaded," Mitch sneered.

"Wanna gamble on that?" We all heard the soft click as "Detective McDougal" cocked the gun.

I remembered Carl Randolph noting that the fake gun did cock, for effect, but couldn't shoot anything. Had Ed gone completely nuts? He appeared to hold his mock weapon completely steady, while I thought Mitch's hand trembled a bit.

I could shove the dress dummy into him from behind, but what if that made him fire? Even a stray bullet could graze Ed, or worse.

I scanned the cluttered table next to me…and spotted a possible weapon of my own.

Mitch's confidence seemed to return, and he squared his shoulders in the blue polo shirt. "Yeah, I'm game. Maybe you can pull the trigger, but at that distance you'll probably miss by a mile. Or hit the pretty costume lady, instead."

That felt like my cue. I snicked my blade open, stepped silently from behind the dress form, and jammed the tip into Mitch's lower back. He gave a yelp of surprise and, I hoped, a little pain.

"This is a nine-inch tailoring shears," I hissed at him, from a tight throat. "It's aimed at your right kidney, and at this distance, *I* can't possibly miss. Drop your gun, now!"

Mitch still balked for a second. If I'd been the only threat, he might have tried to wrestle me for the shears. But I guess taking his eyes off Ed's realistic weapon felt like too big a risk.

His automatic pistol dropped to the floor at his feet, and he raised his hands.

I could see Ed's shoulders relax just a little, though he held his pose. "Kick it away," he barked at Mitch, who complied.

I wondered if I should pick the gun up, for good measure, when we heard a baritone bellow from down the hall. "Police! Did somebody call?"

"In here!" Lauren screamed at the top of her lungs.

Chapter Nineteen

O nce Officer Bharani had taken Mitch into custody, we gathered in the theater's Green Room to give our statements to Gorey. Though he wasn't happy with the chances any of us had taken, all he did was scold us. After all, we had to do something while we waited for the police to arrive, and at least we'd kept the "perp" on the premises.

As it turned out, Lauren's and Ed's bold tactics toward Mitch weren't quite as daredevil as they'd seemed.

They both had received my phone messages, earlier that evening, and conferred about how to handle any possible threat. Lauren concocted the story that she had already returned the pearl-and-emerald necklace to Ronnie; in reality, she'd locked it in the box office safe. She also had alerted the theater's security firm, but was told the guard might take some time to respond. Agnes, the director, had agreed to pause the dress rehearsal until the situation was resolved, one way or another. Ed had retreated to his dressing room where he could keep an eye, or an ear, on the costume shop next door.

Everyone hoped it would turn out to be a false alarm, or at least that the intruder would show up unarmed and could be easily overpowered. They hadn't anticipated Mitch donning a makeshift uniform and toting empty pizza boxes along with his pistol. When those tactics caught them by surprise, Kiernan called 911 from his dressing room, and then he and Lauren had fallen back on the time-honored theatrical skill of improv.

It was after nine when the cops left with their captive. The three of us wandered out to the main stage. Ed prepared to go back to work. But Agnes saw no point in continuing that evening's rehearsal and, for their own safety, had sent the rest of the cast home.

Meanwhile, I got to preview the completed set of "Gloria's" living room, with its plume-y barkcloth drapes, my coordinating throw pillows on Adrian's rose sofa, his sleek deco coffee table, and my jardinière spilling artificial ferns in one corner. Not to disturb any of this, we sat around at the edge of the stage to drink coffee. We explained to Agnes—a slim, erect woman with short gray hair and cat's-eye glasses—the real-life melodrama that had taken place in the costume shop.

"You sure had me fooled," I told Lauren. "I couldn't believe you kept arguing with Mitch, even after he pulled the gun!"

"That did scare the crap out of me," she admitted. "I kept telling myself the cops would probably show up at any minute, which turned out to be a little too optimistic! But Ed took the biggest chance—"

Sitting next to me, he mimed wiping his brow, under its fringe of wavy hair. "I didn't expect him to be packing, either, but when he got hold of Lauren, I had to do *something*. I figured he wouldn't have any idea that the replica gun wasn't real, and otherwise I told him the truth—that it was a vintage police revolver and I'd been trained to use it."

"You were excellent," Lauren said, with a tight laugh. "Pat Harrigan from *Boulevard Blues* couldn't have handled it any better."

Agnes shook her head in disbelief. "Kiernan, there's such a thing as identifying too much with your character!"

Still a bit dazed, I could only stare at him. "I thought you were out of your mind, and I was *so* scared for you! I wish I'd known the cops were already on their way."

"Speaking of nerves of steel..." His warm, steadying hand closed upon my shoulder as he told Agnes, "This lady was *fierce*, poking that guy in the back with a scissors! In another second, he might've called my bluff, so Viv probably saved my neck."

Though that had been exactly my goal, I fanned away the credit. "I only got the drop on Mitch because you still had him, technically, at gunpoint."

The director surveyed us all with a guarded smile and toasted us with her takeout coffee cup. "Sounds like great teamwork—ensemble work, you might say! Now I'd suggest you all get a good night's sleep, because we'll have to make up for lost time tomorrow." She realized that she had to make one exemption. "Except for you, of course, Vivian."

"I'm exhausted, anyway," I admitted. "And I'll sure sleep better knowing Mitch is behind bars...at least for now."

Almost on cue, Officer Gorey chose that moment to call Lauren's cell phone. She put it on speaker so the rest of us could hear.

"Wanted to reassure all of you that Mitch Rubello is spending the night in custody, and so is his accomplice. I gather that guy's also his cousin—we grabbed him in the parking lot. Ms. Joyce will be getting her phone back, too."

Tough luck, Gerry, I thought. *You should be more careful about the company you keep.*

"Gerry Rubello works at the antiques center," I told the officer. "This is all about a valuable necklace, from last week's pawn shop robbery, that got mixed in with a vendor's costume jewelry. And I'm pretty sure it also ties in with the store that was hit in Delaware."

"We suspect so, too." Nevertheless, I heard a pause as if he were making some notes. "Thank you, Ms. Joyce. You're related to that reporter with the *Herald,* aren't you?"

"My older sister," I acknowledged.

"Well, you've been helpful, if a bit reckless. Speaking of which, is Mr. Kiernan there?"

Ed leaned in Lauren's direction to respond, "Yes, sir."

"Young man, you're lucky we don't fine you for impersonating a police officer and threatening to discharge an unlicensed firearm."

L0auren gaped at her phone. "You've got to be kidding, Officer! He wasn't wearing a uniform, or even a badge, and the 'firearm' was a harmless stage prop."

"The theater holds a permit for that gun," Agnes chimed in, from two seats away. "Ed and Lauren both work for us. So even if it had been real, he would have had the right to use it to protect her, same as in a home invasion."

173

This took some of the self-righteous wind out of Gorey's sails. "Still, if the gun couldn't even shoot, all the more reason why he shouldn't have risked his life—and maybe other lives, too—by confronting an armed robber."

Ed took his lecture with good grace. "As I explained earlier, I knew you were on your way, but meanwhile, I was concerned about these ladies." (That was a stretch, I thought, since at first he hadn't even known I was in the room.) "I wanted to keep the guy's attention on me until you got here, and luckily it worked. But I get your point, Officer, and I'll avoid such a crazy stunt in the future."

"I hope so." Gorey's voice turned grim once more. "Remember, taking down the bad guys is *our* job, not yours. A civilian has no business running around playing cop. We get paid to do that, you don't!"

We all exchanged looks and bit our tongues. Agnes, of all people, was the first to giggle.

Ed finally cracked a sly smile and leaned toward the phone again. "Well, actually..."

* * *

The next day, Wednesday, the police visited the antiques center and went through Ronnie's stock, with her assistance. They wanted to check whether Mitch or Gerry could have mixed in more pieces from the pawn shop. Ronnie did find a few more items that she did not remember purchasing, and the cops took them to be checked by a certified jewelry appraiser. I hoped any merchandise that had been stolen from the Kramers would be returned to them.

Needless to say, all of this took a heavy toll on Ronnie's relationship with Gerry. He and Mitch both faced serious jail time, and the cops expected that once they tracked down the second gunman from the Delaware store, they could crack a multi-state ring.

Mona followed the case every step of the way, firmly establishing her credentials as a hard-news reporter. At the same time, she helped to keep the names of the civilians involved in the playhouse standoff out of the paper. Her initial story just stated that police responded to a 911 call from the theater. They found Mitch Rubello in the costume shop, demanding a necklace and threatening two members of the company. (No lie—I wasn't a member of the company, and he never directly threatened me.) They also had found his cousin Gerry waiting for Mitch in the theater's parking lot.

Mona did mention that Gerry worked at the antiques center, and that Mitch might also be implicated in the recent break-in there and the suspicious death of a vendor. Because Ronnie had known nothing about that earlier crime, and cooperated fully with the police, her name was also kept out of the story.

But the official coverage in *The Herald* was one thing, and the Addamsville gossip mill was another. Word soon got around that three civilians had foiled the armed, would-be robber by calling his bluff. Once the rumor spread that the show's star had actually threatened him with a harmless revolver, and the trick had worked, *Murder Most Noir* sold out for the rest of its run.

Probably to cover the costs of his legal defense, Gerry liquidated almost his whole stock of kitschy merchandise. The buyer, an older man who had just retired, happily purchased everything except some borderline-pornographic stuff, and even took over Gerry's old booth. I was glad, because I actually would have missed seeing that colorful display in the rear corner of our floor. And while Gerry always had struck me as a bit cynical about the Baby Boomer memorabilia, new vendor Sal grew up as part of that generation and seems to harbor a genuine affection for it.

I didn't witness any blowups on the job between Gerry and Ronnie, but even while he was clearing out his stuff, she seemed to have little to say to him. At least she mustered the courage to stick around and continue to staff her booth, though she probably kept a closer eye on her inventory from then on.

Lauren offered to return the genuine pearl-and-emerald necklace immediately to the Kramers. But having also benefited from the spate of publicity, they offered to let her keep it for the run of the show. The theater, in turn, promised to keep the piece in a locked case when not in use and to post a security guard backstage while it was being worn. (Also great for publicity!)

* * *

Despite all the extra drama happening in the wings, *Murder Most Noir* remained on schedule to open the first Saturday in June. My most pleasant shock came a few days before that, when Ed called and asked me to be his date for the afterparty.

"If you'd feel awkward, I understand," he added. "It'll be mostly the cast and crew, their close friends, and maybe some press people. But I'm sure you went to some of those things in college, so you know the drill."

I had attended some, though I'm sure the afterparties at our small college couldn't compare. This would be at The Station, Ed explained, in the upstairs banquet room. No way did I intend to pass up that invitation! Poor, troubled Janet had dragged Ed down with her shyness and jealousy, but Vivian the Vintage Vixen wouldn't make that mistake.

"I'd love to go," I told him. "And I'm flattered that you asked."

"Don't be silly. I can't think of anyone I'd rather have by my side." No trace of flip humor in his voice, this time. "You're beautiful, you're smart, you're funny, you're brave...and best of all, as far as I can tell, you have no desire to ever become a thespian!"

I laughed and assured him, "I definitely don't."

"See, you are smart. Half the actresses I knew in Hollywood would have thought that was some kind of insult! Listen, I've got another call, but I'll be in touch soon with more specifics about that party, okay?"

After he hung up, I pondered my silent phone a minute longer. In my almost-forty years, I had sometimes been called cute and even pretty. But this was the first time anyone besides a fawning relative ever had called me beautiful.

Then I recalled something less pleasant. Ed had mentioned, early on, that he was only under contract for the run of *Murder Most Noir*. I wondered if Kaplowitz was considering him for some role in the theater's next show, or if it would be just a one-shot deal. Maybe his other phone call had been from his agent, scouting out another gig that might take Ed farther afield?

* * *

There's a drawback to having investigative reporters in the family. Once word got out that Kiernan might have personally helped to foil the robbery at the theater, assisted by the costume designer and an unnamed visitor, Mona and my father quickly connected the dots. The pearl-and-emerald necklace had come from the antiques center, therefore…

"I hope you weren't involved in any of this, Vivian," said my father on the phone. He falls back on my full name when he's pissed with me.

"Did I steal the necklace from Ronnie and hand it over to the theater? No, of course not!"

"That's not what I mean, and you know it. I know you'd never do anything *illegal*, but you're mixed up in it somehow."

After a deep breath, I explained how the evening had gone. That Mona helped me realize the necklace was genuine, but Lauren wasn't returning my calls, so I went to the theater to warn her in person. I skipped over the part about seeing Mitch go into the building disguised as a delivery boy. Let Dad think I had no clue that I'd be walking into such a dangerous scenario.

Still, he insisted, "It wasn't your problem, Viv! You tried to warn the costume lady—if she ignored you, that was on her. Nah, that actor guy got you involved, somehow."

"Absolutely not. I left him a message, too, but he had no idea I would come to the theater."

"Mona did. She told me, 'Viv would never take the chance that something bad might happen to Ed Kiernan!' "

Boy, was I that transparent? And even if I was, did my sister really have to give Dad more ammo?

"It's like I said," he went on, "these theater people get themselves into crazy situations…"

"Kind of like reporters, right, Dad?" I parried back. "Maybe you'd better get used to the idea that your daughters don't mind taking a few risks, if it's for a good cause."

I seldom talked back to him like that, but amazingly, it worked. At least I heard silence on the line, followed by a reluctant "Welll…"

"Besides, sometimes there are perks," I pointed out. "Mona got a string of front-page stories, and I've been offered free tickets for te opening night of *Murder Most Noir*. Front-and-center, for me and any family members I want to bring along. So maybe you'll want to stay on my good side."

An uneasy chuckle from Dad. "I guess I'd better!"

He probably wondered how I'd suddenly toughened up so much. He couldn't know that, in a way, I'd honed my skills on Mitch Rubello.

Mrs. Peel, eat your heart out.

0

Chapter Twenty

Mona joined me on opening night, of course, and we dragged Dad along. For the occasion, my sister wore an actual if tailored dress; my father spiffed up in a buttoned-down shirt, khakis, and a navy blazer. I think by the end of *Murder Most Noir,* they both accepted the idea that, at the very least, Ed Kiernan stood a good chance of making a living as an actor.

When the curtain first went up, I re-experienced one of my greatest thrills from my college years—the audience applauded the set! Tom Richardson had designed the living room of "Gloria's" home as a parody of old-Hollywood excess that still had a certain visual harmony. My dramatic drapes formed a backdrop across the rear wall, with a gap that brightened or darkened to suggest day or night seen through windows. My campy flamingo print hung above a déco bar that saw a lot of action during the play, as did Adrian's sleek mahogany coffee table. His elegant sofa stood out mainly for its deep-rose hue, and two of my exotic throw pillows pushed things even further overboard.

Still, when Marsha-as-Gloria first swept onstage with her flaming red hair, scarlet lips, and ivory satin peignoir, it all faded into the background, as it needed to. You knew from her first dialogue with her butler that she was a cliché, spoiled, self-absorbed celebrity, worried that she might be slipping past her prime. One by one, other 1940s-mystery stereotypes arrived, such as her bitter ex-husband, her callow lover (obviously after her money), a sexy ingenue eager to step into Gloria's shoes, a burly and surly gardener, and other associates Gloria had treated badly for many years.

Act One ended with the first attempt on her life, made to look like an accident, which she survived. Gloria still called in the local police, a couple of bozos who declined to take the threat seriously. So she hired her own gumshoe, Private Investigator Dan McDougal, who made his entrance at the start of Act II.

This was the Ed I remembered from college, but of course, more polished after eighteen additional years of honing his craft. (No glasses that night—he'd told me he wore contacts most of the time when he was working.) At first, his character came across as more intelligent, sensible, and potentially heroic than any of the others. Though his lines were still clever, he tossed them off in a dry, officious way that made them even funnier. This worked well because most of the other characters emoted more broadly.

But when somebody "offed" Gloria for real, the police still declined to investigate, and all the suspects scrambled to implicate each other. "Danny" even lost track of who, exactly, he was supposed to be working for, and ended up hilariously overwhelmed. At one point, he got so desperate that he did pull his realistic revolver—so knowledgeable folks in the audience could appreciate its authenticity—but of course never actually "fired" it.

Justice triumphed at the end, but less through Danny's efforts than because the assorted guilty characters turned on each other or sabotaged themselves. I listened with satisfaction to the whole audience laughing as heartily as I was…including my sister and my father. They gave the cast multiple curtain calls, one extra each for Marsha and for Ed.

Planning ahead for the evening, I had finally worn the form-fitting, dusky-purple cocktail dress I had bought years earlier from Sally Lederman. The scalloped neckline, fairly modest, was appropriate to sit next to my father and sister during the PG-13 stage play, but also retro and artsy enough, I hoped, for the afterparty.

It must have hit the right note, because when Mona and Dad said their good-nights to me in the theater lobby, he wore a rueful expression while she smiled suggestively.

I really cared only about one opinion, though, and when Ed finally emerged from backstage—all of McDougal's makeup washed off, but still no glasses—

his eyebrows lifted in obvious approval. "Classy!" he said, a word his detective persona might have used, and pecked me on the lips. (Aramis would have wolf-whistled, but coming from Ed in the middle of a crowd, that might have been overkill.)

He had changed into a snappy dark teal blazer, gray slacks, and an open-necked, striped shirt.

"You, too," I told him. "I like you better out of uniform." A second too late, I heard the double-entendre and blushed. "I meant..."

He grinned. "Whatever you meant, I'll take it."

The party crowd swept us along to the parking lot. Ed kept an arm around my waist, though, even as his fellow actors, audience members, and other strangers shot comments back and forth to him.

Just as Dad warned, Viv, you'll never have this guy completely to yourself. Even if he doesn't crave all of this attention to prop up his own ego, he still needs it for his career.

But at the moment, I didn't mind. In college, it made me miserable when Ed and the other actors would head off to a party, and I could only tag along as a lowly member of the backstage crew. Tonight, he kept me by his side, and a fair number of the other ladies might have been jealous of *me*. We rode together to The Station in his leased PT Cruiser, but to me it felt like a chauffeured limo.

I'd never been to the Banquet Room on the restaurant's second floor, and that also felt magical. Windows all along two sides offered views of the river at twilight. The minute we entered, some local media people ambushed us, and I panicked briefly when I realized they were also taking pictures of me! Suddenly, random folks might start asking who I was, and no doubt, they'd be confused to learn I had no show business connections.

We ran into Marsha Fuller, who seemed slightly tipsy already (champagne in the dressing room?). Eager for a photo op, she grabbed Ed's arm and struck a pose for the cameras. I stepped aside, feeling relieved. She and Ed were the leads, so they *should* be in the pictures. I'd be glad to remain a private citizen!

Lauren soon came to my rescue, asking me about my dress. We chatted about vintage clothing while the actors offered pithy comments for the press and local theater bloggers.

I overheard Ed smoothly deflecting a few questions about the would-be thief who had broken into the costume department.

He insisted, "All we did was distract the guy until the police arrived."

Lauren whispered to me, "I have to give Ed credit, he's been willing to take all the heat for what went on that night. Kept our names out of it as far as possible." I explained that my sister also had helped with that, at least in terms of the *Herald*.

A little later, when the media folks had gone, I noticed Lindsy, the sexy twenty-something blonde who had played the ingenue, batting her fake eyelashes at Ed. I made my way back to his side just as she purred, "So you bluffed that robber—held him at bay all that time—with an empty gun? Weren't you scared?"

"Pfft, are you kidding?" he tossed back. "Scared? I was *petrified!*"

I smiled to myself. Whatever roles Ed might play onstage, in person, there was no macho b.s. When he spotted me, he added, "Of course, it helped that I had a couple of really gutsy ladies to back me up."

Even blondie got the message then, and knew enough to step away.

The buffet dinner offered selections from The Station's usual fine fare, and though Ed had a couple of glasses of wine, I was glad to see he didn't imbibe as heavily as some of his castmates. Of course, maybe they had drivers to take them back to their accommodations.

Just before dessert, the theater's managing director, Joel Kaplowitz, stepped up to the podium. I'd never seen this tall, fiftyish figure before, but he looked both prosperous and a bit Bohemian with his gray-streaked, fluffy hair, dark-rimmed glasses, seersucker jacket, and colorfully patterned tie. He congratulated the cast and crew on a great opening night and overall production, "despite some unusual challenges over the past couple of weeks." And that was all he said about the break-in that had threatened at least two of their lives.

"Tonight I want to focus on the possibilities for our bright future," he went on. "I'm sure we'd all agree that two drawbacks of a life in the theater are the need to continually be looking for new work and to travel wherever the best prospects are. Some playhouses of our size have managed to meet those challenges by becoming resident theaters with repertory companies. This system provides its actors with stable employment, while 'new blood' can still be brought in for some productions.

"I want to let you know tonight that we have applied for an Eleanor Newcastle Foundation grant that would enable the Addamsville Playhouse to become a resident theater for this region. Though there are other strong contenders for the grant this year, at least it's a goal for our future. If we continue to mount productions of the caliber we staged tonight, I think we have a good chance. I'll be keeping Agnes and the rest of our in-house staff abreast of any further developments. Meanwhile, everyone, cross your fingers!"

From the hearty applause that greeted this announcement, I sensed many of the playhouse's cast and crew would welcome such a stable arrangement.

The party wound up with dancing, of course. Mostly the fast kind, and I wasn't surprised to see that most of the playhouse folks really had the moves. The band was live, probably friends of someone in the cast. Ed and I occasionally danced with other partners, but some of the partygoers were a couple of decades younger, and keeping up with them was a challenge!

By the end of the evening, I think we both welcomed a slow dance together to the Aerosmith ballad "I Don't Want to Miss a Thing."

With the quieter background music, I told Ed that I'd overheard what he said to Lindsy about the confrontation with Mitch. "I'm surprised you were scared. You sure didn't show it!"

A dry chuckle. "I've had a lot of practice. Hey, I was scared to walk out onstage tonight, too! First night, new show, everyone counting on me? But you just focus on what you have to do. And with Mitch, it was life or death—I *had* to keep him from shooting you or Lauren. So I needed to convince him, and even myself, that my gun was real and I could take him down."

I guessed I understood that. "Thank God it worked."

"Really, though, you probably saved all our butts. The way you snuck up behind him with those shears and made him drop his gun...I dunno, Viv.

You just might have some acting talent, after all!"

A lump rose in my throat. I remembered Mitch aiming his pistol at Ed, and felt again that same primitive blend of fear and rage. "I wasn't acting."

My dancing partner pulled back a little and studied me almost warily. "You mean, you really would have stabbed the guy?"

I'd never asked myself that question before and thought seriously about my response. "I'm not usually a violent person, for sure. It was just on impulse that I grabbed those shears. But if he had shot *you*...yeah. I would have stabbed him."

A startled look came into Ed's eyes, as if he were seeing me for the first time. I don't think it was my bloodthirsty side that appealed to him, but maybe something else I'd kept hidden for too long. After the music ended and we found ourselves in a shadowy corner, he kissed me for real—a serious upgrade from his usual peck on the cheek. I returned the gesture with equal enthusiasm.

As the party started to wind down, I invited Ed back to my place. And there...let's just say our relationship finally moved well beyond the Friend Zone.

Not even Aramis could squawk about that.

Chapter Twenty-One

O ften we look back on decisions we made when we were younger, the movies and music we liked, the people we admired, and wonder *What was I thinking?*

In this case, though, I had the opposite reaction. Back in college, the timing might have been wrong for me and Ed, but my instincts about him had been right on target.

I won't go into all the ways we seemed to be in sync, once we finally got together, just the PG-rated ones. Where most other guys found my condo a little too quirky for comfort, Ed Kiernan—a man totally at home around stage sets and costumes—seemed amused and intrigued. He introduced himself formally to Aramis and even got the musketeer reference of my pet's name. However, to encourage a cordial relationship between the two males, I rolled the cockatiel's cage into my work alcove for the night and covered it with a lightweight, "breathable" cloth to muffle any worrisome noises.

I am also glad to report that the chenille bedspread and other "granny" touches in my bedroom had no ill effects, that I could see, on Ed's libido. (Okay, maybe that detail was more PG-13.)

While I made us breakfast the next morning, I know he subtly emailed his ailing father to explain why he'd been out all night. I squirmed just a little to imagine that retired Councilman Glenn Kiernan, whom I had never met so far, would probably be quizzing his son about me.

Don't get ahead of yourself, Viv. One terrific night does not a long-term relationship make!

I tried to keep that in mind even after Aramis started shrieking for attention. I brought his cage into the kitchen to feed him, and Ed decided to chat him up. I knew actors had to master different accents and even languages for some roles, but I didn't imagine that they could learn cockatiel. Pretty soon, though, Ed began mimicking the bird's clucks and twitters so well that at the kitchen stove, with my back to both of them, I could hardly tell the difference.

"Something else to add to your resumé," I told him. "Bird whisperer!"

Since his overnight visit had been so spontaneous, it was lucky that I could offer him an old beach robe from my heavier days—short, but just broad enough to accommodate his shoulders.

I plated our omelets, and the aroma lured Ed to the kitchenette table. "I actually haven't been around birds much lately," he said, "but my mom liked parakeets and we always had one or two when I was a kid. This guy's a character, though. Does he talk at all?"

"Not so far, and I haven't really pushed that, since he makes such a cool range of sounds on his own. He's better at whistling tunes."

While we ate, Aramis proved my point by providing a background of happy twittering. I took this as a sign that he approved of my houseguest.

I knew Ed had to get back to the theater for his matinee, so I let him have the first shower. Later, while toweling off from my own, I overheard him—still in the bedroom—talking quietly on his phone.

"Wednesday? Yeah, I can make that. I'll catch the train right after my two o'clock show winds up...Dinner? Depends on who's buying!" He chuckled. "Okay, thanks. See you then."

I eased my bedroom door shut to dress and wondered about this conversation. He couldn't possibly be making a date with another woman for next week, could he? If he had to take the train, it wouldn't be anyone involved with his current show. And his father and stepmother lived nearby...

I pulled on jeans and a lightweight sweater before I joined him again in the kitchen. Ed, of course, wore the same clothes he'd had on the night before, with the teal blazer over the back of a chair.

Trying to sound casual, I asked, "Were you and Aramis having another chat? I thought I heard you talking to someone."

"Oh, just Rory, my agent." Ed slipped the phone into his pants pocket. "He's trying to line up auditions for me. After all, I've only got two weeks left at Addamsville, sad to say. All good things must come to an end, and it's always best to have some new prospect in the pipeline."

This was perfectly sensible in regard to his career, but I was feeling pretty vulnerable just then. I hoped Ed didn't take the same attitude toward his romantic relationships.

As he pulled on his blazer, I told him, "If you do get any auditions, be sure to wear that jacket! It looks great on you."

"Oh, thanks." He ducked his head almost shyly. "Before I hit the theater, though, I think I'll swing by Dad's place and change my clothes. Don't want to make it obvious to everyone that I didn't sleep at home last night!"

I grinned. "Gee, I didn't realize the 'walk of shame' was also a guy thing."

He put his hand over his heart. "And here I was thinking about preserving *your* reputation. I wouldn't want people gossiping behind your back, about how a smart lady like you could do so much better."

"From what I saw of that party crowd, they'll all still be hung over today. They won't even remember what *they* did last night, never mind you and me."

"Well, I'll sure remember." He took me in his arms for a warm good-bye kiss. "Call you later, okay?"

I wished him a killer matinee. Aramis had the good taste to wait until Ed had left, by the front door, before letting out an especially noisy wolf whistle.

* * *

Unlike my overnight guest, I had no real obligations that day except the usual sewing and writing projects. That might have been just as well—I felt a bit hung over myself, though in a good way. Dizzy and mellow at the same time. My first night with Steve didn't affect me like this...nor had very many of our nights together.

This is how a person should feel at the start of a new relationship, I thought. *At least a good relationship, one that has potential for the future!*

But did it have potential? Even if we really cared about each other, would Ed's erratic career come between us? Already he had to face up to the end of his run in *Murder Most Noir* and start auditioning for other roles. Those weren't likely to turn up here in western New Jersey.

Maybe this is just too good to be true, after all. There were reasons why we never connected in college, and maybe there are reasons why we'll never be able to make it work long-term. Our lives are just too different...

Except they weren't, anymore. I'd spotted qualities in Ed, back in college, that he still possessed eighteen years later. He was just the kind of guy I needed in my life! And by some miracle, he also seemed to feel we meshed well with each other.

I had almost reassured myself along that line when I got a call from Mona, around noon. "Hi, Sis," she began, a teasing note in her voice. "Where are you? Can you talk? I didn't want to call too early..."

"It's fine, Mona. I'm just cleaning up the kitchen."

"Really? I thought maybe—"

"Ed's gone to work. He has a matinee today."

"Ah! I assumed you two—"

"We did, and that's all the information you'll get for now. Let's just say, a good time was had by all."

She laughed. "I'm so happy for you, Viv! Better late than never, right?"

"The timing is probably better for us now. Except, of course, for certain career issues..."

I confided my worries about where Ed's job searches would take him, how far away, and for how long. "But I've resolved not to worry about any of that for at least another week or two."

"Probably smart. I should warn you, though, Dad's still a bit leery about the whole business of you dating an actor. I don't know if he'll be calling to nag, but if he does, don't let him rattle you."

* * *

As it turned out, in the days that followed, my father didn't harass me at all, but my own paranoid imagination did. Ed seemed very busy working on and helping to promote *Murder Most Noir*, so we couldn't get together as often as we would have liked. All that, I could accept. Still, when we made a lunch date for Monday, our one mutual day off, and at the last minute, he asked for a rain check, I felt hurt and confused. He apologized but gave no real explanation, just that "something important" had come up.

Oh well, I told myself, it was probably just another promotional thing they wanted him to do, for the playhouse. Or maybe an audition for one of those future gigs. *He doesn't want to talk about it because then he'll have to explain to me if it doesn't work out. Maybe that kind of thing is hard on his ego.*

Fortunately, my business picked up, too, probably because of the ad in the theater's program. I noticed one day that Adrian Marcus had propped up a copy of that publication on a small easel in his booth. If a browser mentioned it, he would inform them that he had loaned two pieces of furniture to be used in the main set.

At first, this struck me as kind of tacky, but after a while, I thought, *Why not?* Ed had actually autographed my first-night program, as kind of a joke, but when I placed that at the front of my booth, it got even more attention than Adrian's. At least he didn't ask any nosy questions about what I'd done to get the star's autograph.

Some browsers actually wanted to call dibs on pieces I had loaned to the production. Soon I had to tell many that the plume-festooned drapes, some throw pillows, the big flamingo artwork, and the Roseville jardiniere were already spoken for.

I lied about that last one, though. I figured I was entitled to keep one significant piece from the show, and that Boho planter had played a big part in bringing Ed and me together. It also carried subtle reminders of Kaye's murder, but I tried to disregard those.

* * *

Between Mona and the gossip grapevine at the antiques center, I kept up with the latest developments regarding that investigation. Mitch remained in custody and maintained that although Kaye Burrell had surprised him that morning at the antiques center, her death had been an accident. Questioned about the blood on the crystal candlestick, he first claimed to know nothing about it, then confessed that he'd hit her, but only to knock her out. Even so, the Addamsville police finally got as much as they needed to hold him, if only for manslaughter.

They also were able to link Mitch to the robberies of the Delaware jewelry store and the pawn shop, so he was sure to go away for a long stretch. What they hadn't gotten out of him, so far, was the identity of his partner in those crimes. They offered him various deals, but from what Mona could learn, Mitch seemed less afraid of prison than of retribution from someone he refused to name.

"Whether he's really afraid this other guy will find a way to get back at him, or that some boss higher up will think he's a snitch, the cops aren't sure," she told me one night on the phone. "But the other thief is still on the loose, and if he's smart enough to lay low for a while, he could stay that way."

"Unless somebody recognizes him from the sketch that ran in the paper," I reminded her.

Mona sniffed. "They'd really have to have memorized the drawing, which was just based on a witness's description as the guy was running away. And the dude isn't all that distinctive-looking. He's still likely to get off unless he screws it up in some way."

This got me thinking along ominous lines. Just how vengeful was this mystery man? *He must know that Mitch failed to get the emerald necklace and got arrested because three of us at the theater outsmarted him.* Word already had gotten around that Ed was involved—would this nasty character come after him? Back here on his home turf, and appearing at a regional theater, he'd never seen the need for a bodyguard, but I wondered if he should consider one!

I thought of asking him about that, but over the next few days, we still didn't see much of each other. I knew his schedule at the theater and tried to call him during off times, but even then, I often got voicemail. Once, when we did have a leisurely phone conversation—on a slow afternoon for me at the antiques center—he eventually got another call. Though he apologized, he "had to" take it.

I couldn't help wisecracking, "Don't tell me, Starflix had a change of heart and they're picking up another season of *Boulevard Blues*."

"Nah, I wouldn't do that again for any money." But again, he switched to the other call without telling me what it was actually about.

Maybe I was my father's daughter, after all. When I couldn't be with Ed, I started worrying about him…not only whether he was seeing another woman on the side, but whether by going onstage six days a week and leaving the theater so late, he was vulnerable to an attack. Some nutcase might easily blame him for foiling the attempted robbery at the theater and getting two members of that ring busted.

I didn't worry much about my own safety until a week later, when I got a call at work from the security guard at my condo community. He reported that a man in a black SUV had driven up to the front gate, saying he had an appointment with me.

"He had your address," the guard explained, "and some kind of company name on his vehicle that said 'Sales and Service.' Seemed legit, but of course I'd never let him in without checking with you. When I started to dial your number, though, he backed up real fast and drove away! Just thought you ought to know, Ms. Joyce."

Maybe I was getting paranoid—maybe it was just a repairman who realized he came to the wrong community—but that made me wonder if someone was out to settle a score with me. Or just to tie up any loose ends? With the antiques center doing a brisk business lately, Fred had invested in higher-quality security cameras, better located to show more of the activity on both floors, as well as in our parking lot. So, at least I started to feel a bit safer there…but less safe elsewhere.

Even while reading or hand-sewing on my patio, I flinched and glanced around at any unusual noise. I grew conscious of how many spots in our unfenced community would permit an intruder to secretly spy on me, or even slip through the shrubbery and show up at my door. These dark imaginings made me wish Aramis were a bigger, louder parrot, so I could train him to screech on command, "Nine-one-one! Nine-one-one!"

Once, I did see a dark-haired, bearded guy in a trucker's cap loitering across the street from our complex, as if scoping it out. He wasn't familiar as a neighbor, but I also couldn't say whether he resembled the other, unnamed robber who had partnered with Mitch on the jewelry heists. In the drawing based on the eyewitness account, that man had been clean-shaven. Had he grown the beard on purpose to hide his distinctive, square jawline?

The next time Mona stopped over for dinner, she agreed that it would be smart for me to take as few risks as possible. "You're absolutely right that there's at least one other guy out there who could be ticked off that you and Kiernan foiled their plans to steal that necklace. If he's sensible, he'll leave well enough alone...and leave this area! But if he's a hothead, he could be out for revenge."

At least as much as the idea of this character stalking me, I dreaded the notion of someone going after Ed. He was more exposed, appearing onstage most nights of the week and leaving the theater near midnight. The day after I sighted my possible prowler, I did phone Ed and float the idea of his hiring a bodyguard. But once again, I left a message, and I suspected he'd find the idea ridiculous.

As the days wore on, even if I still didn't talk to Ed as much as I wanted to, at least I didn't get any more alerts from the Hunterdon Village security post. I tended space No. 17 at the antiques center, worked on my blog, and drafted another article for *Vintage Quarterly*. On Saturday, I even got up the nerve to head out on my own to a big flea market, almost an hour to the south of me. I spent most of the day there, though I picked up just a few more small collectibles for my booth.

On my drive home, around dusk, a chime from my phone told me I had a text. That didn't startle me, but the message did. Tersely, it said *Stupid car broke down. Hanning Park, by the River. Can U pick me up?*

It must be from Ed, I told myself, because he had that ancient PT Cruiser. There was no phone number, but he'd signed it *Officer McDougal*. Since it was Wednesday, he would have done his matinee at the theater, and supposedly, he had another mysterious appointment right after that.

Odd, though. When I got a message on my phone, the sender's number usually showed up, unless it was deliberately blocked. And fictional Danny McDougal was a private eye, not an "officer" of any kind. Ed would know that detail in his sleep. Besides, why wouldn't he just call the company that leased him the car and ask them to send a tow truck?

Hoping to get answers to these questions, I pulled to the side of the road and returned his call. Once more, though, I got his recording and left a message.

After that, I sat parked for a moment and wondered what else to do. It seemed an awfully flimsy reason to call 911, but what about the Addamsville PD? The park should be within their jurisdiction, and they knew all about our recent tangles with bad guys.

Still, it took me a few minutes to convince the cop who answered the phone that Ed's text sounded suspicious. "Maybe he had a couple of drinks."

Even drunk as a skunk, Ed would remember the character he played onstage every night! But that still might not convince this guy, so I reminded him that both Kiernan and I had been involved with preventing the attempted robbery at the theater a couple of weeks back. I told him if he wasn't familiar with the incident, he should check with Officer Gorey.

"I'm going out there," I told him. "You'd better hope it's not a trap of some kind, or you may find the two of us…"

"All right, lady, all right. We'll notify the park police."

Better than nothing, I thought, dropping the phone back into my purse. I had a general idea of where to find the park and how to get into it. The text hadn't told me, of course, exactly where inside its borders Ed had supposedly broken down, and I worried that someone might try to ambush me en route.

I was driving through the twilight slowly, straining by the widely spaced post lights to scan both sides of the road, when my phone rang. This time I saw Ed's real number and heard his actual, worried voice.

"I got your message," he said. "What's up?"

"I'm guessing your car didn't break down in Hanning Park, and you aren't waiting for me to pick you up."

"No-o-o…I'm not even sure where that is. I'm at the train station, just got back from the City. *You're not at the park, are you?"*

His mind was obviously running along the same lines as mine. "I am, but I should be connecting with the park police soon. Don't worry. I won't take any stupid...*damn!"*

A black SUV filled my rearview mirror, revving its engine as if about to ram me. My smaller "crossover" vehicle couldn't withstand that kind of attack, so I floored it and tried to escape.

The park road was fairly wide and well-paved, with no other traffic at this hour that I could see. I swerved left, then right, erratically; even with a faster vehicle, my pursuer had a hard time staying on my tail. I flew past signs that politely reminded me the speed limit within the small park was 25. Meanwhile, I heard Ed's frantic shouts from the phone, calling my name and asking what was going on.

I can't keep this up for long. Sooner or later, this jerk's going to catch up and drive me off the road. In such a densely wooded spot, I'd probably hit a tree. My fingers ached from their death-grip on the steering wheel.

Suddenly, a white sedan, branded *Hanning Park Police*, cut across in front of us with its roof light flashing. I took a chance, and at the next level spot, veered off the road.

That left my purser exposed, and he made a desperate try at a U-turn. Before he could pull it off, though, I heard the welcome wail of a police siren; a black-and-white also arrived, with more flashing lights. Two armed cops jumped out and hollered for the driver of the SUV to exit with his hands up.

Watching from a safe distance, I recognized the guy with the short beard whom I'd seen hanging around the fringes of my condo community. I'd been right all along—he was scoping out my place, and probably tried to get past the security gate, too. My nauseating terror eased, though, as I watched a young officer I didn't recognize snap handcuffs onto the stranger's wrists.

I picked up my phone to put Ed's mind at ease, but he'd already hung up. *Huh! Did he have something better to do than find out if I'd survived the car chase?*

Neither cop was familiar to me from my trip to the Addamsville police station, but no doubt they were night-shift guys, both younger than either Gorey or Bharani. When one began to question me about why the driver of the black SUV might have wanted to harm me, his partner interrupted.

"It's connected to the jewelry-store robberies and the holdup at the theater," he said, matter-of-factly. "Gorey knows all about it."

That surprised me, but I guess some message reached the right person, after all. "I'm so glad you guys came," I told them. "The person I spoke to on the phone just said they were going to notify the park police."

The better-informed young cop just shrugged. "Gorey got a call, too. He said you could be in danger, and we should get out of here right away."

Yet another vehicle sped onto the scene, but though it masqueraded as a "cruiser" from many decades ago, its driver had no law-enforcement credentials...except on TV. Ed leaped out, slowing his pace only when he saw that I seemed to still be in one piece and under the protection of real lawmen.

The glare of the squad car's headlights blanched even his freckles of all color. He wrapped an arm around me, and I could feel his fear. "Viv, are you okay?"

"Fine, really! Just a little shaken up." I explained that I couldn't respond to him on the phone because I'd been swerving madly, to avoid being rammed into a tree.

Ed glowered in the direction of the squad car, as if he wanted to dish out some justice of his own on the handcuffed captive.

"You sure got here fast," I noted, with gratitude.

"Like I said, I was right up the road at the train station."

At the cop's request, Ed gave his name and address. He explained that he had phoned Gorey and that both of us had been involved in the standoff a few days earlier at the theater.

The young officer noted this information in his official notepad, then his face suddenly lit up. "Hey, I thought you looked familiar! Weren't you in that series about the L.A. cops..."

Kiernan's lips twisted in either annoyance or amusement. Maybe both, due to the ironic circumstances. "*Boulevard Blues*, yeah."

"My wife and I loved that show! We both were so pissed when it got canceled." He flipped the notepad to a fresh page. "I don't wanna be a total dork, but…could I have your autograph?"

Chapter Twenty-Two

Ed's father was expecting him back at the lake house, and meanwhile, Mona happened to call me. They each ended up hearing, by phone, about the car chase in the park, and each reacted protectively. Mr. Kiernan sounded so stressed that Ed felt he should go home, and Mona insisted on spending the night at my place. It seemed ungrateful to tell her she wasn't my first choice for a bodyguard.

"We'll have lunch tomorrow," Ed told me, after a parting kiss.

I nodded. "Say, I forgot to ask…you went into the City today, again? Anything exciting?"

With a slight frown, he downplayed this. "Let's talk about it tomorrow."

I drove back to my condo much less worried about homicidal jewel thieves, but concerned about my new relationship with Ed. He'd gotten a couple of mysterious phone calls, the last few times we'd been together, and now he was running into New York again on his only free evening? I'd been mostly jealous of the other women in the cast of his play, but could there be somebody else I didn't even know about?

By the time I reached home, Mona, who had "permanent visitor" status at the gate of my community, was already parked in my extra space and standing on my patio. She gathered me into a big-sisterly embrace that soothed my still-jangled nerves. In my kitchen, over glasses of wine, I filled her in on the details of the evening's escapade, against asking her to keep my name and Ed's out of the story if she possibly could.

"I should be able to," she reassured me. "People will care mostly about the robber, since this is his third offense. The important angle is that all three

197

guys in the local gang are finally in custody. But really, you and Kiernan *have* had a lot to do with that."

"Even without publicity, though, my involvement with Mitch's capture provoked this last guy to come after me, and he did it by pretending to be Ed. So I'd rather remain anonymous, and I'm sure Ed feels the same way."

As we made up the sofa bed in my studio for her, it dawned on Mona that maybe I'd had other company in mind for that night. "Oh, Viv, I'm sorry. Are you and Ed…did I…?"

"Don't worry about it, we're getting together tomorrow. He seemed to have something else on his mind tonight, anyway." I told her about his secretive behavior lately, and that he'd spent the afternoon in Manhattan but put off telling me why.

"Now, don't jump to conclusions," my sister advised me, with a wry smile. "It's not necessarily another woman. Maybe he has a gambling problem…or he's secretly doing stand-up comedy at some rathole in the Village."

I considered only the second a real possibility. "But why would he keep that from me?"

"Maybe his act really stinks!"

Soon after that, we both turned in. Though I did have one brief nightmare about the headlights of the big, black SUV looming in my rearview mirror, I eventually got a decent night's sleep.

After breakfast, Mona took off for work at the *Herald,* and I changed into something suitable for staffing Booth 17. Just before I left for the antiques center, I got a call from Ed.

"Hope you didn't feel like I deserted you last night," he said. "You seemed like you were in good hands with Mona. And Dad's been having some more health issues—he went to his doctor yesterday for some heart arrhythmia—so I wanted to make sure he was okay."

"No problem at all," I told him. "Backing me up with the cops was help enough. I appreciated that."

"Can you get away for a quick lunch today? Maybe Pablo's again? I'll explain about my trip to the City yesterday."

* * *

This time I also ordered the *huevos rancheros*, because they'd intrigued me on our first visit. While we sat waiting for our meals, Ed began.

"I know I've been kind of secretive about some of my phone calls lately, and why I wasn't very reachable yesterday. I had dinner with my agent, Rory."

Before I could envision some vamp in a slinky business suit, Ed continued, "He's been planning ahead, trying to line up work for me after *Noir* runs its course."

Naturally, I thought. The play only had a run of three weeks. Then, after a short break, the Addamsville would mount a totally different production with a whole new cast.

"And was he able to?" I tried to keep my voice and emotions level.

"He's got a couple of things in the works. He was looking into another series on the West Coast, a comedy, but I told him I'd rather keep on doing live theater for a while. There's a revival of *Company* touring the Midwest this fall…"

A spicy mouthful lodged in my throat, and I swallowed it with effort. *It's just like Dad predicted…no sooner do Ed and I get together than he'll land a role that takes him away for months at a time.*

"The best option Rory suggested, I think, was an Off-Broadway revue that starts around Labor Day," Ed continued. "It's by a new playwright, so it's kind of a crapshoot—could be the next big thing or a complete bomb! But he thinks I should read for it, so I'm going back to do that on Wednesday."

My gloom lightened a bit. "That shouldn't be such a wrench. At least you'll be working in Manhattan. And off-Broadway would be a pretty big deal, right?"

"It would for me. But I realize that for *us*, it's kind of good news/bad news. I'd probably have to stay in the City a lot of the time…"

True, that would be a hitch, but I heard a more positive subtext. Ed was already taking "us" so seriously that it was influencing his decision to go after the role.

Time to prove you're not Janet, honey. That you won't try to stand in the way of his career, or even fret about what other women he might meet on the job.

I reached across the table to take his hand. "You've got to go after it, of course! We'll still find time to see each other, even if I have to take the train into New York a couple of times a week."

He looked relieved. "I was afraid you'd be upset."

Yep, he still had bipolar Janet on the brain. "At least we've both got phones and laptops, so we'll be able to talk face-to-face no matter where you are."

"That is lucky. But I might not be able to come to your rescue, next time, if you get chased through the park by another bad guy."

I squeezed his hand. "I'll try not to get myself into any more hair-raising situations, at least until the run of your revue is over."

"Anyhow, I shouldn't count my chickens, as they say. I haven't got the part yet."

"Well, promise me you'll give it your best shot," I told him. "Don't bungle it on my account!" And I found that I really meant it.

Chapter Twenty-Three

Mona's career, on the other hand, got a big boost later that week. Before even hearing it from her, I saw the morning headline of the *Herald* on my phone: KINGPIN OF JEWELRY THEFT RING APPREHENDED.

The Delaware cops had traced the robberies in their state and New Jersey to an older guy based in Pennsylvania with mob ties. He recruited small-time, local crooks in each area to do the dirty work of robbing assorted retailers and fencing the merchandise. Mona reported that the ring had netted well over a million dollars for its kingpin in just the past year.

No wonder Gerry and his cousin feared screwing up, and the third guy even tried to get rid of me! Their "boss" sounds like a man you wouldn't want to disappoint.

I called my sister, left a message, and headed out to my workplace. I had settled in for the day by the time she called me back.

"Great job!" I congratulated her.

"Oh, thanks." She sounded a bit breathless. "I've been on the phone all morning, as you can imagine. It's a big rush, helping to break a story like this, though I'm just glad criminals don't usually blame newspaper reporters when they get bad press."

"I hear you on that. Once again, I appreciate your keeping my name and Ed's out of the stories."

"Of course, even though it's kind of a shame. You two not only connected a lot of dots for us, but kept Mitch Rubello from doing some serious damage that night at the theater."

"I'll tell Ed you said that. He's a little bummed right now, trying to line up his next gig. His contract for The Addamsville was for just the one show. They do have a musical scheduled for the end of June, but Ed doesn't know yet if there will be a decent role for him. He says for some reason they're playing things very close to the vest."

"Gee, that's too bad..." Mona started to sound distracted. "Anyhow, speaking of gigs, I'd better get back to *my* work. Maybe dinner at Applegarth's later, to celebrate?"

We made it a date. After that, I checked the time on my phone—about noon. It was Wednesday, so Ed would not have a show at the theater, but supposedly he had gone into Manhattan that morning to read for a part in that Off-Broadway revue.

Will he be annoyed if I phone him? Well, if he's busy, he doesn't need to answer...

My call did go straight to voicemail. "Just wondered if you heard the good news yet," I said, being deliberately mysterious. "It's on the front page of the *Herald* and also got picked up by one of the Philly papers. Guess this means neither of us has anything more to worry about—what a relief! Call me when you have a break..."

Even past noon, foot traffic through the antiques center continued to be light. Out of boredom, I straightened a few pillows that a browser had knocked askew. Meanwhile, I couldn't help wondering how Ed's audition that day had gone—and whether I really wanted him to get the part, or not!

In the general quiet, I heard the whine of a pneumatic drill from the first floor. I wandered out to the head of the stairs and looked down. Near the Randolph brothers' booth, a workman from a security service, on an extension ladder, attached something small to a rafter. Fred stood below to survey the progress.

I called to him, "Finally upgrading the security cameras?"

"Kind of like closing the barn door after the horse has run off, I know," Fred admitted. "Next week, they're also wiring any windows that can be reached from ground level outside. I squeezed some money out of our insurance company. The fact that we actually had a break-in helped me make my case."

I grinned. "I'm sure it did." All of us vendors would probably feel a lot safer in the future, though.

On my way back to my own booth, I heard Cindy's clear voice pipe up, "There's Vivian now!"

Recent events had left me a bit paranoid, so I braced myself for some new accusation or outrageous request. Not that Cindy had ever given me a hard time in the past, but I'd learned recently that even my fellow vendors could not always be trusted.

The zaftig blonde bustled across the aisle, towing along a slimmer, dark-haired woman of about the same age. "Viv, this is the friend I was telling you about," Cindy said. "She's being very brave today, coming here. She thinks it might help to desensitize her a little."

The pieces clicked into place, and I put out my hand. "Oh, you must be the psychic…"

Despite her smile, the brunette hesitated to accept my handshake. "Actually, I'm clairsentient."

"Nice to meet you, Claire," I said.

Cindy laughed aloud. "No, no, her name's Marilyn. I told you that, remember? 'Clairsentient' means that she picks up information from things, and people, that she touches."

My hand still hovered in mid-air, unshaken, but at least now I knew why. I dropped it back to my side but smiled at the visitor. "In that case, you may want to avoid me, Marilyn. I've been in touch with some rough characters lately!" Though I wasn't much of a believer in the paranormal, I wouldn't want her to get a flash of me poking a nine-inch blade into Mitch Rubello's back. Not the greatest first impression!

"I briefed Marilyn on some of the problems we've had here," Cindy told me, though in her usual upbeat manner. "I warned her to not, under any circumstances, ride up in the freight elevator."

"I did walk past it, though," the other woman admitted in a soft tone. "If it's any comfort to the rest of you, I don't think that Kaye woman ever knew what hit her. The end was fast."

Very easy, I thought, for Cindy's friend to tell us what she probably knew we wanted to hear. I could appreciate the gesture without totally believing in her psychic abilities.

"So, how do you like our antiques center?" I asked. "Not too overwhelming for you?"

Beneath her loose, floral tunic, Marilyn squared her shoulders. "I'm trying a new technique for visiting crowded places, letting the vibrations bounce off without absorbing too much. I do think it's working! But an environment like this can be *very* challenging. I pick up impressions not only from the people working here now, but from all of these objects and their histories— their different periods and owners. If I'm lucky, the impressions are pleasant or at least neutral, rather than too disturbing."

To my surprise, I could identify. "I get that. Being in this business, I can't help wondering about the backstories of my merchandise. I inherited a few of these items from my grandmother, but most of them I picked up third-hand and know nothing about."

Marilyn looked me in the eye, and her calm gaze seemed to pierce all my normal defenses. "Yes...and you're the type who *would* like to know more, aren't you? Especially if there was anything mysterious about the source of the object."

Her comment felt so on-target that I had to laugh. "I never thought much about it, but I guess that's true."

Cindy told her friend about the estate sale we had visited together, and the wide assortment of possessions left behind by the various family members. Meanwhile, I noticed Marilyn's attention drifting toward the autographed *Murder Most Noir* program, propped on a small easel near the front of my booth. Without a word, she picked it up.

Cindy explained, "Vivian's loaned quite a few things for the set of that show."

As if in a light trance, Marilyn commented to me, "And you know this person, the man who signed the cover. He's a good friend."

Impressive...unless Cindy already had told her about Ed? "Yes," I confirmed.

"The two of you were in danger, recently. Probably because he's got the same trait as you —can't resist a mystery, has to get to the bottom of things."

That startled me, and I realized it might be so.

Intuitive enough to notice my reaction, Marilyn backed off a bit. "Sorry, Vivian! I hope I didn't say anything that upset you. Sometimes when a message comes through very strongly, I end up putting it into words before I consider the consequences. Just be careful, both you and your friend Ed, in the future. Things worked out well for you this time, but they might not always in the future."

"That shouldn't be a problem, should it, Viv?" Cindy asked cheerfully. "According to today's paper, all of our recent troublemakers are safely behind bars now!"

"I'm very glad to hear that," said Marilyn. With a parting glance around my booth, she added, "You have a lovely display here. And now that the play is over, I'm sure you'll be glad to bring back that big, flowered piece of pottery, won't you? Maybe to fill in that empty corner."

Confused, I looked at Cindy. At first, she also wore a puzzled expression, but then the light dawned. "Oh, Viv, she must mean the jardinière!"

"Is that what it's called?" Marilyn asked.

This woman could picture the old-fashioned Roseville planter, without even knowing its exact name or function? I smelled a trick. After Marilyn had strolled farther down the aisle towards her friend's booth, I whispered to Cindy, "I didn't know you two went to see the play."

"We haven't, so far! By the time I tried for tickets, they were sold out, so we're on the wait list for a cancellation." She must have seen suspicion in my face, because she swore, "And no, I didn't even tell Marilyn about the jardinière!"

After the two of them returned to the Shabby Chic booth, I still saw no prospective customers hovering near mine, and resigned myself to a lazy weekday afternoon. I had packed a sandwich in my tote and ate it at that point, less from hunger than from nerves. I worried about how Ed's audition had gone and whether the outcome would affect our shaky new relationship.

Meanwhile, the drilling and hammering had spread from the lower level to my own floor. Looking across the aisle, I saw an installer mounting another camera near the Ledermans' booth. I also thought I glimpsed a familiar figure talking with them, half-hidden by the curtained partitions.

205

My suspicions were confirmed when I heard the man's buoyant laugh ring across the space. What was Ed doing there, at almost two in the afternoon? Had he auditioned in New York and gotten back already? At least he sounded cheerful.

Maybe he nailed the "revue" job and stopped by to tell me—?

Nonchalantly, I hoped, I wandered over to investigate. When Sally Lederman spotted me, she asked, "Viv, did you hear the news? Isn't it great?"

Ed spun to face me and looked a bit taken aback. "No-o-o." he told Sally. "Viv wouldn't have heard…"

"I have, though," I assured him. "It's in the *Herald* and a couple of other papers. You might want to add, 'Helped bust a tri-state drug ring' to your professional credentials."

"Huh?"

We went around like this for a little longer before Ed realized I was talking about the arrest of the top guy in the jewelry-fencing ring. Then he visibly relaxed. "I'm glad they caught him, Viv, but I hope the paper downplayed any involvement on our parts."

"Don't worry. Mona saw to that, as usual." I remembered his confusion when I'd first mentioned the 'good news.' "Why, did you think I meant something else? Oh, wow, did you get the part you were trying out for this morning?"

The Ledermans also looked at him expectantly, so I figured that had to be it. But Ed just dropped his gaze and shook his head. "No, no. Actually, I never even made it to that audition."

"Oh no, why not? Did you miss the train, or…"

I noticed that Tony faced away from me, as if to straighten an overcoat on its hanger, while Sally appeared to stifle a smile.

Ed just shrugged. "I decided it wasn't the right career move for me just now. Running in and out of the city…and the playwright's a real unknown…"

I tried to comprehend this, but as a good actor, Ed had perfected his poker face. I knew he wouldn't have thrown away the opportunity on a whim. Besides, the Ledermans were doing their best to not meet my eyes, and I didn't think it was because they felt Ed had made a boneheaded decision.

"C'mon, Kiernan," Tony finally said. "Don't torture the poor woman! She saved your damned life a couple of weeks ago."

Ed finally cracked a hint of a smile. "That's a fact, isn't it? Okay, okay, Viv. Truth is, I got a better offer."

"Better than Off-Broadway?" I heard a skeptical note in my own voice.

"In some ways, yeah."

Sally couldn't take it anymore. "The playhouse got the grant, Viv. To start a resident company!"

"Oh, wow, that's terrific! But still…"

"And Agnes already asked me if I was interested," Ed explained. "I thought it over for about five seconds, then said 'Hell, yeah!'"

"Hardly fair, though. You had the inside track," Tony scoffed.

"Well, they want people with roots in the area, which I have…" Ed began.

"And you can play a range of character types and roles," I added, with mounting enthusiasm.

"Not to mention, he can always double as a security guard," Sally reminded me, "if the theater gets any more shady characters backstage."

I put my arm protectively through Ed's. "Now, that's a role I really don't want to see him taking on again!"

"We agree on that, babe." He gave me a squeeze.

"At least, thanks to the Philly cops, those particular guys shouldn't be coming around anymore." I told the three of them about Mona's front-page story.

"Even more great news," Ed agreed.

The Ledermans left us then, to help two teenaged girls who were browsing through 1960s minidresses. Meanwhile, Ed escorted me back to my booth, his arm around my shoulders.

"Listen," he half-whispered, "not everybody at the theater will be part of the resident company, so keep it quiet until after Sunday, okay?"

"Sure," I promised, "but what's Sunday…oh, the wrap party?"

Ed nodded. "That's when Kaplowitz will make the official announcement. You can come with me, I hope?"

Since he had taken his time explaining to me about his "loss" of the New

York job, I felt entitled to also torment him a little. "Well, I dunno...I have had kind of a busy week, and Sunday is usually my day of rest."

"What, you've got somebody else on the side?" He frowned and shook his head. "It's that bird, isn't it? The flashy dresser? I thought the two of you seemed a little kissy-poo."

"Aramis and I do have a long history." After a quick glance around for stray browsers, I pulled Ed behind my booth's wicker screen and gave him a quick kissy-poo of my own. "I think you made the right career move," I whispered.

He grinned. "I think so, too."

"I'll make sure you don't regret it." Stepping from behind the screen, I picked up the folded newspaper and stuffed it into my all-purpose tote. "Since I already made plans to meet Mona at Applegarth's tonight for dinner, why don't you join us? We can celebrate everyone's good news."

On our way out to the parking lot, I recalled Ed telling me he still had a few serious offers waiting in the wings, in case the playhouse couldn't find a role for him in its next production. I wasn't just thinking of Kaplowitz and the other theater bigwigs when I asked, "They aren't worried about losing you back to Hollywood?"

"I did have to convince them I was committed to sticking around," Ed admitted, straight-faced. "I gave them the full pitch. Told them I really like working at the playhouse, and that if I can stay here, I'll be able to keep an eye on my aging dad...plus, I just started dating this hot Addamsville lady, which also might have future possibilities."

My heart jumped in my chest. "You didn't—!"

Ed creased his nose. "They told me that was too much information, but they gave me the job anyway."

As we headed for the highway and the restaurant, I could hardly comprehend the changes in my life over the past month. Not only had I finally started dating my "unrequited" college crush, and helped him foil a violent robbery, but he had actually passed up a lucrative career move to... what?

Spend more time with me?

Maybe I had finally evolved into one of the gutsy, glamorous "gals" from those old movies I had watched as a kid.

208

CHAPTER TWENTY-THREE

Thanks, Nana Vivian—wherever you are!

Acknowledgements

Thanks to Pat Marinelli for her tips on realistic police procedure; to Joanne Weck for her expert tips on the behind-the-scenes machinations of community and regional theaters; and to fellow authors Chelle Martin, Elizabeth John and Jo-Ann Reccoppa for their valuable input on the nuts-and-bolts aspects of the writing. All of the above are fellow published members of Sisters in Crime Central Jersey/Jersey Sleuths.

For info on how regional theaters arrange to borrow props for their productions, I'm grateful to Robert Klein of the Players Guild of Leonia, NJ, and Midge McClosky of the Shawnee Playhouse, Shawnee On Delaware, PA.

I also owe thanks to my neighbors Irene and David Fritzinger, for allowing me to spend time with their two pet cockatiels Frankie and Mikie. Much gratitude to Anne-Marie Cottone, for patiently accompanying me on many, many jaunts through the Antiques Center of Red Bank and similar emporiums; also to the vendors at those establishments, for sharing background on how such a large retail collective functions and how the individual vintage dealers manage their businesses.

All of these folks have contributed greatly to the authenticity of this book's setting, plot and characters.

About the Author

Eileen Watkins came to her fiction career from a long background in journalism, writing and editing articles on visual art, architecture, interior design and home improvement for two major daily newspapers. During that time, she interviewed artisans, designers and collectors, and acquired a taste for the type of quirky décor that fictional Vivian Joyce offers her customers.

Early in her fiction career, Eileen published eight stand-alone mystery and suspense novels with Amber Quill Press, several of which won EPIC and Indie book awards. She went on to put out the Cat Groomer Mystery series with Kensington Publishing. All six books received Certificates of Excellence from the national Cat Writers' Association, and both *Claw & Disorder* and *Night of the Were-Cat* won that organization's MUSE Medallion for Mystery Fiction. Also a horse lover, Eileen published the women's fiction novel *Reboot Ranch* through FreedomChaser Books.

She belongs to Mystery Writers of America and national Sisters in Crime, and serves as publicity officer for Sisters in Crime/Central Jersey, a.k.a. the Jersey Sleuths. Visit her online at www.efwatkins.com.

AUTHOR WEBSITE: www.efwatkins.com

SOCIAL MEDIA HANDLE:
  Pinterest: www.pinterest.com/eileenw1987

Also by Eileen Watkins

From Amber Quill Press:
  Dance with the Dragon, 2003
  Ride a Dancing Horse, 2004
  Black Flowers, 2004
  Paragon, 2005
  Danu's Children, 2009
  One Blood, 2010
  Dark Music, 2013
  Hex, Death & Rock'n'Roll, 2014

From Freedomchaser (WCY) Books:
  Reboot Ranch, 2020

From Kensington Mystery:
  The Persian Always Meows Twice, 2017
  The Bengal Identity, 2018
  Feral Attraction, 2018
  Gone, Kitty, Gone, 2020
  Claw & Disorder, 2021
  Night of the Were-Cat, 2022